JOHN L. MONK

HELL'S CHILDREN

A Post-Apocalyptic Survival Thriller

HELL'S CHILDREN
A Post-Apocalyptic Survival Thriller

Cover Design by Yocla Designs

ISBN-13: 978-1535181495
ISBN-10: 1535181494

For Dorothy

ACKNOWLEDGMENTS

My friend had to go to his daughter's elementary school for a conference with the teacher. The school wasn't teaching the sixth graders "order of operations." The students were learning to add, subtract, multiply, and divide in whatever order the operators happened to arrive.

My friend asked the teacher why she was instilling bad habits in children who might never fully break them.

"It's too hard to remember all those rules," the educator said.

So I'd like to thank my friend for that troubling story—which formed the basis for *this* tale of a world without adults.

Yes, that sounds like a terrible world, I know (and it is). But look on the bright side: it's also a world without Wal-Mart fights on YouTube, Smart Phones at the dinner table, and teachers who don't teach. When you add up the good, subtract the bad, multiply X and divide by Y, what do you get?

Yeah, I don't know either. I went to public school.

JLM

ONE

Fourteen-year-old Jack Ferris shoveled another scoop of dirt onto his mom's grave. Two feet to the right was his dad's shallow plot, dug weeks ago by his mom while she still had the strength.

He leaned on his spade and surveyed the work through eyes red from crying. Neither grave was even close to deep enough, but he doubted if such things mattered anymore. The world had gone to Hell, it liked it there, and it wasn't coming back.

"Love you Mom and Dad," he said.

Jack grabbed his coat and the .40 caliber pistol resting on it and climbed the short flight of stairs to the deck of their modest corner townhouse in Centreville, Virginia. Standing there in his t-shirt, breath steaming in the frigid November air, he scrutinized the road that looped through the neighborhood. Nothing to see but a row of cars on either side covered with leaves from months of sitting idle. Well, that and a Volvo the Asian kid five doors down had plowed into a tree. That was yesterday. Jack hadn't seen the crash, but he'd heard it. Scared him to death. He'd run out with his pistol thinking it was the food gang coming to make a go at the house. Instead of the food gang, he'd seen his neighbor climb out of the car, fall down, get up, and then stumble out of sight.

1

Jack hadn't bothered to check if he was all right. What would be the point?

All the townhouses in their row of eight had sliding glass doors. The neighbor's door two units down had been smashed in long ago. After that, Jack and his dad had boarded up their own door using fencing from houses where people had died. They'd run the boards vertically, allowing only a narrow opening to get in and out.

After a last look around, Jack slid the door open, then carefully stepped over the dark towel stretched over the floor like a mat. Lurking beneath it were three boards hammered through with about fifty nails.

Months ago, in noble acceptance of their looming deaths, nuclear workers everywhere had preemptively shut down reactors. Weeks later, the coal plants followed when nobody was well enough or willing to work. With the electricity out going on two months, the house wasn't just dark, it was cold. About forty degrees.

Jack tried to imagine the small kitchen without his mom standing there in her apron doing three things at once. His dad should have been sitting in his leather recliner reading out loud from whatever he'd picked up, regardless if anyone was interested. That's how he'd been—couldn't enjoy something unless everyone was involved. Both parents had been Jack's world in ways other kids could never understand. And though he'd known since his seventh birthday that they'd die one day—because they'd told him so—that knowledge didn't ease his pain one bit.

Jack grabbed the flashlight from the stainless steel island and stalked angrily through the living room. With barely a glance at the boarded-up windows, he went upstairs to yet more shuttered darkness, in search of the rest he needed but wouldn't get in that too-quiet house.

***

In the beginning, when his parents stopped going to work for fear of getting sick, they'd guessed rightly that trucks would stop delivering food to the supermarkets. They'd further assumed desperate people might take from others if it meant their families could eat. As the Sickness raged, it quickly became obvious the quarantines were

2

useless. In the end, the news people on TV—visibly sick through their heavy makeup—as much as said so. Everyone got sick, but only kids ever recovered, and only about twenty percent. That's how it worked. Adults and the older teenagers wasted away over a course of weeks and months, and then they died.

The electricity lasted a little longer than the newscasters, whose final broadcasts turned bleaker and bleaker. Scientists had learned a little bit—the Sickness was a metabolic disease that attacked the mitochondria in cells, interfering with their ability to turn fuel into energy. But though they got better at describing in detail the effects of the disease, they never found a cause. No pathogen or poison had been discovered, leading one flustered contributor to refer to it as a *curse*, and not a virus.

As the adults disappeared, gangs of kids emerged, going door to door demanding food from those too sick to resist. In response, Jack's parents—still in the early stages of the disease—hammered up the boards, established a watch rotation, and made sure all three floors had a gun: rifles upstairs, and pistols on the main floor and basement. An emergency hoard of beans and rice kept them fed while most of the world slowly died from not just the Sickness, but starvation.

If only the Sickness had killed in a week, the adults would have left behind a world of packed supermarkets and pantries. But the disease could take months to kill, and the food disappeared.

***

Pounding on the front door shook Jack from his troubled doze. He knew instantly who it was, but peeked out his parents' bedroom window to be sure. Standing in the street facing the house was a group of teenagers ranging between twelve and fifteen years old. There were also three cars and a yellow Humvee that hadn't been there before. Each boy or girl was armed. One of them—a tall, redheaded boy—had a carbine of some kind slung around his neck like a Marine. Probably an AR-15, like the one Jack's dad had. Serious firepower.

The redhead cupped his mouth and shouted something.

3

Jack unlatched the window and raised it all the way up.

The boy shouted again: "Hey! In the house!" He reached through the window of one of the cars and honked the horn.

Some laughed at that. Some didn't.

The boy was so big, it was amazing he'd survived the Sickness, unless he was just a really large fifteen year old. His voice carried a sense of confidence and power, and his friends seemed to defer to him in their body language. It also helped that he had the coolest gun.

Jack's father had taken him deer hunting four years straight, the last time a year ago. He'd let Jack bring down a buck of his own on his tenth birthday and then made him field dress it. Shooting the older boy with his dad's rifle would have been the easiest thing in the world. The thick boards over the windows were spaced for concealment and protection while allowing a clear view of the front yard and street. If he shot him, the rest would scatter, and he'd be safe. Sooner or later, though, standing watches alone with no sleep and trying to guard two entrances would take its toll. Also, he wasn't sure he was ready to kill someone. Not in cold blood. Which was why he'd decided to leave. With the burials concluded, he'd hoped to slip out early tomorrow, start fresh, but there was zero chance of that now.

"I know you can hear me," the boy shouted.

"Yeah, I hear you," Jack yelled back.

The boy smiled, big and showy. "Someone said you buried your momma. I would say sorry to hear it, but I'm not. Their time is over. I'll make it simple: we want your food. Guns, too." He laughed. "We know you have at least one. Also, you're gonna join us. Do what I say, no questions, and you get to eat. If you don't, you need to get out and keep going. That's the rules."

Beside him, a wild-looking girl held up a gas can and shook it. "Better hurry, too, or we'll burn you out!"

The crowd around her hooted and yelled and punched their fists in the air. The older boy seemed oblivious to that. He just stood there confidently, staring up at the window.

4

"And who makes the rules?"

"That'd be me," he said, head cocked to the side as if trying to figure something out. "Come on out. You know it makes sense."

"Tell you what," Jack said. "You stay there while I think about it. Maybe invent some fun new rules while you wait."

The girl's shrill voice carried over the mob. "We won't warn you again!"

After a quick look out the back window—kids there too, just outside the fence—Jack tugged down the stepladder to the attic, climbed up, and pulled it shut behind him. He turned on his LED flashlight and moved to the wall they shared with the next-door townhouse. A month ago, before the two neighbors there died, that wall had been smooth plywood blocked by boxes of old stuff. Now there was a hole in the middle barely wide enough for Jack to slip through in an emergency.

He'd known for a while now the house was being watched. His dad's AR-15 leaned against the wall next to the jacket he planned to take and the backpack of supplies his mother had packed for him. She'd called the pack a *bugout bag* and had stuffed it with so much food it nearly tipped him over the first time he'd tried it on. Since then, he'd replaced some of the food with fishing gear, a book his dad had wanted him to read, and a small selection of family photos. He'd also packed extra ammo for the rifle and the .40 caliber on his hip. Both guns were about half metal, half plastic, and he hoped he wouldn't be forced to shed more weight when he started walking. He liked the rifle and hoped to use it for hunting.

The sound of shattered glass carried from downstairs. Quickly and quietly, he passed the rifle and pack through the hole and climbed through. Then he pulled the big box with his mom's old wedding dress in front of the opening to hide his escape.

The neighbor's attic wasn't nearly as packed as Jack's. Just a few boxes stacked up near the floor entrance. Jack stepped around those, careful to place each foot squarely on the wooden planking so as not to bust through the ceiling, then made his way to another wall with a hole in it.

With no electricity, it had been a chore cutting these holes with his dad's various tools, but he'd managed to bust through four houses. He'd stopped there because the Asian kid lived in the fifth one.

Thinking back to yesterday's spectacle, he wondered if the kid was still alive. Maybe he was out there with that mob, right now.

In no time at all, Jack traversed each of the four connected attics. After listening for half a minute, he lowered his gear down to the second floor and followed after. The family who'd lived there had fled early on, before roadblocks made that nearly impossible for anyone else. He felt bad for them. They'd had a baby.

"Focus," Jack said quietly, then flinched at the crack of automatic gunfire outside. He revised his earlier assumption—it was an M4, not an AR-15.

What the hell is he shooting at?

Looking around the room, he wrinkled his nose at the sour stench of condiments rotting in the fridge. He'd searched the house before and found it empty of food, people, and pets. The family hadn't taken much. Mostly clothes, it looked like. A waste of space. One thing the world would never run out of was clothing. And if the Sickness didn't take him one day, he'd have an endless supply sitting on store shelves waiting for him to find.

"You survived it already," his weakening mother had said when he'd broached the subject. "That makes you immune."

Jack had just nodded. If it wasn't a disease—if it really was a curse like that news guest had said—none of the old rules applied.

More shots sounded from outside, back-to-back like the grand finale of a Fourth of July celebration.

He slipped out the back door and crept to the gate. At the last second, he stepped onto the horizontal rail and pulled himself up for a look. Four houses down, a group of boys stood on his deck. One of them opened the sliding glass door—purposely left unlocked—and went inside. A second later, pained yelling issued forth, bringing a grim smile to Jack's face. Another boy ran in after him, and then he screamed, too.

Jack hiked his pack a little higher on his back and ducked out into the common area between the houses. As he trundled along the fence deeper into the neighborhood, he wondered how anyone could be so stupid as to follow someone into a nail trap.

He shook his head. *What do you expect from a bunch of cabbages?*

TWO

On his seventh birthday, before they cut the cake and gave him his presents, Jack's parents sat him down for the *talk*.

"We're going to die one day," his mother had told him, quite simply.

"What?" Jack said, staring uncomprehendingly between them.

His dad smiled gently. "Hopefully a long time from now, but yes, we're going to die. You will too, but that's a long ways off. With a little luck and lots of brains, you'll be just fine."

Jack knew what death was. His parents had explained the process at his *last* birthday, when he'd turned six. In the years that followed, they'd continued the pattern of shocking reveals at every birthday. And even though he always got cake and presents, he'd quietly come to dread each year's passage.

Seven-year-old Jack's eyes welled with tears. "Why do we have to *die*, mom? What for?"

She pulled him into her lap and hugged him. "It's just what happens." When he cried harder, she made him face her. "Jack, listen. Your father ... and me too ... we believe we go somewhere when we die. Do you understand?"

"Like Heaven?" Jack said, staring between the two in wonder. He'd heard about Heaven from his new friends,

8

Greg and Lisa.

Jack's dad cast her a surprised glance, then looked at him and smiled. "Uh ... you bet, mister. Heaven. Right, hon?"

His mom nodded. Then she nodded again, more emphatically. "That's right. But that's not what we wanted to talk to you about. Not about Heaven. Okay?"

"Okay," Jack said, shifting in her lap.

They went on to explain how they'd never planned to have children. They'd been too busy doing other things and had decided against it. Then one day, after they had done all the things they wanted to, they changed their minds. But then they had a problem: their bodies were too old. To *conceive*, she'd said. Rather than give up, they went to the doctor's office to get help. When they found out no doctors would help them—because of her age—they left the country to find one who would.

"You're not old," Jack said, shaking his head at the absurdity.

"Maybe not to you," she said. "How old do you think I am?"

Jack thought about it for a good while, then shook his head. "I don't know. But not a lot."

"I'm sixty-two," she said. "Your father's sixty-five. If he lives to be eighty, I'll be seventy-seven and you'll be twenty-two."

He started to cry again. "And then what happens? You die?"

His dad laughed kindly and ruffled his hair. "Your mother and I could live to be a hundred years old, buddy, but that's very difficult to do. With our healthy diet, I'm pretty sure at least one of us will make it to ... oh, eighty-five at least. But then we wouldn't be able to take care of you. So you'll have to be your own man as soon as possible. You need to be a survivor. Do you know what that means? A survivor?"

Jack shook his head.

"That's okay, son. There's still plenty of time to teach you."

"That and more," his mom added.

Over the years that followed, up until the Sickness came and everyone started dying, they prepared him against the day they wouldn't be there. When other kids were playing video games or watching TV, Jack was learning advanced math, science, and history, and he took karate classes. His parents didn't trust public schools to teach him to be a survivor, so they taught him at home and drove him to take the state's required tests. That's how he'd met Greg and Lisa Mitchell—fraternal twins, and his best friends.

In time, his parents included Greg and Lisa along on family hikes, and his friends invited Jack over for dinners and sleepovers and bike riding. Sometimes they'd go to an outdoor range where his parents liked to shoot targets. His mom had been an Olympic shooter in her younger years and liked to stay in practice.

While on hiking trips, his parents would call out times tables and advanced vocabulary words. Instead of ghost stories around the fire, his dad would talk about the ancient Greeks, or the terror of the Mongol empire, or World War Two and the tens of millions who'd died. A great storyteller, his voice could be loud and scary, or low and soft, as if confiding a terrible secret. The children would hardly interrupt for fear of derailing the stories.

When they weren't learning terrible and important secrets, they'd look in their plant books to identify the various species they found along the way, pointing out which ones were edible and which were poisonous. Every outing was like a new book filled with unknown adventures. Each trip a journey into a dangerous and magical world.

There were other trips Jack took—with his dad or mom and nobody else. He always felt a little uneasy about those because they didn't talk about history, or math, or science, or even war. Nothing so concrete or entertaining. Instead, they talked about the people around them.

***

Jack and his dad were sitting outside a coffee shop at the mall, resting their feet after a little shopping. His dad had coffee—no sugar, lots of cream. Jack had tasted coffee before and decided it wasn't for him, so he settled for hot chocolate.

"So what's their story?" his dad said.

"Uh, whose?"

His dad nodded pointedly *that way*.

Jack, ten at the time, followed the look and saw three big kids shoving a smaller kid and punching him in the arm. The smaller kid laughed like it was no big whoop, though he did rub his shoulder. Jack watched them carefully, knowing he was expected to think before offering an opinion.

A minute later, a couple of girls—very pretty—walked by carrying purses and bags, and the roughhousing settled down. One of the boys said something and the others laughed. In response, the lead girl turned her head and replied back in anger, bringing more laughter. When the girls were gone, the boys pushed rudely through the crowd and disappeared.

His dad looked over at him. "Well?"

"They seem like jerks."

"That's obvious enough. Why are they here?"

Jack sighed. "Probably just shopping."

"Is that how people shop?"

"Maybe they're resting. Like us."

"Is that how people rest?"

He smiled and shook his head. His dad never gave an inch. He'd ask questions like that all day until Jack got serious and engaged them properly.

"I guess they want to be here, even if they aren't shopping. And yes, I'm trying to figure out why." He'd almost added *sheesh* to the end of that, but stopped at the last second.

He closed his eyes to prove he was thinking about it. Now he was curious—just what the heck *were* those big kids doing here? Then he had it.

"They're here because they're bored?"

"Are you asking me or telling me?"

"Telling. I mean, why stand around hitting that kid? Why bother those girls? I think it's because there's nothing to do here if you don't have money. Maybe they don't have money."

"So why are they here if it's so boring?"

Jack shrugged. "I guess wherever they came from is even *more* boring."

His dad didn't say anything for a moment, content to sip his coffee and wait on his son. Jack worried he'd find some other group to ask him about.

"Were you afraid of them?" his dad said suddenly.

Jack grinned. "Not from over here. I'd sure hate to be that one kid, though."

"What if you'd walked over near them? Would you have been afraid then?"

The obvious answer was they liked to hit smaller kids, and Jack was a smaller kid, so of course he'd be worried. They'd stared around at the bustling crowd with a troubling intensity, as if willing something dramatic to happen. And when the girls walked by, they'd treated it like a challenge, invading their peace for no other reason than the entertainment value of a few hurled insults.

"Yeah, I'd be afraid," Jack said at last. "They're big kids. And they're bored. They might hit me or call me names. But it makes me mad."

"What makes you mad?"

"If I want to walk over there, or anywhere, I shouldn't have to worry about them. If they're not shopping, they should go home."

Finally, his dad got that look in his eyes that said the questions were done with.

"Well, son, here's an encouraging thought: when you grow up, you won't have to worry about cabbages like that hitting you in the arm. In fact, they'll probably fear you more, no matter how big they are."

Cabbages.

His dad liked to split the world into two groups: cabbages and weeds. Cabbages, he'd once said, needed farmers to take care of them. They grew in rows and would die quickly without water and fertilizer. Weeds, on the other hand, were prickly and tenacious, and if you wanted them dead you had to dig out the roots or they'd come right back. Weeds were survivors.

Jack said, "Why would they ever be afraid of me?"

"Because you'll be their employer, or you'll employ people like them. Now, on that note ..." He groped around in his bookstore bag. "I bought you something. Trust me, it's good."

He took out a thin paperback with a boring cover titled, *The Autobiography Of Benjamin Franklin*. Jack's heart sank a little, but only for a moment. His dad was many things, but none of them were boring.

"You know the rule, Dad," he said, grinning. "If I read one of your books, you have to read one of mine." He pulled out a book from his own bag and set it on the table.

Looking at the book, with lasers and giant robots fighting on the cover, his dad grimaced. "Megabots?"

"You'll love it," Jack said, smiling impishly. "Lots of symbolism. You know how much you love symbolism."

"Is that right?"

The two of them laughed and enjoyed the moment. A bit later, his dad's face grew serious. "I think you'll like learning about old Ben. Not much symbolism from what I remember, but he ran away from home."

Jack blinked in surprise. He wanted him reading about runaways?

"Are you and mom trying to cut back on bills?"

At the sight of his father's frown, Jack realized he might have pushed too far.

"Young Ben ran away because he wanted to start a business. He was fourteen years old. Think about that."

Jack thought about it, frowning in concentration for added effect.

His dad leaned over and fixed him with a considering eye. "In my opinion, Ben was a slacker. Your eleventh birthday is next week. That's the day you start your own business. It's a lot of work, but I think you're up to it."

Jack shook his head, not quite believing what he was hearing. His parents had moved their yearly bombshell announcement up by an entire week.

THREE

Jack entered the clearing where the main path diverged in the direction of Chantilly and shrugged off his heavy pack. Despite the cold, he'd removed his jacket before crossing the bridge over the creek near the park entrance. The steady wind painted his back in bands of chilled sweat.

Though he hadn't traveled more than half a mile, he needed to rest. Shaking his head in frustration, he forced himself to accept the sorry fact that his pack was still too heavy by at least fifteen pounds. Most of it from food, but he didn't want to shed any more of that. Now that he no longer had his mom's survival pantry, he regretted his original decision to try living off the land. He should have brought more food and less ammo. If he hadn't been so concerned about someone breaking in while he was out, he would have relocated the pantry out here and buried it in trash bags. Woulda-shoulda-coulda.

"Christ, it's cold," he said, mostly to hear his own voice.

A new and unfamiliar sense of vulnerability swept over him, and he mourned his parents' fate from a different perspective. If they'd lived, he wouldn't be out here in the cold faced with starvation, forced to flee an armed-to-the-teeth gang of cabbages.

He immediately regretted the unworthy thoughts, and tried not to hate himself for having them. His parents had helped him understand he couldn't always control how he felt about things. It was part of being human. All he could do was confront those feelings, sit with them, and try to disarm them.

His mom had called it *tracing it back*—a way of figuring out how he felt way down deep and peeling his emotions away one layer at a time until he uncovered the truth. The first time he used it, he'd traced back why he was angry at a neighborhood friend who'd played a mean trick on him. He'd learned it wasn't the trick, so much, but rather the shame of having trusted someone so easily that they *could* hurt him.

Standing in that clearing, Jack did his mom's old exercise and traced it back, digging down to why he felt so angry at them. He'd gotten pretty good at figuring out why he felt things. Having parents like his, with their crazy-but-not-so-crazy questions, had done it to him. A blessing and a curse, he figured. This time it was a blessing, because he hated feeling like they'd abandoned him.

If only they hadn't waited so long to have him. He could have spent more time with them. They could have been like normal parents who didn't turn everything into a survival lesson. Now he was stuck with their unfair expectations. He had to survive—had to be strong—and if he couldn't, then everything they'd done and said would get sucked away into the nothingness of death, and nobody would remember who any of them were.

"There you go, Mom," he said huskily, looking back the way he'd come. "It's traced."

Way off over the trees, an oily column of black smoke curled into the sky. Though he couldn't be sure without going back, Jack knew what it was. Those idiots had poured gasoline onto his house and lit it. Probably because of the nail trap he'd set, or maybe because they had gasoline and wanted to burn something and any reason would do. Anyone still alive in the last four houses would have heard the gunshots and noticed the fire, so he wasn't *too* concerned about that.

Despite losing his house and all their stuff, he wasn't angry. He hated the idea of people pawing through their photo albums and family heirlooms. This way, the smoke was carrying it to Heaven.

Jack smiled at that. In the years following his seventh birthday, he'd figured out his parents didn't really believe in Heaven. And yet, for some reason, Jack still did. Well, a little. He never talked to them about it, and they never broached the subject. It felt good believing. And because he liked how it felt, he'd never traced it back to find out why.

When he glanced down along the path, Jack saw the Asian kid walking his way from their neighborhood. Too far to yell at, but at the boy's pace they'd meet in a few minutes. Making it seem casual, Jack snapped the loop free on his holster and rested his hand there.

"That's far enough," he said when the kid was about ten yards off.

The boy stopped. Up close, he looked about twelve or thirteen.

"Where are you going?" the boy said.

"Somewhere. Why are you following me?"

The boy shrugged. "Because you're not with those freaks back there. They're nuts."

Jack grew alarmed. "Did they see you coming this way?"

"No," he said.

"Did they burn down my house?"

He shrugged. "Didn't see. Probably." He looked around the clearing. "Why are you out here?"

"What's your name?"

"Pete. What's yours?"

A moment passed where Jack struggled with what to say next. Trust had to be earned, sure, but people still needed a chance.

"Jack Ferris," he said at last. "I'm off to see some friends of mine, see if they're all right. After that, who knows?"

In truth, he and his parents had already planned out his destination, but he was keeping that to himself until he found his friends.

Pete bit his lip. "Can I come with you?"

The boy was scrawny from lack of food. Possibly near starvation. Scared, certainly. Other than that, he looked healthy, despite having crashed into a tree yesterday. Still, he could be unbalanced. His parents were almost certainly dead by now.

Looking down at his too-heavy pack, Jack realized that with help he wouldn't have to shed any more weight. He could divvy it up.

"What are you doing?" Pete said.

"If you're going to come with me," he said, digging through his pack, "we have to share the load. You okay with that?"

Pete frowned as if puzzling over a bizarre concept. Then he nodded.

"Here, eat this."

Pete caught the protein bar Jack tossed him and tore into it without saying thank you.

For the next five minutes, Jack split the contents of the pack into two uneven quantities. He kept his flashlight, his clothes, his collapsible fishing rod and tackle, all the ammunition, and half the food. He stacked the rest of the food, the tent, his sleeping bag, the rechargeable batteries, the fuel for the camping stove, and the mess kit onto a lightweight tarp and then cinched it up with a length of cut parachute cord.

"When we get into the woods," Jack said, "we'll find a stick you can tie it to. Kind of like a hobo."

"A what?"

"A hobo. You know what a hobo is, right?"

Pete shook his head.

He stared at him in disbelief. *How could someone not know about hobos?*

Jack picked up the tarp, hefted its weight, and handed it over. "Hobos are people who carry stuff on sticks. Got it?"

Pete nodded, holding the bag out in front of him.

"It'll be easier if you sling it over your shoulder, like Santa. You know who Santa is, right?"

"You still believe in Santa?"

Jack smiled. "No, but I like the holiday specials. You okay, man?"

Pete nodded and slung the makeshift pack over his shoulder. "Which way to your friend's house?"

Jack showed him a nearby signpost describing the trails

in the area. It had a little mark showing where they were. They'd barely made a dent into the park.

"We'll go this way," Jack said, following one of the paths with his finger to where it met a squiggly blue line. "There's a road just beyond where the sign ends. We'll cross the highway and stick to this creek here. It cuts between a bunch of neighborhoods. My friends live in one of them." He stared at the kid thoughtfully. "You sure you're okay?"

"Why do you keep asking me that?"

"Because you crashed a car into a tree yesterday. What was that about, anyway?"

Pete looked at him like he was crazy. "I was trying to learn to drive. I'm fine."

Jack didn't push him. He'd watched his parents drive countless times, so he knew the theory behind it. When the Sickness swept the world, they'd pushed to teach him, sensing he'd need to know how. He'd resisted. Stupid of him, he now realized. But at the time, learning felt like giving up on them. Then his dad died and his mom got sick. After that, leaving the house meant leaving his mom and their food unguarded, so he hadn't bothered.

Together, they set off down the trail. The clearing fell away and they entered a stretch of woods. From time to time, houses popped into view through the trees, and twice they had to cross bridges over the creek that twisted through the park. During the summer, every opportunity to look in that creek revealed turtles, frogs, and water snakes.

They didn't see people, and as cold as it was, there weren't any animals other than squirrels. An hour later, they came out of the woods onto a single-lane road.

"You might feel like following the road," Jack said. "But we can't get caught out during the day. Not with all our stuff. I don't feel like shooting anyone, and I honestly don't want to get shot. We'll cut across and stick to the plan. All right?"

"Why do you keep talking like that?"

Jack frowned in genuine puzzlement. "Like what?"

"Like an adult or something. Because you're not."

Jack smiled sadly. "Too bad for us, huh?"

Pete opened his mouth to reply and then closed it.

Together, they resumed their march on the other side, this time without a path to travel by.

FOUR

The creek they followed was called Big Rocky Run. It was neither big, nor very rocky. And if it didn't exactly run, it made up for that by meandering around neighborhood after neighborhood, hiding them safely from sight. The way was thick at times with brambles they had to skirt, and other times they could walk easily beneath evergreens or through fields of tall, dry grass. Jack and his parents had hiked up and down this stretch of secluded parkland countless times, so he didn't need a trail or even a map.

He couldn't believe how slowly they were going. He kept having to stop, turn around, and go back to make sure Pete was okay. He was never okay—usually, he was resting. Once, Jack found him following a split in the trail leading to a neighborhood of single-family homes.

"Where the hell are you going?" Jack said.

Pete turned around dazedly and said, "How did you get behind me?"

After that, Jack made sure to stick closer for fear he'd wander off again.

When they finally made it to another road—Route 28—it was a half hour past dusk and too dark to see unless they used Jack's flashlight. Beyond the road, the creek continued through more scrub and woods. From there, it would carry clear out to Fairfax. Greg and Lisa lived considerably closer than that. A good two more hours of hiking and he'd be very close to the twins' apartment complex.

"When are we stopping?" Pete said for perhaps the tenth time, swinging the pack to his other shoulder. He'd tried the hobo thing, but reverted back after five minutes, complaining the stick hurt too much.

Also for the tenth time, Jack said, "Just a little farther."

"It's freezing out here."

Jack turned and regarded the heavily breathing boy in the meager light.

"The more you move, the warmer you get. Didn't your family ever go hiking?"

"Are you kidding?" Pete said. "We didn't do stuff like that. That's how you get ticks. Ticks have Lyme disease."

"You never did Boy Scouts?"

"*Lyme* disease, man. No way."

In truth, Jack was laying it on a bit thick. He'd never been in the Boy Scouts either, even though he'd wanted to. He'd launched a pretty good campaign to join. But just when he thought his parents would relent and let him sign up, they went out and bought a bunch of hiking gear, instructional videos and books, and that was the end of his merit badge dreams.

"We'll start our own Boy Scouts," his dad had said. "You can bring as many of your friends as you want with us. By doing it yourself, you can get in more hiking, and you'll learn more."

Being the good and dutiful son of his *doomed-to-die parents*, Jack had relented—but not before getting them to agree to let him attend public school. At first they'd said no. Then, a few days later, they came back and said they'd talked it over. If he wanted to try high school, it was his decision.

High school was five years off. They probably hoped he'd forget about it, but he never did. For some reason, he was fascinated with the idea of having his own hall locker.

Four years later, the Sickness happened, and high school became just another dream in a long list of stuff he'd never get to try.

One thing Jack's homegrown Boy Scout troop hadn't done was hike at night. Too much that could go wrong. Too hard to get help when something did. It was particularly foolish to try it *now*. But Pete's easy life and tick-phobic parents rankled him, and he didn't need to trace anything back to know why. Plain and simple jealousy. Not the smartest reason to stumble along in the dark and risk breaking an ankle in a world without paramedics and doctors, but there it was.

"All right, fine," Jack said. "But we're not staying in any houses. We'll go up the road and find an office or something."

"A house might have a fireplace. And blankets. Just saying."

"And food gangs looking for smoking chimneys," Jack said, though his will weakened at the thought of a fire.

"We'll put it out in the morning," Pete said. "There's a trail to that neighborhood like ten minutes back. Remember?"

Now that they weren't moving, the cold began to creep into Jack's bones. The wind whipped up and carried down the empty four-lane highway, making the world seem that much colder. Jack hated the thought of walking down that wind tunnel for three miles, but he didn't want to show indecisiveness in front of Pete.

"We need to find you a backpack," he said, sizing the other boy up. "That has to hurt your shoulders."

Pete grunted. "*Big* time. So we gonna go back or what?"

Jack paused in quiet reflection, as if mulling over a particularly thorny math problem. Then he nodded. "Sure. You lead the way."

Pete breathed a sigh of relief, turned around, and headed back down into the scrub.

Jack felt a different kind of relief. A year ago, he'd read the harrowing tale of Sir Ernest Shackleton, the polar explorer trapped with his men in Antarctica in the early twentieth century. Facing certain doom, if not for the man's legendary leadership, he and his crew would have died. One of the things he did was make sure his men stayed busy, and that he never showed indecisiveness.

Everything he did had a purpose, or at least he made sure it seemed that way.

As they made their way back, Jack marveled that he suddenly thought of Pete as *his men*.

***

"What the hell is he doing?" Pete said.

They were lying under a truck in front of the house they'd chosen. Someone was walking down the street busting out car windows. Every time he came to a car, he'd smash a window and howl. Thankfully, he was moving away from them. Jack saw curtains move in one of the houses, but nobody came out to challenge the boy.

"No idea, and I don't want to ask him. Come on."

As they approached the house, his heart sank. The front windows were broken in. The house had a perfectly good chimney, too, but all the chimneys in the world were useless without windows to keep in the heat.

"Shit," Pete said, shaking his head. "You think it was that kid?"

"Who knows?"

The windows in the next house were also smashed in. Same thing with the one after that. Meanwhile, the sound of smashing glass carried to them every minute or so. Also, a terrible stench was growing the farther they went—the smell of decaying bodies. By busting open the windows, the kid had allowed the smell of the dead to seep out into the night.

"God, it stinks," Pete said, retching involuntarily.

"That kid's a menace," Jack said in a tight voice, nose wrinkling at the stench. "We need to get out of this area. We'll see which way he goes, then go the other way."

The two observed from a distance as the destructive kid worked his way to an intersection. A second later, a car appeared and stopped in front of him. Jack and Pete crouched down behind a parked car and watched.

Angry shouting carried from the car. The boy with the bat laughed a loud, fake laugh and ran. Then the car pulled away.

When Jack thought it was safe, they stood quickly and jogged up the street. A different neighborhood began farther on.

"Hey, you two," someone said behind them.

Jack turned and saw the bat-wielding vandal standing alone on the sidewalk. In height and build, Jack pegged him at thirteen.

"Hey yourself," he said, hand resting casually on the butt of his pistol.

"What's in that backpack? How about that bag? Probably something to eat, right?"

Jack shrugged, then realized it wasn't visible in the gloom. "Just some junk we found. No food."

Pete said, "Go on, leave us alone."

The boy issued a weird giggle. "Maybe I will and maybe I won't."

Pete whispered, "The dude's schizo. Let's go."

Jack nodded, and together they started walking. When they looked back, the boy was gone.

They continued into a less upscale neighborhood composed of duplex dwellings. On the bright side, it appeared the kid with the bat hadn't progressed this far in his lonely rampage. Nothing looked smashed up. Sadly, none of the houses had chimneys. They passed through quickly and moved into a better neighborhood.

The house they eventually chose was down a long, looping stretch of single-family houses that ended in a cul-de-sac. The front door had been pried open at some point, judging from the marks around the jamb and the missing doorknob.

Pete sighed. "I bet everything good's been taken."

Feeling like a scavenger and not liking it, Jack said, "Come on," and pushed inside.

Upon entering, the rank smell of putrefying flesh invaded from everywhere, causing him to cover his nose.

"Jesus!" Pete said, and backed out of the house.

A few seconds later, Jack followed him.

"I'm ... not ... staying in there," Pete said between retching sounds.

Jack nodded. "I know what you mean."

Just as he decided to cross the street and try another house, there came a brightening in the distance followed by a flash off a stop sign.

"Quick, back inside," Jack said, prodding him.

Pete started to argue, then gasped when a car appeared.

Jack shoved in behind him and peeked out the peephole. Twenty seconds later, the street got brighter, then darker as the car passed in front of the house. There were two people in the front seat and two in the back. Light flared suddenly from the side window, blinding him briefly, and then they'd passed.

There was a window next to the door with the curtains pulled shut. Jack nudged them aside and peeked out for a better look. The backseat passengers had a couple of those million-candle flashlights used by rescue teams and police. They were sweeping the huge beams here and there, as if searching for something.

In time, they rounded the little cul-de-sac and started back. As the lights from the car passed over the house, Jack shut the curtain—then mentally swore. He held his breath, willing the car to continue up the street. It crept slowly along and stopped with its headlights angled toward the house. A long, steady car horn issued forth, causing them both to flinch. Then someone got out and came around to the front of the car.

"What's going on?" Pete said.

"You know how to shoot?" Jack said, unslinging his dad's rifle.

"Just in video games. My mom said I'm a pacifist."

Before he could reply to the absurd statement, the boy outside shouted, "Who's in there?"

The AR was loaded, but not chambered. Jack drew his pistol—finger off the trigger like his mom had shown him, barrel safely pointed ahead of him and down.

Cracking the door an inch, he yelled, "Who are you?"

"Doesn't matter," the boy said. "How old are you?"

Jack thought quickly. Too young and they'd probably storm the house. Too old and they wouldn't believe him.

"Fourteen—and three quarters."

He'd invented that last part.

"What are you doing here? You're supposed to be at the school. Didn't you hear?"

Jack looked back at Pete and said, "You know what he's talking about?"

The boy nodded. "They went door to door telling people. I guess they skipped your house."

Or maybe they saw us outside with guns.

To keep the conversation going, he shouted, "What school?"

"The high school. Where you from, man?" Before Jack could reply, the boy added, "Come on out. We're supposed to round up everyone and meet there. There's food. We'll drive you. Anyone's with you, they can come too—except, no little kids. They gotta stay. That's the rules."

The rules.

For the second time that day, Jack said, "Who makes the rules?"

"Blaze makes the rules."

Jack couldn't help but laugh. "There's actually someone who calls himself *Blaze?*"

"He's in charge. He can do what he wants. That's also the rules. And don't make fun of his name."

"Sounds sort of dumb. I think I'll stay here. Thanks anyway."

Someone in the car asked what was going on and the boy waved him off.

To Jack, he said, "You're that guy, aren't you? The one at the house we burned. I recognize your voice from earlier. Man, Blaze was pissed when you snuck out."

Then it dawned on him: Blaze was that bully with the red hair and machine gun who'd threatened to burn his house down—and had actually done so, apparently. Probably had to burn a lot of houses to live up to his invented name.

The boy outside glanced furtively back at the car, then took a few steps forward. From Jack's vantage, he was even skinnier than Pete.

Another kid climbed stealthily out of the back window of the car and approached behind him.

In a quieter voice, the skinny kid said, "Some guy with a bat said someone came this way with a bunch of food. It was you, wasn't it? Listen, if you stuff something for me in

26

those bushes"—he indicated the decorative shrubs in front of the big bay window—"I'll tell the guys you don't have anything. Then I'll come back later and get it. No one has to know."

"Mitch, you're a useless backstabber," the kid behind him said. "Get back in the car!"

Jack witnessed a look of sheer terror cross Mitch's face before he fled back to the car and got in.

"I want all your shit," the newcomer said, holding up a gun for him to see. "Now, or we mess you up *big* time and take it anyway."

Gritting his teeth, Jack cracked the door wider, took aim with his pistol, and blew out one of the car's headlights. In the enclosed space, with no ear protection, the blast surprised him.

Pete screamed.

The gun had twelve more rounds. Jack shifted his aim to the other light and shot that out, too. Now it had eleven.

The boy fired wildly and ran for the suddenly moving car. He leapt for the swinging door, then slammed into it when the driver hit the brakes, bashing him edge-on and sending him sprawling. The car started moving and stopped again when the boy got up. This time, he succeeded in getting inside. The driver swerved back and forth as if dodging bullets. At one point, the car went up on the sidewalk, and sparks shot out from where the undercarriage struck the curb. A second later, it was back on the street again and speeding away.

FIVE

Jack shut the door and turned to Pete. "They'll be back. Pretty soon, I think. Especially after they tell this Blaze person I'm here."

"After what you did?" Pete said. "You shoot like a boss. No way they'll come back."

"Humans like to hunt," Jack said. "Those guys have nothing else to do, and this leader of theirs probably wants to keep them busy. You ever hear of Shackleton?"

"Shacka-who? What's that have to do with hunting?"

Jack dug out his flashlight, clicked the switch, and pointed it at the ground. Pete looked badly shaken, but still in control. His shirt was pulled up over his nose against the stink. A brief look around showed no bodies, just furniture, confirming the owners had likely died upstairs.

"Those video games you played had guns," he said. "You chased people around trying to shoot them, right?"

"Yeah," Pete said, "but that's not the same thing. Video games aren't real."

"Even better—you had no good reason for committing violence except for the thrill of violence. You were hunting and shooting humans for no reason. For fun." He snorted. "Some pacifist."

"They weren't *real* humans. Just animation. It's not the same thing."

Jack's parents had never bought a video game console for him, though he'd once played a little at a mutual friend of Greg and Lisa's. It was really cool ducking around things and sneaking up on people, or trying to hide from people so they didn't shoot him. Weeks later, his dad asked why he enjoyed their hunting trips so much, and Jack made the connection.

He shook his head. "Fine. Listen, these kids out there— they've lost their whole world. They don't have video games anymore, or adults to tell them to leave people alone. Just the opposite. If you were listening, this Blaze freak is telling them to go out and bring home the dinner. You ever get bullied in school? Someone ever hit you in the arm a bunch of times because you were littler?"

After a brief hesitation, Pete nodded.

"Those are the people we're up against," Jack said. "Except *these* kids have guns, cars, and hunger. They probably wish they'd died but don't know it yet."

Pete shivered in the darkness. Though the house was just as cold as outside, at least there was no wind.

"If you're right," Pete said, "what can we do?"

"We leave. The high school is about five minutes away by car. That's five to get there, five to gather more people, and five to come back. You want something from here, I suggest you go get it. I recommend a blanket. That jacket of yours is kind of skimpy."

In barely more than a whisper, Pete said, "Maybe we should have gone with them."

Jack was about to snap something back when, from out of the darkness, a girl's voice said, "Can I come too?"

Both boys whipped around and stared at the figure of a young black girl crouched behind a sofa chair, blinking in the beam of Jack's flashlight. About eight or nine years old, she had on green pants and a puffy pink jacket, and her hair was collected in a cascade of glossy tails bound in fat white beads.

"Who the hell are you?" Pete said, fists raised protectively.

"Ease up," Jack said. He took a knee and smiled. "I'm Jack. What's your name?"

"Mandy," she said. "My mom and dad died." She said it flatly, as if delivering a trivial piece of news.

Jack nodded sadly. "Mine too. Do you live here?"

She shook her head. "Uhn uh. All the doors are open, but everywhere stinks inside."

Jack looked at her closely. She was thin like Pete, except more pitiful for her youth, and he felt guilty for having eaten so well during the Sickness.

"Are you hungry?"

She nodded vigorously. "Do you have something?"

"Sure," he said. He nudged Pete, who got a protein bar from his bag and handed it to her. "Now listen, Mandy, we need to get out of here. But we can't take you. Lots of hard walking ahead. You need to group up with the other kids your age and—"

"And what?" Pete said in a sharp tone.

Jack glared at him.

Mandy's eyes welled with sudden tears, and her face grew tense. "I had a friend named Courtney. She did my hair like this. Then some boys got her and she told me to run. When I came back, she was gone."

Pete said, "You hear that, man? You just gonna leave her?"

"No, Pete. Obviously I'm going to save the world. Is that what you want to hear?"

Immediately, he regretted his tone. Bringing anger to the situation wouldn't help.

Mandy watched the exchange with a frightened fascination on her face, as if everything hung in the balance. Which, in the new way of things, it did.

"I can keep up," she said. "That's how I got away. 'Cause I'm fast."

"You need to be," Jack said, already working out how they could do this. "You're not a pacifist, are you?"

Mandy shook her head, *no*.

To Pete, he said, "Hurry with that blanket, and meet us out front."

***

Pete came out with the makeshift bag wrapped in a blue blanket snagged from upstairs. Instead of Santa, he looked more like The Grinch after he'd stolen Christmas.

"We can't walk with her the whole way, not through those woods," Pete said. "And also, hey: I'm not sure you're right about that gang. Why would they come back after you shot at them? They're not stupid. I think you're just making it up as you go along."

"I *am* making it up as I go along," Jack said. "So what, you want to wait for them?"

Pete surprised him when he said, "Yeah, actually. If you're right, we'll keep following you. If you're wrong, Mandy and me are leaving."

Despite being a pain in the ass, Jack couldn't help but admire the other boy for his natural suspicion. He also appreciated his regard for the girl, but thought it was misplaced. There were way too many orphans now for anyone to help. Winter hadn't officially started yet. When it did, Jack's parents had predicted millions of so-called "survivors" would die from exposure and starvation.

"All right," he said, pushing those thoughts away. "We'll hide between those houses across the street. When they come back, we'll slip off to the next neighborhood and find a car. Then you'll finish learning how to drive."

"What?"

"You said it yourself: we can't walk the whole way, and definitely not with Mandy. So we need to drive—*without* crashing into any trees."

"I can keep up," Mandy said.

Jack smirked at Pete's sudden loss for words and started across with Mandy. A second later, Pete joined them.

"We'll wait here," Jack said, indicating the waist-high power transformer. "If they come, we'll hide behind it."

"*If?*" Pete said.

Jack sighed. "Just be ready to move if you see headlights. *When* you see headlights."

Ten minutes went by with the three of them sitting there on the military green transformer, waiting in the deepening cold. To her credit, Mandy didn't complain. Pete, when he wasn't talking, punctuated the silence with huffs and resigned sighs. Very irritating, particularly because it ramped up the situation more than it needed to be. Suggesting the gang was coming back hadn't been some divinely inspired prediction of a future event. It was a hedge against a dangerous possibility—that they might return and want to get even. Anyone who called himself *Blaze* had to have a huge ego, and that kid, Mitch, had said he was mad at Jack for escaping.

"It's been like an hour," Pete said at one point.

"Twenty minutes, tops," Jack said. "If they don't come, you're really leaving on your own?"

"I might."

Jack snorted. "Not with my stuff."

"You can't carry it all—that's why you need me."

True enough. Also true he'd make sure they left with half the food, for Mandy's sake, but Jack kept that to himself.

More time passed, and Jack began to think he'd been wrong. Just as he decided they should find a car with a full tank, light flared at the end of the street and a car roared their way, rap music thumping through the rolled-up windows. Then came another car. Then another. Now four cars were parked outside the house where they'd found Mandy. The music stopped and a group of about fifteen boys and girls with guns jumped out from every door and took up lazy positions around the cars.

Jack looked back at Mandy and held a finger to his lips: *shh.*

She covered her mouth and nodded.

He pointed behind them and whispered to Pete, "Head out that way and keep walking until you reach those houses. Can you see the playground?"

"Yeah."

"Hang out there until I come."

"You come too."

"In a minute," he said. "I need to see this. Don't worry, I'll be along."

Pete nodded, took Mandy by the hand, and slunk away. Jack watched them go, making sure they were headed toward the distant playground equipment, then turned to the food gang.

One of them was the girl from earlier today—the one

with the can of gasoline. All of them were of the older variety. About twelve to maybe fifteen years old. The news had said the older someone was the more likely they were to die of the Sickness. Gathering this many must have taken a lot of searching and a good amount of organization.

Jack's year had been spent worrying about his parents and watching them slowly die, so he hadn't had much time to think about himself or his friends, Greg and Lisa. The scientists said siblings had a better chance of either both dying or both surviving. With everything in him, he hoped for the latter. He couldn't imagine one twin without the other.

A minute later, another vehicle pulled up behind the others. A shiny, yellow Humvee. The door opened and Blaze got out. He made an impatient circling gesture with his hands, and his people fanned out in front of the house.

"Hey, kid," Blaze shouted, "you in there?"

He said something to one of the girls, and she approached the house. Hesitantly, she looked back.

"Get in there!" Blaze shouted, and she went in. He pointed at two nearby boys. "You and you, check those houses."

The boys nodded and grabbed tools from the back of one of the cars, then ran to the houses bracketing Jack's hiding place. He listened carefully for sounds of splintering wood, but didn't hear anything. Then he remembered the door to the house they'd gone in had been pried open.

The section between them was dark, and he was mostly hidden behind the transformer. Still, when Blaze swept the area with his gaze, Jack thought his attention lingered a fraction longer on his hiding spot, as if sensing his presence the way a dog might.

Several minutes later, the girl and the others came back and gave their reports.

Blaze raised his voice. "If you're there, come on out. You're smart, and a good shot from what I hear." The redheaded boy paused, waiting—for Jack to come rushing out with open arms, apparently. When that didn't happen, he added, "Maybe you ran again. Or maybe you're hiding somewhere listening to everything I'm saying. If you are, come by the high school and check out our setup. If you can find stuff and bring in good people, you eat. But if you cut deals behind my back, well ... I'll show you."

Blaze said something, and a bound and gagged figure was dragged from one of the cars. Jack was fairly certain the prisoner was Mitch, the skinny kid who'd offered to let Jack go if he hid food for him.

The gasoline girl pointed and laughed, but she was the only one.

It was dark out, so Jack hadn't seen the weapon strapped to Blaze's hip. When he reached for the sword and pulled it from its decorative scabbard, Jack could hardly believe his eyes. It was a rapier—long, sharp, and deadly. *Jack's* rapier.

Blaze grabbed his prisoner by the shirt and shouted, "If you're with us, you're with us. If you're not, you get to rot!"

Jack winced at the boy's muffled scream as Blaze drove the blade into his back. After he fell down, Blaze kept at him, stabbing him again and again to the cheers of the crowd around him.

SIX

For his eleventh birthday, a week after learning he had to one-up a runaway founding father and juvenile entrepreneur, Jack got a gift certificate to Atlantic Knives & Swords, a box of old kitchen knives, and a ledger book.

"Can I buy a sword, Dad?" Jack said, looking at the certificate for two hundred dollars in store credit.

"You thinking of chopping someone up?"

Jack rolled his eyes. "Is this about that business you wanted me to start?"

His dad nodded. "It sure is."

"How am I going to start a business?" Jack said. "Who wants to buy anything from me?"

That's when his mom chimed in. "I do, actually. I'll pay you twenty dollars to sharpen all my kitchen knives."

Jack shook his head. "How am I supposed to do that? I don't have, um ... the uh, what's it called again?"

"A *whetstone*," his dad said. "You can also use sharpeners, but they won't last very long, and they don't do a good enough job."

"I don't have a whetstone."

"That's why you have that gift certificate."

That afternoon, father and son went to the same shopping mall they'd seen the bullies in the week before. And even though there were lots of Saturday delinquents to question Jack about, they went straight to the shop and asked the man working the counter about whetstones.

The man, whose name was Henry, said they had a number of great stones, both coarse and fine. Perfect for restoring a blade from "death by a thousand broccoli cuts to factory perfection."

Though his dad seemed fascinated by the whetstones, Jack had eyes only for the swords.

The *swords!* Big and small. Wavy or curved or straight. Double-bladed or hooked near the end. Some were fantastical, with cool glyphs embedded in the steel and sparkling jewels in the hilts. Others were simpler in design, like out of history books. One wall had a bunch of samurai swords and tanto knives with wavy lines running up and down the blades.

"Can we get a sword?" Jack said when his dad came over to drag him back to the boring whetstones. "Please?"

Frowning in thought, his father turned to Henry. "How much is that stone you were telling me about?"

"That one's sixteen ninety-nine," Henry said. "It's double-sided. You're gonna want to level it first, and I recommend buying two for that purpose."

"You *do* have instructional books, am I right?"

Henry nodded. "Yep. Books are ten dollars each."

His dad bit his lip as if trying not to smile. "How much is that gift certificate again?"

"Two hundred dollars," Jack said.

"Well, then, we have to spend the rest on something, don't we?"

Jack's delighted grin was easily the brightest thing in the store that day. When they returned home, they did so with a book titled "Techniques In Sharpening," two double-sided stones, and a wickedly sharp rapier.

"What are you going to do with that sword?" his mom said when they got home.

Jack shrugged. "Hold it sometimes."

"And?"

He sighed. "Hang it on the wall in my room. Dad already said."

***

As neat as the sword was, Jack had to admit it wasn't much use except as a curiosity.

The front of the book directed him to a website with a video on sharpening. Totally fascinating. By the end of it, he wanted to start on the box of dull knives his dad had picked up from a thrift shop, but he had to read the book first. It wasn't long, and he skipped the section on serrated knives because he needed a file for those.

When he was ready, after soaking the stones in water the required amount of time, he set to work penciling a grid over each. Then he rubbed them together, just like the video had shown. Gently at first, and then with more force when he looked at the lines and saw uneven erasures in the pattern. It took about five minutes for the grid to vanish from each stone. It took longer to do the same for the fine stones because, being fine, they tended to remove less material.

Out of nowhere, his dad came up behind him and yelled, "*Boooooo!*"

Jack seized up, yelped, and nearly dropped a whetstone. "*Jeez*, Dad, what gives?"

His expression was serious. "What if you'd been holding a sharp knife just now?"

As irritated as Jack was at the childish prank, he had to concede the point. By concentrating so hard on grinding, he'd put himself in a position to be startled.

"It's not fair," Jack said. "I didn't expect you to do that."

"Of course not. I'm too sneaky. So what's the lesson?"

Jack shrugged. "You want me to lock the door?"

"And what if you cut yourself and fainted from loss of blood? How would we know?"

Jack thought about that.

"Your back was to the door," his dad said, relenting. "Turn your desk around and face it. Put your back to the wall, just like in the Old West. And try not to get so wrapped up in one thing you tune out the world. Very dangerous, not knowing what's going on around you. Got it?"

Jack smiled. "Yep. Got it."

The methods involved in knife sharpening were similar

across the world, with a few subtle differences. All traditions required the knife be raised at a twenty-degree angle. But the Japanese preferred a perfectly straight, back-and-forward approach, whereas the Europeans held theirs at a slant to the stone. More surface area per pass meant more muscle, and Jack quickly decided the Japanese approach would work best for him.

For the next two hours, he practiced the first stage of sharpening the various knives in his thrift store collection. He found he could get the blades a lot sharper the more he practiced. It was all about turning his body into a kind of a machine. If he thought about it too much, he'd mess up and press too hard on the forward slide or throw his angle off. But by rocking forward and back—this side, then that side, every ten passes—his knife got so sharp he could easily cut notebook paper into strips.

When he applied the same methods to the finer stone, he could cut a tomato in half, lay it flat, and then slice off super thin pieces without holding it. That kind of perfection took three more hours of sharpening, and by the time he was done, his muscles ached and his hands were trembling from fatigue. But he'd done it—he'd sharpened all the knives in the box.

"So what do we do now?" Jack said. "Sell them?"

His dad shook his head. "They're sharp, but they're not pretty, and we don't have a knife shop."

"So how do we start a business?" A second later, when his dad didn't answer, Jack's eyes widened. "Oh, yeah, I see. Hey, that's a cool idea."

His dad smiled. "It's what I did when I was your age. Pretty good money, too."

***

When his parents were kids, the world had been a lot different. Back then, children could buy cigarettes and work in coal mines. These days, an eleven-year-old who showed up at someone's door asking for knives to sharpen would warrant a frantic call to Child Protective Services. But nobody would object to a kid stuffing doors with flyers printed at an office supply store, so that's what he did. Even his mom helped out, doing one side of the street while he did the other.

For a mere twenty dollars, the wording promised "Ferris Knives" would sharpen up to eight knives to factory-milled perfection, smooth out notches, and drastically reduce the drudgery of food preparation.

By the end of the day, the Ferris family had handed out all three hundred flyers. By the middle of the next day, four people called the number on the flyer. Some of them wanted more than eight knives done. Some wanted serrated knives, and Jack's dad—who took the calls—said they were working on adding that to their list of services.

"We don't mind helping with your business," his mom said at one point. "But you can't pick up knives from people's houses."

Jack pulled a snarky grin. "Why not?"

"We'll get them for you," she said, ignoring him. "But that's a lot of driving, and your dad and I don't work for free. So you'll pay us five percent of whatever you make. That should cover gas, wear and tear on the car, and compensate us for our time. Deal?"

Jack stroked his chin like a shrewd businessman. "Would you take four percent?"

"No."

Jack rubbed his chin some more, then stuck his hand out. "Okay, deal."

Solemnly, they shook hands.

For the next month, he didn't remember a time when his fingers weren't sore. The flyers worked well. *Too* well. Satisfied customers told neighbors, friends, and family members, and rather than a slump after the initial canvassing, business increased. Pretty soon the home phone was ringing ten times a day, prompting another dip into his earnings to pay for a separate phone line and voicemail system. Jack was seriously considering telling his dad he'd learned his lesson—whatever that lesson was— just so he could take a break.

A week later, the new phone rang and his dad answered. He glanced at Jack, turned around, and spoke quietly for several minutes.

Before hanging up, he raised his voice. "Sure, Henry.

Great idea. You got a deal."

Jack—sensing he was somehow the topic of conversation—said, "What was that about?"

"That was Henry, from the knife shop. Seems he got an anonymous flyer in the mail. One of yours. His shop has a sharpening service, mostly for chainsaw blades and tools. He wanted to know if you'd be interested in picking up a little piecework."

"*And you said yes?*"

"Jack!" his mom said, shocked at his tone.

Jack swallowed. "Sorry, it's just ... ugh. I mean, this is a lot of work. I was hoping I could take a break. My fingers hurt."

His dad sat across from him with a perplexed look on his face. "Then why are you still doing everything by yourself?"

Jack opened his mouth to answer and then closed it again. It was a good question. A *great* question.

Greg and Lisa were fast learners, and just as enthusiastic about earning a few extra dollars as he had been. They split the commissions 25/25/50, in Jack's favor. After all, he had to pay for his parents' time, the phone line, advertising, new whetstones, and a set of sharpening files, apparently. To their credit, his friends didn't seem to mind.

Eventually, his dad created a sole proprietorship to keep the business as legitimate as possible—child labor laws notwithstanding. Jack, for his part, hastily learned double-entry accounting and helped with the taxes.

For the next two years, up until the Sickness went from a vague concern in the news to a full-blown panic, the three friends grew and managed their burgeoning business.

SEVEN

Jack lay motionless in the darkness, paralyzed with fear and disgust at the cold-blooded murder he'd just witnessed.

"Come on, dudes," Blaze shouted, waving Jack's sword over his head. "Fun's over."

The mean-looking girl jumped up on one of the cars and howled like a dog, bringing disgusted looks from the various boys and girls.

Blaze barely glanced at her. "Alice, quit screwing around and let's go," was all he said.

Alice stuck her tongue out, hopped down, and joined him in the big Humvee. After they left, Jack stood up and stared silently at the body in the street, stabbed through with his own sword. Something made for looking at, not for killing.

He turned around and started walking.

As he made his way across the field in the direction of the rendezvous playground, he thought about what he'd seen. There was more to it than simply Blaze being a crazy murderer. The violence had been controlled, with a purpose: to keep everyone in line, to instill fear. Saying he was nuts was a shortcut to a satisfying conclusion. In the new reality, where every house was a mausoleum, labels like *crazy* became harder to apply to people.

41

Then there was the matter of the sword. Jack would have loved to have brought it with him, but weight was an issue, and a sword was useless against a gun. So he'd left it on his bedroom wall. Now Blaze had it and was going around stabbing people. It turned Jack's stomach.

When he arrived at the playground, the place seemed empty at first. Then Pete crept out from behind a slide with Mandy and said, "Hey, what happened back there?"

Jack looked briefly at Mandy but didn't hold back. "Bunch of people our age, same ones from earlier today. That dude with the red hair was there."

"Blaze?"

Jack nodded. "He killed that one guy for trying to make a deal with us. Left him dead in the street."

Mandy gasped.

Jack said, "Looks like Blaze is making some kind of army. Wants as many older people as he can get. On the plus side, you'd probably get to eat regularly. On the other hand, you'd have to steal food, and you might get killed."

Pete snorted. "Screw that guy."

"Yeah," Mandy said.

Jack smiled briefly at her serious expression. Any reason to smile was good. "Hiking's out of the question, and I'm freezing. We need a car."

"Just one problem," Pete said. "To get the keys, we need to go into houses—maybe houses with other kids in them, or some adult who hasn't ... you know. *Yet.*"

Jack kept his face carefully neutral. His mom had died only yesterday. "We'll do what we have to."

Together, they slipped into the next neighborhood, this one filled with high-end townhouses. Jack's house had been built in the eighties. His parents had alternated semesters teaching at the university and mostly rejected extravagant living, preferring to save as much money for their son as they could.

"How about there?" Mandy said, pointing at the closest house—a corner unit with leafless rosebushes in front and on the sides.

Jack nodded. "Sure."

Mandy ran up and checked the door, then ran back.

"It was locked," she said.

The next house was also locked. As was the next. The one after that was wide open. A second later, they knew why. Lying in the tall, frosted grass was an emaciated man in his underwear, gnawed on by animals and dead for who knew how long.

"Jesus," Pete said, backing away from it. "If he lived here, I'm not going in."

"Me neither," Mandy said staring at it with a worried expression.

Jack shook his head. "Fine, stay out here with the dead body. I'll be right back."

Cautiously, he went in and shut the door behind him. After waiting a minute, listening for sounds, he turned on his flashlight and squinted against the too-bright light. The air smelled fresh when he lifted his nose and sniffed. It would have been nice to stay, but there wasn't a wood fireplace, and he had to admit the comfort of a warm car beckoned to him.

Quickly, he searched all the places someone might put a set of keys and found them on a hook in the kitchen.

"Got 'em," he said when he came out.

Nearly all the parking places were filled, and Jack was momentarily at a loss to find the right car.

"There it is," Pete said unnecessarily when Jack pushed the lock button, causing a newish four-door to beep and blink its lights.

Jack tossed him the keys, and Pete climbed behind the wheel. When he turned the key, it made an unhelpful clicking sound and the dashboard lit up, but that was it.

"Now what?" Pete said.

"We keep trying."

For the next thirty minutes, they went door to door looking in houses that had already been broken into. Well, Jack did, and sometimes Mandy. Most of the houses stank of death, and a few had bodies in the living rooms. Pete refused to go into any of them. Which was fine. The keys were usually easy to find, so Jack was never inside for very long.

Every car they found was dead, but the last one—a

newish four door—had started to turn over before running slowly down.

"I think we got something," Jack said. "Now we just need jumper cables and ..." He popped the hood and looked at the battery. "And a screwdriver. My knife has one built-in. Search the other cars for jumper cables. My parents used to keep a set in the trunk."

Pete's eyes were a little wild. "Are *you* gonna get the keys? I'm not going in any houses. I told you!"

Jack raised his hands for calm. "Relax, will you? Just bash the windows, like that kid we saw. Then look for a button. Or just unlock all the doors."

"But I don't have a bat."

"You can use a rock," Mandy said. She ran over to a lamppost with a ring of garden stones around it, grabbed one, and brought it back. "Like this!"

She threw the rock through the driver-side window of a nearby car. Predictably, it smashed in.

Jack smiled. "Yeah. Like that."

Ten more minutes and they had jumper cables. Another five, and Jack had a spare battery. He connected it the way his dad had shown him: red to red, black to black, but it didn't start. They found another battery, but that didn't work either. Two more cars and the results were the same. The rushing around kept them warm, but Jack was starting to feel like they were wasting their time.

"One more," Jack said, hooking up a battery he'd snagged from a big SUV, thinking maybe it had more oomph. This time *he* got behind the wheel. "If it doesn't work, we're walking."

It worked. A little sluggish, but it started.

"Yay!" Mandy shouted, jumping around.

Jack let it idle and got out. "I figure with half a tank, we should be good." He stared at Pete curiously. "How did you start that car yesterday?"

"My mother made me run it every three days, that's how. It was almost out of gas."

Jack was impressed. *Score one for Team Pete.*

Five minutes later, happy with the charge, Jack put the SUV battery in the trunk and their packs in the back seat with Mandy. Then he and Pete got in front, with Pete behind the wheel.

"You sure about this?" Pete said. "I almost got killed last time."

Jack looked at him steadily, taking his measure. "You'll be fine. How did you mess up before?"

"I tapped the gas when I meant to push the brakes. I was trying to use one foot, like you're supposed to."

"So use two this time," Jack said. "Figure out the other way later. Also, no lights. Just drive slow. *Real* slow."

Pete nodded, put the car in reverse, and jolted them out into the lane. Jack and Mandy jerked forward against the seatbelts, then back again when Pete slammed on the brakes.

"At least I didn't hit anything," Pete said sheepishly.

He put the car in drive and jerked it forward again while turning the wheel. Just barely, he managed to avoid hitting the bumper of a red minivan.

"Slower," Jack said. A second later he added, "And stop jerking it back and forth."

"Do you wanna drive?" Pete said, voice rising.

"No. Take a right up there."

Pete took the right up there, then a left, then drove for a mile and took Route 28 when instructed to. They hadn't seen any roadblocks yet, and Jack wondered if Blaze and his gang had been dismantling them. Most were civilian-made, not government. The government had mostly gone the route of the grocery store workers—stayed home, hid, and hoped the plague would pass. It was the regular citizens who'd blocked everything off. This had the benefit of keeping anyone with the Sickness out, but it also kept people trapped in their homes. And in the end it wasn't a benefit at all, because everyone still got sick.

"There's a car coming," Mandy said, pointing between the seats.

It took him a moment to see it, but she was right. Down the road, heading their way in the opposite lane, was a car with its lights off. Blaze and his gang had driven with their lights on, rap music thumping through the closed windows like they were on vacation in a world with no parents. This other car seemed more like their own—kids hiding out from the predators of a world with no parents.

The two vehicles slowed as they converged. The other driver was maybe ten years old, his face a mask of fear. There was a smaller boy in the back seat, his face pressed against the glass, staring at them.

"Freaky," Pete said after they'd passed. "How does he even reach the pedals?"

"Maybe has something tied to his feet," Jack said. "But yeah, that was weird. Now pay attention—we're coming up on the next turn. There, on the right."

Pete took the turn and found his first roadblock: two cars parked across the exit ramp between concrete walls.

"Shit," Mandy said.

Jack looked back at her. "Hey, no cussing."

"But I always cuss."

"Well, not anymore. You too, Pete."

Pete stared at him. "I didn't say anything!"

Jack pointed between the first two cars and said, "See if you can nudge it open there in the middle."

Pete swallowed nervously, then gingerly edged the car forward until the front bumper was very close to the gap. When the three cars touched, they rocked forward against their seatbelts, but the cars didn't move.

"More gas," Jack said.

Pete grunted and gave it some more, bringing a frightening crunch from the front as the hood buckled under the strain. A little more and the tires started spinning, then smoking, and then he gave up.

"Wait here," Jack said and got out. He approached the cars and scooted over the hood of the lowest. On the other side, running along the ground, were long wooden beams jammed through the drainage holes of each wall. Concrete had been poured messily on the other side—uphill— creating a four inch berm that tapered off with the grade. The tires on that side had been removed, leaving only rims, and the rims were jammed up against the beams. If they wanted to pass, they'd need a jack, or possibly a sledgehammer. And lots of time.

"It's no good," Jack said when he got back to the car.

Quickly, he described the situation. "Let's try the next exit."

The next exit had a barricade, though not so thorough. A school bus was angled across the lane. Sometime in the past it had been pushed aside, creating a barely passable gap. Pete scraped through it, setting Jack's teeth on edge. After that, they continued at an easy clip and didn't run into any more roadblocks.

Five minutes later, Jack pointed and said, "Take a right up here, back towards 50."

"What's 50?" Pete said, slowing to take the turn.

"How long have you lived around here?"

"Since I was little."

"And you don't know 50? It's a major road."

Pete shrugged. "I don't know road names. I'm not old enough to drive, remember?"

Jack didn't know a lot of public schoolers—cabbages, he reminded himself. Most of his interactions with them were at his karate classes, and even then, very limited. Those kids had been brash and whiney, and sometimes shockingly stupid. They didn't talk about the same sorts of things as Greg and Lisa. Usually stuff about football, or video games, or YouTube. Whenever he'd tried talking to them, they'd smirked or outright laughed every time he said something with three or more syllables.

Eyeing Pete, Jack had to remind himself the boy was cut from the same cloth. A decent enough guy, but ultimately clueless.

"What?" Pete said, looking faintly offended.

"Nothing. Just keep driving."

"Who died and made you boss?"

"Everyone who mattered died," Jack said, feeling tired. "I might not be your boss, but I'm going to find my friends. You'll like them. Whether they like you, we'll see."

"Will they like me?" Mandy said.

Jack smiled. "Of course."

Minutes later, they arrived at a garden-style apartment complex called Rolling Meadows. Unlike many of the other neighborhood entrances, there weren't any cars blocking the way, so they had no trouble. Greg and Lisa's apartment was around the back through a security gate that had been removed since the last time he was there.

"You sure your friends are here?" Pete said after they parked.

"No," Jack said.

"I'll keep the car running."

Jack glanced at his new friend, Pete, then back at Mandy, and then at the two packs on the seat next to her. Everything he owned in the world was in them.

Keeping his face blank of expression, he reached over and turned off the car.

"Best not to waste gas," he said, and carried the keys out with him.

At the third floor, he stopped outside the Mitchells' door. There was a note taped to it: *Friends, family, we're at the Welcome Center.*

Jack knocked anyway, then tried the door and found it locked. He sniffed the air and noticed two things. The first was the faintest tinge of death in the air, but it could have come from any of the apartments. He didn't think the twins would let their parents rot in the house unless they were forced to. The second was the smell of burning wood.

Back in the car, Jack said, "We need to go around front."

Pete, who'd dozed off, blinked tiredly and simply nodded. In the back seat, Mandy lay curled up, fast asleep.

They drove around and parked in front of the Welcome Center—a large, one-story building that Jack knew had a big room with lots of comfy couches and chairs, as well as a foosball table, a kitchen, and a community pool. Great for birthday parties.

After they parked, the smell of wood smoke had gotten a lot stronger. They left Mandy in the car and approached the front doors. No light came from inside, or any sign of people.

Just as Jack was reaching for the door, a girl's voice behind them said, "Hands in the air, and don't move."

EIGHT

Pete issued a high-pitched yelp of surprise, and Jack sighed with relief.

"Lisa, it's me. Jack."

"Shut up! Why are you ... what? *Jack?* Turn around!"

He turned cautiously around and looked at Lisa Mitchell for the first time in five months. She'd always been pretty, with long blond hair and intelligent blue eyes. Older than her brother Greg by thirty minutes, and Jack by a month, she'd somehow outpaced them when they played soccer and other sports together. For a girl, she was remarkably strong. At twelve years old, she could crush fresh apples in the palm of her hand, spurting juice everywhere.

It was about that time, Jack figured, that he'd secretly fallen in love with her. Because nothing was more attractive than the willful destruction of farm-fresh produce.

In the meager light of the half moon, Lisa appeared thin, tired, and fearful. Something he'd never expected from the brave, brilliant girl who got off on trouncing public schoolers at the national spelling bee.

"See?" he said. "It's me. I'm here now."

Lisa leaned in close for a look, blinked in surprise, and then collapsed into his arms crying—which freaked him out a little. Not only had he never hugged her before, but he'd

49

never seen her cry. Then again, the world had never wasted away in death before, either.

"Um ... did Greg, uh ... you know. Make it?" he said, staring around, seeing it was only her.

"Yes," Lisa said. "Both of us recovered quickly. Mom and Dad faded fast." She stiffened in his arms abruptly. "Who the hell is he?"

"I'm Pete."

Jack said, "Relax, okay? He's with me. Are you all right?"

The moment passed and she shook her head. "Sorry, I'm ... just tired. We sleep in shifts—kids everywhere stealing, too many mouths to feed. Come on, let's get out of the cold."

"One minute," he said.

He went back to the car for Mandy and the gear. It took a while to shake her awake, and when she got out she nearly fell over. She was too big for him to carry both her and the packs the whole way, so he waited until she was steady.

The Welcome Center was about twenty degrees warmer than outside. After the power had gone out, Jack and his dying parents had been forced to wear jackets or blankets most of the time. It felt strange removing his coat.

"Everyone sleeps in the party room," Lisa said. "There's a fireplace, but we don't burn anything in it."

That was odd. "But I smelled wood smoke."

"It's a gas fireplace. We drained the hot tub out back and keep a fire going in it at night. Every few hours, we drop in dumbbells from the exercise room till they're good and hot, then wheel them inside."

"How do you move around all that hot steel?"

She smiled tiredly. "We cut the wires from the exercise machines and tied them up. We swing them in when they're cold and drag them out when they're hot."

"Where does the wood come from?"

"Furniture. Pretty easy to break it apart. Pain in the ass to haul it back here. Not to mention dangerous."

"Because of the gangs," he said.

She nodded.

He laughed quietly. "Looks like you're doing all right."

"I'd rather have my parents back. Other than that, we do our best. I wish you'd come sooner."

Jack just nodded. Not much he could say to that.

Pete staggered suddenly and righted himself. He looked exhausted. Jack told him to take Mandy in and get some sleep. For once, Pete didn't give him any lip. He just did it.

"So, the gangs," Jack said. "How bad are they?"

"Pretty bad. All they do is take. The other day, they came in a group of eight, telling us what to do." She went quiet a moment, her expression cold. "Six of them left, and Greg and I got two new pistols for our growing collection."

"Jesus," he said. "Was it Greg who—"

Lisa held up a hand, cutting him off. "Doesn't matter. Give me a second. It's time to wake him up. I'll tell him you're here so he doesn't blow your head off in the middle of the night. Or Pete's. Oh, and if you need to pee, there's buckets of water in the bathroom. Just fill the tank and flush. Down that hall and to the right." She pointed off into the gloom. "If you get thirsty, there's jugs of boiled water in the kitchen."

They walked into the party room, and Jack relaxed. He found a spot near a group of children spread around a wheelbarrow full of hot dumbbells. There was a candle burning on the fireplace mantel. In the meager light, the children looked Mandy's age and younger.

Lisa approached a larger shape lying at the edge of the circle in a sleeping bag. She nudged it with her foot. When it didn't move, she kicked it, bringing forth a muffled curse, then whispers.

A moment later, Greg said, "He is?"

Lisa shushed him angrily and whispered something else. Greg got up and came over.

"Hey man," he said quietly. "Glad you made it. Knew you would, what with your doomy parents and ... ah crap, man, I'm sorry."

Jack smiled. "I know, man. It's cool. Glad you're okay."

"You too, man."

They talked briefly, catching up a little, enjoying the good news of their mutual survival. For Jack's part, he was happy he wasn't alone, and glad there was someone else alive who'd known his parents.

Before leaving, Greg lightly punched his shoulder and said, "Later on, okay?"

"Sure, man."

The front door opened and closed and the room fell quiet. Jack lay back and shut his eyes.

***

In the morning, everyone wanted to know more about the new arrivals. Lisa and Greg quickly introduced Pete, Mandy, and Jack to the group. She introduced each child and gave their ages.

Kimberly was a two-year-old girl with fine blond hair.

Brian was four years old.

Two sisters, Riley and Jessica, were seven and eight, respectively.

Not everyone was so young. The twelve-year-old black kid with the pistol on his side was named Tony. Of them all, he appeared the most well fed, if not slightly plump.

Wondering if he'd come from a gang, Jack gazed steadily at him and said, "You're eating well."

Tony smirked. "I used to be pretty fat. Now I'm starving. You got something to eat, I'll show you."

Jack smiled. He'd forgotten how overweight people were before the Sickness.

"That reminds me." He turned to Lisa. "I brought some food with me. Is there somewhere ...?"

Lisa nodded. "I have just the place for it."

Jack grabbed his backpack and Pete's makeshift pack and followed her into the rental office near the entrance.

"There's a safe under here," she said, pulling aside a blanket. "I cracked it."

He stared at her in amazement. "You crack safes now?"

She smiled, basking in the attention. "I learned last year on my grampa's floor safe. Easy, once you know how they're made. There were lots of videos online showing how it's done. Grampa said if I ever robbed a bank I'd have to pay him hush money." Her smile faltered and she glanced away. "Anyway, it wasn't too hard."

Jack nodded at the safe. "So what was in it?"

"A little money, blank checks, papers, stuff like that. We used it for kindling. How much food did you bring?"

Jack broke it down quickly: ten packs of dehydrated trail food, five pounds of rice, five pounds of beans, seven protein bars, and a pound of beef jerky his parents had made from the meat in the freezer after the power went out.

"Dang, Jack," she said in awe. "It's a treasure trove. You're basically a millionaire now."

"What's mine is yours."

For the second time in less than twenty-four hours, she hugged him and cried again. Jack wasn't sure whether to put his arms around her or thump her on the back like they did on TV, so he just stood there awkwardly and felt guilty for liking it so much.

"Uh, hey," he said. "You okay?"

She nodded and wiped her eyes. "Yeah. I'm just ... I miss my mom and dad, you know?"

He nodded, feeling his own eyes stinging now. No way was he going to cry in front of her, though.

From the doorway, Greg said, "Hey, you two. Everyone's asking about breakfast. And by everyone, I mean *me*."

"Who's watching the road?" she said.

"Tony and the new girl. What's her name?"

"Mandy," Jack said.

"We'll be there in a minute," Lisa said.

The safe was nearly empty, but for a few cans of chili and some boxes of spaghetti. Lisa took out the chili, deposited Jack's contribution, then locked it back up. She cooked the chili in a cast iron pot hanging over the fire pit out back. Ten minutes later they were sitting around a circular table enjoying their meager meals and chatting to fill the silence.

At one point Pete, who'd been quiet the whole morning, said, "So now what? Just sit here like dummies?"

Greg glared at him. "Why don't you shut up and enjoy the food we just gave you for free?"

Pete shook his head in disgust and wouldn't look at anyone.

"His delivery sucks," Jack said, "but he has a point.

There wasn't a lot of food in that safe. And security's an issue, especially after ..." He looked around at the various worried faces. "I think we should, uh ... Tony, was it?" The boy nodded. "You, Lisa, Greg, and Pete—we should maybe go have a meeting."

"What about me?" Mandy said.

"You get to do the dishes," he said and got up.

Lisa led them to the rental office and shut the door. Though there were several chairs inside, nobody sat. Pete looked nervous, and Greg kept glancing at him with a frown on his face.

"So, Greg," Jack said, "what's the plan to save us all?"

Greg, who'd never volunteered for anything since they'd known each other, and who always deferred to either his sister or Jack, said, "Uh ... how the heck should I know? *You're* the Chosen One."

Jack almost smiled at that. Ever since he'd confided about his parents' plan to fast track his childhood, Greg had ribbed him with the moniker at every opportunity.

"If you don't know how to save us," Jack said, "why did you call out Pete in there?"

Greg shrugged. "Didn't like his attitude."

"I don't see a lot of people signing on to help us," Jack said. "We shouldn't pick fights with each other. Now shake hands."

Greg's face grew momentarily hard. Then he sighed and held out his hand. Pete looked at it like he'd never seen so strange a custom before as handshaking, then reached out and grimaced through the experience.

Jack turned to Lisa. "What's your plan?"

Her lips twitched into a challenging smirk. "I'm waiting to see where you're going with this."

"Me too," he said. "Okay, Pete. You brought it up—got any big plans to keep us alive?"

"Why are you asking me? I don't have guns and stuff."

Jack looked at Tony. "How about you?"

Tony's smiled slyly. "We should make a crew of our own and take stuff, too. If we don't, other people gonna take everything, and then what?"

Lisa gasped and started to say something, but Jack held

up his hand.

"As bad as that sounds on the surface," he said, "it's hard to blame him. And though I'll never steal food from people or force them to join us, I like what he said about forming our own group. We need people, but they have to be old enough to carry a gun."

"None of us are old enough to carry guns," Pete said. "We're not grownups."

"Even though he's talking like one," Tony threw in, laughing and looking around to see if anyone else laughed, too. No one did.

Jack glanced from him to Pete. "We're not old enough to drive, either. Time to face the facts: *we're* the grownups now. We need to act like it."

Lisa pointed outside to the party room. "I'm not kicking out those children, Jack, and you're not either. We have a duty to protect them and anyone else who needs it."

He raised his hands in a calming gesture. "Nobody said anything about kicking anyone out. But we have to be realistic. There's a murderer out there named Blaze, and he's snapping up all the teenagers he can. What's more, he's sucking the area dry of what little food there is. Once he's done, he'll have to branch out or his people will mutiny."

"Can't mutiny on land," Pete said.

Everyone turned to look at him—calmly, as if studying a strange bug that had crawled into the room—then looked back at Jack.

Greg said, "How long until that happens?"

"No idea. When he raided my house, they got enough food to feed three people for a year. Mom had quite the survival pantry. Who knows how many other houses like mine he's found? Or how many people he's killed?"

Jack went on to describe the scene with the gang at his house, the journey with Pete, and the eventual killing of one of Blaze's own people. He left out that it had been with *his* rapier. In an odd way, he felt ... not responsible for it, exactly, but connected to it on a personal level.

After he finished, Tony said, "What if we joined him? We'd be safe then, right?"

Jack pulled a leaf from his learning excursions with his dad and paused, pretending to think about it long and hard.

"Nobody's safe anymore, least of all them. Blaze is like Stalin in World War Two. He thought everyone was out to get him, so he started killing his generals and replacing them with idiots. I'm not joining a guy like that."

"Stalin?" Tony said. "I get it. He's like a drug cartel boss."

Jack didn't know much about drug cartel bosses, so he said, "*Exactly* like a drug cartel boss."

The younger boy seemed to deflate. "So if we ain't joining them, then what?"

Jack smiled. "I thought you'd never ask."

NINE

Their immediate problems, Jack said, were food, secure shelter, manpower, medicine, and a safe and dependable water supply. When Greg pointed out they had a giant pool of water out back, he asked how long it would stay clean when rodents inevitably fell in and drowned. Better if they had something they didn't have to boil every time they got thirsty, like a natural spring, or a well with a pump (though he had no idea how they'd power it).

Jack had a few ideas about how to get more food beyond simple scavenging, but didn't go into that. For now, their hoarded food would have to last them.

Medicine, he said, would have to be scrounged from homes and any pharmacies that hadn't already been looted. He figured looters would have gone for the painkillers, and even then, he wondered how many survivors in the area were pill poppers. He didn't know anything about drug addiction, though he suspected it was one of the reasons his parents hadn't wanted him going to high school.

In addition to drugs, the doctors and dentists of the world were all gone. Broken arms could be splinted. He could learn how to pull teeth. But fillings and root canals and the like were now a lost science. Going forward, he asked that everyone maintain a strict no-sugar policy, and that brushing came second only after staying awake on watches in terms of priorities.

"If I had my way," Jack added, "we'd limit carbohydrates, too. The Inuit never had to brush their teeth. All they ate was blubber and protein and organs, and they had near perfect dental health."

He'd learned that from his mom, who taught in the biology department at the university. Other hunter-gather societies were the same, she'd said.

Pete made a face. "That's disgusting. You're full of it."

Jack just shrugged and continued to the next thing: shelter.

The problem with the Welcome Center was it had eight different entrances, huge windows front and back, and it was sitting in the middle of a large number of other apartment complexes and housing communities. Worse, the smoke from the pit out back was a beacon to the food gangs. They needed to relocate to a more remote location with a fireplace—preferably with a stove, like he'd seen at a cabin with his parents a few years ago. The stove sat inside the fireplace and kept the whole cabin toasty, and there was even a cooking surface on top. Way more efficient use of fuel.

"Is the gas out everywhere, or just here?" he said to Greg at one point. His own house was all electric, and he had no idea if gas was still a viable heating option this long after the Sickness.

"I don't know about everywhere," Greg said. "It turned off here the same time as the water and electricity. Lots of freezing kids out there right now."

Pete grunted. "Most of them are probably dead. I mean, how's a baby gonna feed itself?"

"We can't think about that," Jack said quietly. "Not if we're going to keep going." He turned to Lisa. "How many people our age do you still see around here? Minus the ones who attacked you."

She rubbed her chin. "There's still one or two I know hiding in their apartments that I couldn't get to join us. They're pretty far-gone. The rest float between the supermarkets, restaurants, and houses scrounging for anything they can find. I found a dead cat the other day that looked like it'd been skinned. Messy and wasteful."

Jack nodded slowly to himself.

"He's got that look in his eye," Greg said to his sister. "He's gonna say something Chosen One-ish."

Jack ignored that and said, "Let's do a final sweep of the complex and surrounding neighborhoods—see if we can get more recruits. We'll go in armed groups of two." He recalled that nut with the bat, smashing out car windows. "Nobody crazy, and no troublemakers. And try not to get anyone younger than about ten."

"How do we get them to come?" Greg said.

"If they still have food, offer them security in exchange for sharing. If they don't have anything, offer security, food, medicine, that kind of thing. The basics."

Greg looked at him like he was crazy. "We don't have medicine. Nobody's gotten sick. And if they did, how would you know what to give them?"

"Usually it says on the bottles," Jack said impatiently. "If it doesn't, we find a book on it later and figure it out. Next topic: what do we need that you guys haven't scrounged already?"

Tony said, "Gold and silver. Coins and chains and stuff like that. And diamonds. One day, may have to use that as money."

Jack wasn't so sure about that, considering the world's supply of precious metals and jewels was now available for a tiny population to easily grab. Not wanting to stifle anyone's creativity, he smiled and nodded.

"Good idea," he said. "What else?"

Pete said, "Backpacks? For the children. So they can carry stuff."

"Excellent idea, Pete. Everyone gets their own pack. What else?"

More time passed while they brainstormed ideas, none of them coming up with anything the twins and Tony hadn't scavenged already.

Jack said, "How about fishing tackle? Rods, reels, lures, that kind of thing. I brought a little with me, but we could use more."

Lisa quirked an eyebrow. "You know some place to fish around here that I don't?"

"Not around here," he said, smiling mysteriously. "Later on, who knows?"

Pete started saying how fish had mercury in them, and that's why they couldn't eat them, and they didn't taste good anyway.

With a teasing twinkle in his eye, Tony said he'd never seen mercury in fish sticks. Pete said you needed a microscope to see mercury, and Tony just laughed at him.

"Guys, please," Jack said, and they quieted. "Lisa and I will head out together. Greg?"

Greg shrugged. "I'll go with Tony."

Lisa looked at Pete. "Someone should stay here and watch the kids. How good are you with a gun?"

"I'm a pacifist."

Jack sighed. "What about scavenging?"

Pete looked skeptical. "I'm not going anywhere with dead bodies inside."

"Most of the places have already been opened and searched already," Lisa said. "For any that aren't, we have tools in one of the closets. Should be a crowbar in there. As for the dead bodies: just sniff at the doors. If it's fresh, go in."

Jack said, "We need prescription drugs. Look in the bathroom cabinets. Also, bring back any car keys you find."

Tony said, "Don't forget gold."

Pete sighed with impatience. "Anything else?"

"You should bring Mandy and the kids with you," Lisa said. "They shouldn't be here alone."

Pete snorted and stalked from the room.

"Fun guy," she said.

Jack just smiled.

**

Jack and Lisa spent the rest of the day ranging through three other apartment complexes. As a precaution, he carried his dad's AR-15, and Lisa wore a 9mm on her hip.

They took turns knocking on doors. Every door got three rounds of loud knocking before they moved on. As it happened, they moved on quite a bit. Sometimes they'd hear something inside and knock a fourth time, only to leave empty handed.

One time, they knocked on a door and a rail-thin girl around the right age opened without first asking who was there. Her hair was dyed green with blond roots. Jack had never met anyone with green hair before and felt oddly intimidated.

"Hi," he began. "Uh, I'm Jack, and ..."

The girl turned around and walked deeper inside.

The two friends looked at each other, then into the dark apartment. The girl was gone. Like a ghost.

"We going in?" Lisa whispered.

Jack seriously considered shutting the door and leaving.

Lisa said, "Keep that big gun ready," and walked in.

"Hey," he whispered, but it was too late.

For the first time in a year, Jack chambered a round in his dad's rifle. After applying the safety, he followed her inside.

The sour, ever-present stink of the Sickness intruded from everywhere, assaulting him like hammer blows. At a certain point in the process, people lost control of their bowels, too weak to hold anything in.

"Jack, in here!"

He rushed forward into a candle-lit room, prepared for the worst and wishing for anything but what he saw. Lying on a king-size bed was the paper-thin body of a woman next to an adult male corpse.

"How can she still be alive?" he said in horror.

"She's not," Lisa said. "He is."

Jack jerked back in fright—the so-called corpse was a man in the last stages of the Sickness. His mouth worked open and shut, dragging in painful gasps for air, and his body was covered in sores. The woman on the bed had died some time ago and had simply dried out next to her husband.

Jack's parents had agreed not to let it progress this far. His mom ended his dad's suffering after he'd lost the ability to eat or drink. A few days ago, she told Jack she loved him, zipped herself into a sleeping bag, and followed his dad into death by her own hand.

The green-haired girl was beside the bed on her knees, praying under her breath in a mumbled rush.

"Hey," he said. "You, uh … You should get out of here. There's no … Your dad, he …"

Lisa looked at him and shook her head.

He couldn't say the simple truth: there was no hope here. The girl wasn't paying attention to him in any event. She just prayed and rocked.

Lisa retreated to the living room, and Jack followed her.

"What now?" he said.

Her eyes flashed angrily. "Oh, I'm suddenly in charge?"

Jack started to reply but she stopped him.

"Sorry," she said. "It's just … my parents. They looked that way. Mom … she was so thin when she died. I carried her down three flights by myself. We buried her first. The hole wasn't deep enough for the … to stop the dogs from …" She turned around and shook in a series of short, wracking sobs.

"Let's go outside," he said.

She nodded and followed him out.

"Sorry," she said, wiping her eyes. "I haven't cried this much in years."

"I tried crying, once," Jack said. "Just to see what it was like."

She glanced at him, smiled a little, and slid down into a seated position against the wall. "We can't leave her in there."

"I'd ask her to join us," he said, "but she won't leave her dad. Not until he's gone. The way he looked, it can't be that long. She'd be a good addition to the group." He looked back inside. "I mean, for her age. No idea how her head's doing."

Lisa nodded.

They waited like that for a while, not talking. The girl didn't show up, and the door was still open.

"Lisa," he said at one point, choosing his words carefully. "When you said eight kids attacked you guys and only six left … did you mean that the way it sounded?"

She nodded.

"Can I ask who did it?"

"Me," she said in a light voice. "Greg took the bodies in my dad's car and put them in the dumpster."

Jack nodded thoughtfully. There was probably no delicate way to ask her to kill the man in apartment. And what kind of coward was he, that he couldn't do it himself?

Lisa snorted and glanced at him in disgust. "I'm *not* going to euthanize that man, if that's what you're thinking."

He shook his head. "Totally not thinking that."

A few minutes later, he got up and walked back inside. He found the girl lying on the ground next to the bed, staring off into space. Her father, unfortunately, was still breathing. It couldn't be much longer.

"Hey, you—kid," Jack said. "We have a group, but we need more people. Your dad, though ... He's not going to make it, and I'm sorry about that. None of the adults do. I don't think he has much longer."

The girl didn't reply.

He tried again. "We're a good group. Nice folks. We need more help. If you want to come, there's a spot for you."

He hated how lame he sounded. Insensitive. Lisa would have done a better job.

The girl hadn't been crying when they'd first walked in. Now her cheeks gleamed wetly in the flickering candlelight.

"So, if you're interested," he said. "You know, after ... We're down at the Rolling Meadows Welcome Center. There's heat, food, and other people for protection. We're leaving for a better place soon, so you need to hurry. Two days, tops, and then we're gone. Okay? Can you nod if you understand?"

A minute later, when she didn't nod or get up, Jack stepped quietly from the room. Then he and Lisa left.

TEN

They returned to Rolling Meadows by cutting through a duplex community. Jack had lost the heart to continue their search after seeing the girl and her doomed father, and Lisa clearly felt the same.

When they turned the corner at the end of the long block of garden-style apartments, they saw a group of about ten people in front of the Welcome Center. Boys and girls, and no little kids. For a moment, he thought maybe Tony and Greg had wildly succeeded in bringing in more people. But then he saw some of them had pistols clenched carelessly in their hands. And though none of them was tall with red hair, he knew what he was looking at.

"Do you see Greg?" Lisa said, squinting against the afternoon sun.

Jack said, "Nope. Nobody else, either. Maybe they're still out recruiting."

"I hope so. What do we do?"

"Oh, I'm in charge now?" Jack said, more from a sense of nervousness than a desire to be funny.

Lisa smiled tightly. "We have the drop on them. How many rounds does that rifle carry?"

His mouth felt dry. "Thirty in the magazine."

"Do you want me to do it? I can spare you that."

Jack sucked in a long, steadying breath and shook his

head. "I've had more practice. From a distance I—"

A girl in a puffy orange coat pointed their way and shouted something. As one, her companions turned to look. One raised a pistol and fired, causing Jack and Lisa to crouch automatically. The shooter was too far away for anything like accuracy, but he could still get lucky.

The two friends ran back around the corner to bangs and cracks as more joined in. A short-term solution. The complex was like Swiss cheese, with covered walkways running through the middle connecting parking lots on either side. Unless they fled the neighborhood, they'd be surrounded in no time.

Jack had cleared the rifle back at the girl's apartment and topped off the mag. Now he chambered a new round, this time without engaging the safety. When the first kids appeared—a boy and a girl—he sighted on the boy and fired, jerking some at the recoil. The boy went down and didn't move.

Jack hoped the girl would run, but she didn't. She raised a pistol and fired as fast as she could.

BAM BAM BAM!

Jack grabbed Lisa and pulled her back around the corner under a shower of stinging splinters.

"Over there," she said, pointing across the street at a set of dumpsters nestled in a concrete niche.

Wordlessly, they took up positions on either side of the one labeled "Cardboard Only" and aimed their weapons. There was a terrible smell coming from it—one he recognized from the houses he'd searched for car keys. Supposedly, Greg had dumped two bodies here from the first assault on the Welcome Center.

Not ten seconds later, armed pursuers came boiling around both corners of the building.

Jack didn't hesitate this time—he ruthlessly cut them down. Loud as it was, he could hear Lisa's shots as well. Boys and girls fell dead in the grass. Two who survived the onslaught fired back, their bullets clanging loudly against the steel of the dumpsters. The rest ran away. For the ones that kept firing, he spared none. The shooters quickly fell to the devastating accuracy of the rifle, and soon the field was empty but for the lingering haze of gun smoke and a lawn littered with broken bodies.

The muscles in Jack's neck tightened of their own volition, like when he'd once had a stomach virus, and suddenly he was on his knees throwing up. Lisa came over and held him.

Between heaves Jack said, "Can't ... stop ... puking."

He attempted a humorless laugh, trying to be strong for her. For *them*. Shackleton wouldn't have thrown up. What a disaster for the crew of the Endurance if he had.

"Shh, Jack, just take it easy. We're okay now," she said. "You did what you had to. Those idiots would have killed us."

A minute later, when the spasms had passed, he said, "Was it like this for you the first time?"

Lisa wiped his mouth with her coat sleeve, her expression blank.

"Different," she said.

He waited for her to elaborate. When she didn't, he forced his gaze back to the lawn on the other side of the road. Near one of the still shapes, a little sign poked up admonishing people to clean up after their dogs. Five lives, and a sixth around back. Kids who should have been talking about football and YouTube and "doing it" and whatever nonsense flitted through their stupid, cabbage brains.

"Come on," he said, getting up. "Let's go see."

***

The entrance to the Welcome Center was littered with broken glass, and what glass remained in the doors was riddled with bullet holes. The doors hadn't been locked, but the gang had shot them up anyway.

"I think they're the same ones from last time," Lisa said, nudging a large piece of glass with her sneaker. "Trying to prove a point."

The first thing Jack noticed on entering were droplets of blood scattered in the foyer, but the entryway was free of anything but glass and bullet holes. No bodies. The party room was similarly shot up, with stuffing from pillows scattered everywhere. No bodies, and no blood.

It didn't add up.

"No sign of the children," he said. "Or Pete."

Lisa went to check the rental office. Moments later she called out, "Jack, come look!"

The room had been smashed up. There were scratches and gouges from gunshots on the face of the safe—and a thin trail of blood leading to the entryway.

"They shot the safe," she said. "Looks like a bullet bounced off and hit one of them."

"Least they didn't get it open," he said.

She tried the dial and swore. "Those ... those *idiots!*"

"What now?" Jack said.

"The stupid dial's broken! I can't get in."

"We'll figure it out."

"Our *food's* in there!"

He wanted to reach out and reassure her but thought she'd bite his arm off.

"Your brother's still out there," he said. "That's way more important."

That seemed to snap her back. "Greg—oh, God! Surely he must have heard the shots."

Thinking of the bullet-riddled glass and busted safe, he said, "*We* didn't hear them." It must have happened when they were inside with the girl and her dad.

Lisa opened her mouth to reply, and then the sound of an automobile came rumbling from outside. Raising her pistol, she looked at him, her face angry and set.

"I'll check. You stay here," Jack said and crept to the entryway. A moment later, he called back, "It's Pete!"

Pete got out of the car and said, "What happened to the door? We heard shots. Are those bullet holes?"

Jack said, "Never mind that. Are the children with you?"

"What? Yeah, back seat. And I got that stuff you wanted." He stared fearfully around as if expecting gunmen to parachute in at any moment.

Quickly, Jack explained everything that had happened.

"Have you seen my brother?" Lisa said.

Pete shook his head. "We left before them. I found lots of great stuff."

"I don't care!" she yelled and stormed back inside.

Pete recoiled as if slapped. "What the heck's her problem?"

"Never mind," Jack said. "So what'd you get?"

Pete smiled broadly. "A little food, some nice backpacks. Some pills like you asked for. But check it out: there's a guy five buildings down. He locked his door and left. We *definitely* want this guy."

"What's he look like? I'll talk to him," Jack said. He didn't know what to feel more pleased about. That there was an unaffiliated teenager nearby who wasn't comatose with grief, or that Pete was using words like *we* when talking about their group.

"Tall, black, big muscles," Pete said. "Don't worry, I'll take you there."

Jack shook his head. "We still need to wait for Greg."

Pete stared at him blankly, then nodded in realization. "That girl's brother."

"Her name's Lisa."

"Oh yeah. What do we do with the stuff I got?"

"Leave it for now. I need you to grab your blanket and give me a hand."

Pete ran in to get it. When he came back, they went to the scene of the gun battle. His eyes widened in horror at the grisly scene.

"Oh, Jesus!" he said, cringing away when Jack searched the nearest body.

"Just lay the blanket down and stack whatever you find," Jack said, coming back with a small caliber pistol and an extra magazine.

Pete dropped the blanket in a heap, shaking his head.

"No way," he said. "I'm not touching dead people!" Without warning, he ran back to the Welcome Center.

Jack was both irritated and relieved. Irritated because he could have used the help. Relieved because now he could cringe his way through the ghoulish task without anyone witnessing his distress. A leader had to project invincibility, even if it was just make believe.

Five minutes later, he'd gathered eight handguns, maybe a hundred loose bullets, six more magazines, and no food. The bodies were too large and too many for him to haul to the dumpsters and dispose of by himself. When Greg got back, Jack would ask him to help. He didn't want the little kids finding them.

Pete's haul from the apartments was considerably more lucrative. He'd gotten a pile of key rings, some fishing gear for Jack, gold chains for Tony, a few pistols and boxes of ammo, and a small assortment of boxed and canned food. He'd also brought back a trash bag full of prescription pills, none of which were recognizable as antibiotics. There were a good deal of pain meds, though. Jack stowed those away in his almost-empty pack, left the rest in the garbage bag, and gave that to Pete to dispose of. He didn't want any of the children getting into it and thinking it was candy.

"Any trouble getting in the apartments?" Jack said.

"Most of the doors were already open," Pete said, eyeing him warily, as if any moment Jack would ask him to touch a dead body. "Used the crowbar on the others. Really hard—it's super heavy."

"What about apartments with dead people?"

Pete shook his head. "Mandy went in those. She doesn't mind the smell."

It bothered him that Pete was so quick to risk the girl's health and sanity rather than do it himself, but held off saying anything so soon after the attack. They had enough to worry about.

He found Lisa in the rental office working on the safe.

"How's it looking?" he said.

She'd removed the broken dial from the door and was busily turning the metal rod with a pair of pliers.

"Not as bad as I thought," she said. "It still spins. But without the dial, there's no way to measure each turn. Maybe with some kind of disk and a little superglue ..." She turned back to the safe, twisting the rod around slowly, then sighed and stood up. "So yeah, that's what I need."

"Should be easy enough," Jack said.

A commotion sounded from outside.

"They're here, they're here!" Mandy yelled on the way out the door.

Jack and Lisa emerged to a scene as joyful as it was disheartening. Tony and Greg had definitely brought in new people to fill their ranks. Five of them. The problem was: most were between four and seven years old, and the oldest looked to be about eight or nine.

"I know what you're thinking," Greg said when he saw their faces, "but what could I do? This place we found was full of them. They were wandering in and out. They were starving."

They certainly appeared to be starving. Skin and bones, the lot of them, with dirty clothes and grimy faces.

Quietly Jack said, "We can't save everyone, man. It'll be hard enough saving ourselves."

"Yeah, I know, but ... oh, jeez," Greg said, taking in the shattered front doors. "What happened here?"

ELEVEN

Standing near the door to the teenager's apartment with Pete and Tony, Jack considered the best way to make his pitch—provided the boy was back home. According to Pete, he'd locked his door and left three hours ago.

"Do you remember if he was armed?" Jack said.

Pete shrugged. "He might have been."

"How could you not remember?" Tony said.

Pete sat on the stairs and folded his arms. "Because I don't."

"You're not coming?" Jack said.

He shook his head. "If he has a gun, he could freak out and shoot us."

"If you're so scared," Jack said, "how did find him in the first place?"

"Mandy saw him when she was checking doors."

That was odd. "Where were you?"

"Downstairs waiting. He went out the front, so I didn't get a good look."

Jack couldn't believe it. "You let a little girl roam the floors by herself?"

"I told her to run if she didn't feel safe," Pete said. "Get off my case."

Tony didn't hold back. "Man, you're a little baby, that's what you are."

"Oh yeah?" Pete said, standing up. "Say it to my face!"

Tony shoved him, and Jack had to step between them. "Knock it off. We're here for a job."

The two boys glared at each other a moment more and then settled down.

"Come on," Jack said, and went to stand outside the door. "Keep your gun holstered, but be ready, and ... Wait a minute—you any good with it?"

"I shot it a bunch of times," Tony said, puffing his chest out fractionally. "It's easy."

Jack realized a gun safety lesson was needed if they were going to keep people from accidentally shooting each other. One more task for his ever-growing list.

After a brief hesitation, he knocked on the door. He tried his best to look non-threatening, knowing whoever answered would see him through the peephole. Hard to do with a rifle looped over his shoulder.

They didn't have to wait long for a response. The peephole darkened, and an angry, male voice shouted from inside, "Who the hell are you?"

"Uh, my name's Jack, and—"

"I said I'm not joining! Go away!"

Jack quirked an eyebrow at Tony, who shrugged.

"Right, um, we never asked you to join. Maybe you meant someone else?"

"Don't care—leave me alone."

"No problem, but before we do," Jack said, choosing his words carefully, "why didn't you join that gang or whoever it was that asked you?"

"Because I didn't. And don't think I can't see that gun you're carrying."

Feeling like an idiot, Jack unhooked the rifle and passed it to Tony. Then he unclipped his holster and passed that over, too.

"See that?" he said. "No guns. It's dangerous out here. Only reason we have them. Let me in and we'll just talk, okay? My voice is hurting from all this shouting."

About ten seconds later, the door opened fractionally, secured by a chain. A boy of about fifteen stared angrily out through the crack.

"That's all of you?" he said, angling his head to see if anyone was hiding.

"There's another of us over by the stairs," Jack said.

The boy said, "There's not a drop of food in the house. Even if you search, you won't find anything."

"We don't want your food," Jack said. "That's the point of all this—we have food already. What we don't have enough of are teenagers. Just little kids."

The boy pulled a face like he'd heard something strange. "What do you mean little kids?"

"Not too many," Jack said, wishing he'd kept quiet about them. "They don't eat much. We're leaving in a day or two for a safer place. If you want in, we could use you."

The boy still wore that strange expression on his face. "You have a lot of children?"

Just as Jack was thinking maybe the boy was the wrong type to join them—if he hated children so much—the sound of a crying child carried from somewhere deep inside.

Smiling like he'd solved a puzzle, Jack said, "There's always room for more."

***

The boy's name was Brad, he was fifteen and a half, and he had a seven-month-old brother named Tyler. The apartment they were staying in belonged to Brad's father, who'd died back when hospitals were still admitting victims.

"What about your mom?" Pete said.

The older boy had freely volunteered the stuff about his dad, but no more.

"No need to answer that, Brad," Jack said, throwing Pete an angry look. "Pete's sort of a bull in an etiquette shop. Says the darnedest things."

Brad smiled briefly. "No, it's fine. She got the Sickness a month after my brother was born. I buried her, then came here after we ran out of, uh ..."

A sudden tenseness invaded the room.

"It's okay," Jack said. "Like I said—we're not here to rob you. Tony, place my pistol on the table for Brad to pick up. Be careful with it. Always treat a gun like it's ready to fire."

Tony smirked like he knew everything already. He

73

unholstered the gun and handed it directly to Brad, who took it warily.

Jack bit back an angry retort. He'd deal with it later.

"There you go, Brad," he said. "Your first gun. Even if you don't come with us, you can keep it. I'll show you how to use it before we leave, give you some basic safety—"

Brad released the magazine, cleared the chamber—already empty—put the magazine back in, and racked the slide. It was a single-action semi-auto, so there was no need to decock it. After engaging the safety, he placed it on the table near Jack.

Pete had looked ready to bolt the entire time the older boy was manipulating the weapon. Jack was spooked, too, but hid it better.

"I used to shoot with my grandfather," Brad said, grinning. "He was a police officer way back when. He said if every gun's loaded and ready to fire, may as well keep it loaded and ready to fire." He reached behind his back and pulled out a small, black pistol Jack couldn't readily identify. "Glad you're not here to rob me. Bet you are too, huh?"

Brad laughed, and Jack and the others laughed nervously with him.

"The reason I came here," Brad said, "is because ... well hold on. May as well show you."

He got up and the others followed him to the kitchen. He opened a cupboard and inside were about twelve big cans of baby formula in different brands. "Dad only had one when I got here, for when Mom visited. They were getting along better after Tyler was born, with everything so crazy. It was like their marriage problems didn't matter anymore. Anyway, I was able to add all these cans ... well, you know how. Door to door." He shook his head and his voice grew hard. "Pretty unfair, if you ask me, what happened to everybody."

Jack nodded. "If you join us, there's security and smart people. Good people. You need help. You can't keep leaving your brother alone to go out."

In the end, Brad agreed to come with them, and set about packing the things he wanted to take. Namely, the clothes on his back, the cans of formula, and a stack of cloth diapers. Jack wrapped the cans in three sheets, then split the load up so Brad didn't have to carry anything but Tyler.

Struggling with his burden, Pete said, "Why'd you give me so much? You think because I'm Asian you can make me carry everything around. That's racist."

Jack laughed. "No, Pete. If you were a Sherpa from Nepal, *that* would be racist."

"What's a Sherpa?" he said. "First hobos and now Sherpas. You think because I'm Asian I know everything. I knew you were racist."

"I'm black," Tony said, "and *I* know what a Sherpa is. I read a book about Mount Everest one time. Teacher acted like I did something special, reading a book on my very own. Hey Brad—you believe this guy, thinking he's got it worse than us?"

Brad snorted. "Don't drag me into it."

On the way back to the Welcome Center, Tony and Pete went back and forth about various degrees of racism and which race had it worse, each trying to outdo the other on how they'd suffered over the years. So long as they weren't insulting each other, Jack was content to let them. He did wonder why anyone would care about such trivial things in a world with so many new dangers.

Then, tracing it back, he realized maybe that was the point.

Back at the Welcome Center, everyone gathered around Brad and the baby. It was like Brad was a celebrity, old as he was. What a difference a year made. When he took off his jacket, his muscles stood out starkly. He was tall, too—bigger even than Blaze—and in some ways it felt like having an adult around. That impression quickly evaporated when they talked to him. Despite his size, he seemed unduly shy and embarrassed by the attention, and fussed with Tyler the whole time.

Lisa reached out and played with the baby boy, smiling in a way Jack hadn't seen since before the Sickness.

Out of nowhere, a peculiar jealousy came over him. He watched Lisa's face as she tried to engage the fifteen-year-old. Brad barely looked at her, and her manner switched from curious and excited to gentle and kind. At one point, she glanced at Jack and shrugged as if to say, *I tried.*

"Any news about the safe?" he said.

"Best news ever," she said, smiling proudly.

While he and the others were away recruiting Brad, she'd glued a plastic coaster in place of the dial. After first measuring out the combination locations—extrapolated from a portion of the busted dial—she was able to accurately use the combination and open it.

Everyone cheered and agreed she was a genius, and that night they celebrated with beans over sauceless spaghetti.

The next day, Jack was anything but pleased. Three of the children Greg and Tony had brought home the day before were missing. That would have been a concern all its own. But then they returned with eleven *more* children, all of them between about five and ten years old, bringing the total number of mouths to feed to twenty-seven.

TWELVE

In the months since Jack had last seen the twins, Greg had learned how to drive. The twins had tried to check on him, but the roadblocks—still there at the time—had made that impossible.

"Twenty-seven people," Jack was saying, "and only three of us know how to drive a car."

"But a bus?" Lisa said that afternoon when he told her his plan. "Really? They're huge. It takes practice."

"Then I'll practice."

Before dark, Jack found a number of cars that fit the keys Pete had recovered. Of these, he picked five that had full or almost full tanks, and enlisted Pete to help get them going with the car and jumper cables from the other night.

"I may as well learn to drive a car first," Jack said and got behind one of the wheels. One by one, he drove through the neighborhood and parked them at the Welcome Center so they wouldn't get stolen. Driving wasn't too difficult, he decided, with traffic laws and busy interstates as extinct as the dinosaurs. Like Pete, his biggest problem was not pushing the gas when he wanted to push the brakes.

Nobody knew how long it would take for the batteries to recharge, so they ran the cars all night. Even so, in the morning, one of them wouldn't start after stopping it. The others were fine.

Brad helped him disconnect and carry the four batteries to Greg's trunk. Jack added a bunch of tools selected by Lisa, along with five sets of jumper cables Mandy had scavenged from the neighborhood.

For the excursion, Jack tapped Lisa for her brains, and Pete as a second driver. Greg, Tony, and Brad would stay behind to guard the children.

They left shortly before noon.

**

Since fleeing his house, Jack hadn't been anywhere but the apartment complex and surrounding neighborhoods. The only people he'd seen besides the green-haired girl and Brad were the little kids that kept showing up. Now, during the day, there were plenty—walking aimlessly down the road in the cold, milling outside already looted stores and fast food places, or sometimes driving to who knew where. Usually the ones in cars were alone, but once he saw a car packed with youngsters, with an older girl up front. Tempted as he was to flag her down to see if she'd join them, he resisted the urge. The last thing they needed was more mouths to feed.

The bus they'd scraped past the other night was still on the exit ramp off 28, failing in its job to block sick people from making it to that section of the city.

"Now what?" Lisa said, staring skeptically at the huge vehicle. She looked through the doors. "No keys."

"All your tools and electrical gear are in the trunk. If you can crack a safe, you can hotwire a bus."

Lisa looked at him like he was crazy. Which, he figured, might actually be true.

The folding doors opened with a solid push, and Jack breathed a sigh of relief that they wouldn't have to drive around with a gaping hole in the glass. He'd actually never been on a school bus before, though he'd often dreamed of it. Right up there with having his very own hall locker.

The first thing Lisa did was pound a flathead screwdriver into the keyhole. She clamped an adjustable wrench around the hexagonal handle and tugged hard, snapping something inside the keyhole and causing it to turn. Unsurprisingly, the bus didn't start.

"It was worth a try," Jack said, smiling to show how much confidence he had in her.

Lisa cast him a withering look, got down on her knees, and peered under the dash using Jack's flashlight. A minute later, she popped off the housing for easier access. She traced wires for the next ten minutes, exposing them in places to test with a voltmeter.

Jack had always been interested in electronics. He knew the general concepts, Ohms Law and all that, but had never done anything practical with it. Lisa, on the other hand, had built her own radio when she was Mandy's age. Greg was just as smart, though less competitive, and he tended to follow Jack's lead on what to do, like with the knife sharpening business. In every way, he and Greg were best friends. Despite that, Jack had always felt closer to Greg's sister.

"Be careful," he said. "Much as you'd enjoy my resuscitation skills ... well ... actually, go ahead and shock yourself. I could use the practice." He laughed loudly, broadcasting to the entire world that it was just a harmless joke.

Lisa looked up and smiled at him, holding his gaze a fraction longer than could be considered harmless at all, causing his pulse to pound in his ears.

Before embarrassing himself further, he nodded curtly and went outside to see if Pete needed help with anything important.

Five minutes later, Lisa stomped out of the bus and swore.

"What's wrong?" Jack said, appearing by her side as if by magic.

"The battery's dead. *Too* dead. Doesn't make any sense. It should have at least *some* charge, but the needle's totally flat."

"Maybe there's something wrong with the voltmeter," he said.

To find out, they went to the car and tested it on the battery. It worked fine.

"How about the one on the bus?" Pete said.

They went to the back to find out, but the battery wasn't

there. After some searching, they found *three* batteries in a compartment on the side of the bus.

"What the hell?" she said, looking at the glowing meter when she checked them. "There's a charge."

For lack of options, they went back around to look at the engine. Lisa was pretty good with electronics, but she didn't know anything about engines. Jack didn't either.

"What about that big red button?" Pete said.

Sure enough, there was a big red button in the engine compartment. Lisa shrugged, pushed it, then went back to the front.

"That did it!" she yelled. A minute later, they heard the unmistakable sound of the engine trying and failing to turn over.

"Let's start hauling," Jack said.

Together, he and Lisa hooked the four batteries to the ones in the bus in parallel using Mandy's cables. Probably overkill, but it was a big bus with a big engine. The whole time, Pete stared at them from ten feet away, offering helpful comments like "be careful!" and "are you sure about this?" and "you're gonna get electrocuted!"

Lisa climbed up to try again. Like last time, they heard the engine turn. This time, it kept turning, and a few seconds later the bus sputtered to life.

"I'm letting it run a while," she said and clomped down the steps.

After about ten minutes, they disconnected the batteries and put them back in the car.

Pete crossed his arms defiantly. "I don't know how to drive a bus."

"I told you, I got it," Jack said. "When we're ready to move out, we'll put you in one car and Greg in another. Lisa, how much gas do we have?"

"Tank's nearly full."

Pete said, "You only learned to drive yesterday. You don't know how to drive busses."

"So I'll figure it out."

It took considerably longer to figure out than he wanted. The big problem was learning the air brake system, especially with Lisa offering random advice about all the little things he was doing wrong. Eventually, though, he got the bus moving.

Not hard at all, he thought, feeling confident.

When he arrived at an intersection and turned right, he knocked out a stop sign, and the back right wheel bumped up over the curb. Lisa, who'd been standing beside him, stumbled down the stairs and crashed hard against the doors.

"Lisa!" Jack yelled and slammed to a stop.

He rushed to help her, noting she'd scraped her cheek. Her shirt had pulled up a little from where she'd slid, and there were scratches along her side.

"For the love of ..." she said in a pained voice. "Help me up."

He reached down and grasped her hand. "Are you okay?"

"I think so," she said, inspecting her bruised elbow. "This stupid bus is like a giant, rolling building. You need to plan ahead when you turn like that. Go wider."

"I know, I'm sorry." He felt like dirt for hurting his friend. "A hundred times, I'm sorry."

Ahead of them, Pete got out of the car and shook his head, then got back in. Then, inexplicably, he left them there and kept driving.

"Where the hell's he going?" Lisa said.

Jack frowned. "No idea, but he shouldn't just take off like that."

She snorted quietly. "Take him on a bus ride. That'll teach him."

At her little joke, he felt a wave of relief. If she could joke, she couldn't have been hurt too badly.

Lisa worked her elbow and winced briefly in pain. When Jack opened his mouth to apologize again, she leaned in and kissed him lightly on the lips.

"I'm fine. Now, shut up and get us back."

She went to one of the seats and buckled in.

Why did she do that?

Jack's heart thudded in his chest. He could barely think, let alone drive. But if he didn't do something, she'd know how rattled he was and lose all respect for him.

"You gotta release the air brakes, remember?" she said, voice dripping with bratty amusement.

"Yep!" he said, and pulled out the little knob, bringing a loud hiss of air.

There weren't any more stop sign incidents, and he handled the turns much better, though he'd had to back up once for a second approach. When they pulled into Rolling Meadows, he drove the bus back behind the complex so it wasn't visible from the street. The fewer people who knew they were leaving, the better.

Before shutting down, Lisa showed him the wires he had to disconnect to stop the engine—different than the two she'd used to start it, and which were now wrapped in black electrical tape.

"I'm all out of twisty connectors," she said.

"What if we keep the wires connected all the time, then just hit that big red button in the back?"

She nodded. "I forgot about that. Next time."

When they got to the Welcome Center, Pete acted like he hadn't abandoned them out there with a possibly disabled vehicle and no easy way to return home. It drove home the realization they needed more drivers.

Jack went looking for Brad and found him sitting in the party room near the fire feeding his brother.

"Hey man," the older boy said at his approach.

"Hey. I was just wondering: have you ever driven before?"

"Nope. Why?"

"Because we need more people than Greg and Pete who know how." He smiled to put him at ease. "If I can drive a bus, you can drive a car. In fact, going forward, we need backups for everything we learn."

Brad nodded. "Makes sense. I can show Tony how to use that gun of his without shooting himself."

Jack shook his head. "Leave that to me. I'll set up a class like the one I took with my parents. Speaking of guns: you ever do any hunting?"

"Once, with my dad and one of his friends. We didn't shoot anything, though. Tell you the truth, I was pretty happy about that. I hate killing anything. Even spiders."

Jack smiled. "Yeah, me too. But we're going to have to hunt. You're big and strong, and you're at least safety conscious. If I show you how to field dress a deer, you think you can handle it? It's pretty gross."

Brad looked down at Tyler and nodded. "There's nothing I won't do for my little brother."

THIRTEEN

The morning of the big move, Greg, who was on watch, woke Jack an hour before dawn.

"Is it time already?" Jack said. "Why's it so dark still?"

"Sorry, man," he said with a hint of amusement in his voice. "It's the chick with the green hair you told me about. She's here. Man, she's skinny ... Cool hair, though. I brought her inside. She wants to talk to you."

Jack blinked in the faint light offered by the candle over the fireplace. "Really? That's great."

She was standing in the office just off the entrance. Greg asked if she wanted to sit on one of the plush office chairs. She shook her head.

Jack clicked his LED flashlight and set it down facing one of the walls so as not to blind her. The twins had gathered a box of candles, but they needed more. Lanterns, too, like a hundred years ago. Flashlights made more sense for emergencies and should be spared.

"Hi there," he said, wincing at how loud his voice sounded after the quiet of the party room. He held his hand out for her to shake, then lowered it when all she did was stare at him. "You wanted to talk to me?"

"They're dead," she said in a flat, expressionless voice. For so slender a girl, her voice was deep and resonant. "I got sick like them, then got better. But they didn't."

He looked closely at her and noted she seemed somehow more emaciated than last time. Or maybe his mind hadn't been able to accept it then, just as it balked now.

"Greg, can you bring some of those crackers—the ones with the salt? And some water?"

"Yeah, sure. Gimme a minute."

"What's your name?" Jack said after he'd left.

She stared at him curiously, as if slowly processing the request. "Olivia."

"I'm Jack."

"You said that when you came to my apartment. That's how I knew to ask for you."

He smiled in embarrassment and revised his first impression of her. She may have been troubled, but she wasn't completely gone, or dumb.

"Sorry about your parents," he said.

"And I'm sorry about yours."

He didn't know what to say to that, and felt a wave of relief when Greg finally returned with the crackers and water.

Olivia stared at the meager plate and said, "You and that girl had guns at my apartment. Can I have one?"

He stared at her a moment, his gaze lingering on the hollowness of her cheeks. "Maybe eat some crackers. Then we'll talk about guns. Okay?"

Mechanically, she reached out, took a cracker, and put it in her mouth. When she started to cough, Greg gave her some water, which she gulped down.

"Not too much," Greg said, taking it from her. "You look like you haven't, uh, had anything for a while. They say it's bad if you eat and drink too much after so long."

Olivia wiped her mouth free of crumbs and water and said, "Now can I have a gun?"

"Why do you want one?" Jack said, dreading the answer.

"You know why. Please?"

He watched her quietly in the dim electric light, then sighed. "Greg?"

"Yeah?"

"Give us a moment."

"You got it," he said, sounding relieved, then left and shut the door behind him.

Jack reached out tentatively, took the girl's hand—frail to the point of skeletal—and guided her into a chair.

"We all lost parents," he said lamely.

"Yeah, but I actually loved mine."

Jack stiffened in sudden anger. Sure, he wasn't comatose with grief, but he still loved his parents. With great effort, he forced himself to calm. The girl was suffering and lashing out. He had to remember that.

"How old are you, twelve?" he said.

She shook her head. "Thirteen. Almost fourteen. And this is what I want. Why can't you just give me one?"

"I saw you praying. What would your parents say if they knew their daughter was going around asking people for guns?"

For the first time, her expression broke into something beyond apathetic—she squeezed her eyes shut as her face tightened, and a single sob escaped. Jack's earlier anger evaporated, replaced by a kindred sorrow.

"Why did it happen?" she whispered. "The Sickness?"

"Nobody knows. Some kind of weapon, maybe." He shrugged. "I even heard it was aliens. The news had all kinds of crazy theories before everything went dark."

"Why did I live?"

"I don't know that either," he said. "I do know you could have killed yourself a bunch of different ways, but you came here instead. Do you think maybe you're looking for a reason to keep living, and not for a gun?"

She didn't reply. She didn't let go of his hand, either.

"Olivia," he said, "there's nobody in the world to stop you from doing it, if that's what you want. There's so much death outside these doors I can't even get my head around it. If I tried, I might want to shoot myself, too. Instead of that, I keep busy. That's the trick."

"Busy doing what?" she said, wiping her eyes.

"Living, planning, helping friends. We're leaving in the morning for a place I know about. When we get there, we'll try to make it through the winter and see what happens after that. You're just in time. We could use the help."

"Leaving here?" she said. "For where, exactly?"

Jack knew the girl wasn't a spy for a food gang, unless she was also one of the greatest actresses who'd ever lived. But if she stayed, he couldn't know if she'd get picked up by one of the bigger gangs. He wanted to keep their destination secret until they were strong enough to protect themselves.

"It's hard to explain," he said and hoped she wouldn't press him. "But it's definitely better than here. So what do you say: you with us?"

Olivia stared out at nothing, not saying yes and not saying no. He was content to let her think about it, the same way his parents always waited for him to answer one of their strange and difficult questions.

After sitting in silence for a good two minutes, she grabbed another cracker and put it in her mouth. Then she nodded.

***

Those early November mornings were particularly chilly, warming up around noon almost to where you could say it was merely cold.

With the wheelbarrow full of dumbbells cold for several hours now, none of the children wanted to get up. Jack recruited Greg and Tony to prod them into action, forcing them to take what meager possessions they had—a doll, a picture, a piece of jewelry—and file onto the bus.

While that was going on, he plied Olivia with a small amount of protein-rich food and some water. He then quietly passed word to the others to keep an eye on her, with special instructions to everyone to keep her away from guns. If she wanted to hold one, they were to tell her no and then inform him.

While the bus was warming up, they packed the food from the safe in the car with Greg. They put the blankets and pillows, the big pot, and their supply of candles, tools, and dishes in Pete's car. Lisa got on the bus with Jack to keep the little ones in line, and Brad and his baby brother rode with Pete—to keep *him* in line.

Olivia's ride was a harder choice. Jack didn't necessarily

think of himself as a matchmaker, but his oldest friend had mentioned her green hair twice since she'd arrived. If Greg had a crush, he'd do a good job keeping an eye on her, so she went with him, along with Tony.

"Everyone's settled," Lisa said after buckling in each child.

"Great. Now we try to live through the day with me at the wheel."

The fastest way to the interstate was by way of 50 to 28, but that was pre-Sickness. Right now, he didn't know if the route was free of roadblocks. Rather than risk the unknown, he backtracked to where they'd found the bus, then took 28 back in the direction of his old home and what he now thought of as Blaze's territory.

For all his worry, they didn't see anyone. Jack snorted. If *he* were a homicidal gang leader, he would have posted sentries.

When they got on 66, he blinked in surprise at how open and traffic-free it was. They saw the odd car—stalled or abandoned—but otherwise the way was clear. Which, considering the nature of the catastrophe, made sense. Nobody sick had the energy to leave, and the few that were still healthy had gotten out, for all the good it did them.

Jack hoped the roadblocks were limited to the neighborhoods and side streets. But if they did find one out here, big as the bus was and with his friends helping, he figured they could push through if needed.

***

"Why are you slowing?" Lisa said about ten minutes past the Gainesville exit.

"Look at that," was all he said, pointing at a hillside pasture.

"Oh, wow! Cows!"

The children in the bus pressed against the glass to see.

Squinting, Jack said, "Something's not right."

One of the children confirmed the observation by screaming. Then, because they were little, all of them started screaming, even if they didn't know why.

Jack stopped the bus, stood up, and shouted, "Knock it off!"

As one, the children quieted and stared at him.

"Sit down, face forward, and stay quiet on the bus," he said. "That's an order. Anyone who doesn't gets left behind. Got it?"

Their collective gasps made him feel guilty, but only a little. This way it'd be easier if he had to issue any new orders. He'd be the mean one, the ultimate big kid, and dangerous in his way. He could never be their friend, never smile with them or laugh, or it'd undermine his authority.

"Come on, Lisa," he said, and stepped off the bus.

"Laying it on a bit heavy, aren't you?"

He nodded. "So, what do you think?"

They surveyed the hillside, dotted with about fifty black cows. All were in various stages of decomposition. The smell was awful. The view, ghastly.

"Who would do that?" she said quietly. "Looks like they were ... like someone came through and killed them over the course of ... I dunno. Weeks, I guess. Look at that one." She pointed way off to the side at a wreck of sunken skin.

"Wasteful," Jack said. "They didn't butcher them properly—just took the legs. It's like they got hungry, came here, shot something, cut its legs off, and then left. Part of the reason I brought us out this way was to ... " He shook his head. "I thought maybe *we* could bag a cow or two. Maybe a sheep or something. You know, for the winter."

"I'm sure there's more," she said. "It's a big country."

Jack stared at the mess on the hillside another minute, not saying anything. Then he sighed. "Let's get out of here."

As they continued down 66, it became obvious the interstate was wide open except for the exits, which were mostly blocked off. That was fine. The place they were going didn't have any nearby neighborhoods to worry about, and when they got to the exit—just short of Front Royal—they passed through without a problem.

Jack couldn't stop smiling as they snaked through trees and hills deeper into the Virginia countryside, far away from dead adults and lunatics with guns and swords. Eventually, they pulled off the county road onto a wide gravel lane that led to a gate. Beside it was a sign reading, "Big Timber Model Homes: Join The Log Home

Revolution!"

The children's voices rose in excitement as they pulled into a wide, grassy clearing with a large creek-fed pond in the distance. Situated around it were a number of beautiful log homes, all of them brand new.

Jack stopped the bus and gazed intently at the scene before him. No cars or trucks. Best of all, no smoke from the four chimneys. Not necessarily proof the place was deserted, but he'd definitely take it.

"Jeez, Jack," Lisa said from the seat behind him. "Where did you learn about this place?"

"Last year, with my parents," he said. "They were in the market for a log home they could build themselves, up in West Virginia. We sat in a class in that big one over there." He pointed to the largest of the cabins, with a soaring roof and a wraparound deck. "The brochure showed a retired couple putting one together all by themselves. Said it could be done for something like thirty thousand dollars. My parents looked into it. Way too much work, and only cost that much if you found all the materials yourself." He smiled. "*Or* they could buy one of these lovely model homes, which the company would build for us starting at two hundred thousand. Dad said it was a total bait and switch. They could have bought one, but they wanted me to have the money after they ..." He shook his head. "You know how they were."

Lisa cursed under her breath. "Your parents, I swear. Laying all that on you. It wasn't fair."

He laughed drily. "But they were right. Who knows, maybe it'll pay off."

After they parked, the children practically boiled out of the bus, running between the different model homes or out into the huge field of tall grass. Jack saw a herd of deer in the distance flee from the commotion and wished he'd thought to bring his rifle down with him.

Then, looking at the quiet cabins, he climbed back up and got it for a different reason.

"Expecting trouble?" Lisa said.

"Yep." He grinned. "Mostly as a policy. Let's grab the others."

They met between the vehicles with Greg, Brad, Tony, Pete, and Olivia.

"I'm pretty sure we're the only ones here," Jack said, "but we need to know. So, groups of two. Don't bust into anything. This is our new home and we should treat it that way."

It turned out all the cabins were locked up tight, as was the trailer, and no one was inside when they looked through the windows.

Greg said, "I bet the keys are sitting in there somewhere. We won't be living in the trailer, right? Doesn't have a chimney."

Jack conceded the point. "Pete, where's that crowbar you had?"

"In the car," he said, not moving.

"I'll get it," Brad said and stood in front of the smaller boy. "Keys."

Pete handed them over with a sullen expression. Minutes later, Brad had the door open with minimal effort. When they went in, they found an office with a number of desks laden with computer monitors, brochures, and office clutter.

Sure enough, hanging on the wall as if waiting for them were keys numbered one through four.

FOURTEEN

The four model homes each had different names, chosen by the company to match their sizes or other appeal.

The Paul Bunyan model was the smallest. It had a large bedroom, a loft, and a single fireplace with a stove you could cook on.

The next biggest was the Abe Lincoln. It was like the Paul Bunyan, but wider, and had two bedrooms on the main floor.

Still bigger was The Skyline. Longer in shape, this one had two fireplaces—a stove-free unit in the living room wall, the other in the fancy dining room at the far end. The stove in the dining room had a cook top. The kitchen was in the middle, and like the other two cabins, basically useless without electricity. The Skyline had five bedrooms—two small ones on the first floor, three upstairs, and three bathrooms. Without plumbing, also useless.

The biggest cabin by far was The Saskatchewan. With six bedrooms, it was built up and out, and very much *around*. It had an enormous great room with a nice fireplace, as well as one with a cooking surface set between dining room and kitchen, just like in the Skyline. Everything about the cabin looked super expensive, from the bearskin rugs to the multiple flat screen televisions and exercise room. It also had a kitchen that was bigger than the main floor of Jack's old house. There were huge windows that couldn't open, a soaring ceiling, and a spiral staircase that looked carved by hand.

When Jack had come here with his parents, he'd loved the Saskatchewan the most because of how big it was. Standing there now with Greg and Lisa, he gazed upward and said, "That's a lot of air to keep heated."

"Well, we got all that wood outside," Greg said, a note of longing in his voice.

It was true. Each cabin came with a decorative diagonal sweep of stacked wood just beside the front door.

"That won't last but a week or two," Jack said. "Which brings me to my first concern: sleeping arrangements."

"I want my own cabin," Greg said, grinning at the space around him. "This one will do."

Jack smiled politely, but he was nervous. If people became grasping, that'd make it harder for everyone.

"This one's way too big," Jack said. "We'd be forever chopping wood ... if we actually had something to chop it with. I'm thinking the Skyline makes the most sense. Just like at the Welcome Center—only each of the adults gets a room of their own."

No slouch at math, Lisa said, "There are seven *adults*, Jack, and only five bedrooms. Someone has to room up."

He leered at her. "Well, if you insist ..."

She punched his arm just shy of painfully.

"Violation!" Greg said in a robotic voice. "Do not talk to my sister that way. *Beep!* Brotherly expression of outrage executed. *Beep!* Duty completed."

Lisa punched his arm, too.

"*Beep!*"

Jack peeked outside to make sure none of the others were around, then motioned his friends deeper into the cabin. The little kids were exploring the upper floor and not paying attention.

He lowered his voice. "What I'm about to say will sound self-serving as hell."

"Nothing new there," Greg said.

Jack didn't smile. "I know I've sort of jumped in and started acting like I'm the boss or something. How do you guys feel about that?"

Lisa said, "You're doing great. We're not dumb, we get it. Someone has to lead, and I honestly need a break. Keeping everyone fed without getting murdered in our sleep ..." She shook her head. "I'm worn out."

"And I'm too busy with more important things," Greg said, still trying to tease a smile from his suddenly serious friend.

Jack nodded. "All right. I think Brad and Olivia are on board, but Tony will need to see you two defer to me on things. He'll see that and stay in line. Pete's the biggest problem. That stunt of his, leaving us like that ..."

"Maybe he wasn't thinking," Lisa said, frowning. "Or just assumed we were fine."

"Maybe. If anything like that happens again, we deal with it right away. Agreed?"

As one, the twins nodded.

"Great," Jack said. "Now, for the cabins. I want everyone in the Skyline, with you and Olivia sharing the master bedroom. It sucks, I know, but Olivia's sort of delicate right now, and I'd really appreciate it. Everyone old enough to carry a gun gets a room."

He paused, waiting for Lisa's input, then decided her stony silence meant he could continue.

Swallowing, he said, "The little ones will share the living room. We'll bring in mattresses from the other cabins so it'll be comfortable and warm, and relocate the couches and tables. We'll take the stove from the Abe Lincoln and set it up in the fireplace."

Lisa—who was *still* good at math—cleared her throat. "With Olivia and me sharing a room, and all the *boys* getting their *own*, that leaves us a room short."

"Um, yeah," Jack said. "Okay, so here's the self-serving part."

Greg laughed. "There's actually *more*?"

"If I'm playing as leader, it makes sense for me to sleep in the Paul Bunyan." He paused, gauging their expressions. Then he added, "Alone."

Lisa shook her head, perplexed. "Why would you do that?"

Greg coughed, "*Chosen one*," and covered his mouth with a hastily raised fist.

"Shackleton," Jack said, glancing at him. "You've read about him, right?"

"We watched the documentary," Greg said. "It was cool. You're right, you should totally do that."

Lisa stared from one to the other. "Right about what?"

Greg said, "*He's* the captain. Shackleton had his own room because he was the captain. Captains need to be mysterious. They can't mingle too freely with the enlisted men. Ol' Jack here has to stay aloof. It's a leadership thing. Psychology. Man stuff."

Lisa stared at him like his hair was on fire, her whole manner incredulous. "Well would we be allowed to come *over* sometimes, oh captain, my captain?"

Jack nodded. "Whenever you want. As leaders, we have to maintain our distance a little. That way, when we give an order, the children will be more likely to obey. They won't be little forever. You'll also have your own rooms, for the same reason. We'll take planning meetings in the Bunyan. When I'm alone, I'll be sleeping. Not that big a deal. My biggest concern is wasted wood. Once we get some axes, I'll pull double duty on chopping."

Lisa didn't seem convinced.

Jack said, "Look, if it was just us, it'd be different. But the stakes are too high. We don't want people having to guess who's leader or where their place is in the pecking order. There's a lot of work ahead."

She raised her hands in surrender. "Okay, fine. I think it's stupid, but whatever."

Greg threw an arm around her. "Look on the bright side, sis. You get to bunk with Olivia. You can put in a good word for me."

"How's that the bright side?"

He smiled and patted her gently. "It just is."

***

When Lisa broke the housing arrangements to the others, she didn't give a reason for Jack getting his own cabin. Only Tony seemed to notice the difference, but he stayed silent. The others just nodded.

Olivia was still too frail to do very much, so Jack asked if she wouldn't mind watching the children.

"Only until you get your strength back," he said.

"Sure," she said, smiling shyly and tugging a lock of her green hair. "I'll keep them out of the way."

Ever since she'd decided to throw in with them, Olivia seemed to have perked up a little, and she'd dropped the bad attitude. Both good signs, though Jack wasn't so naive as to think she was suddenly all better.

For the next few hours, Jack and the others moved mattresses, bedding, and chairs from the other cabins. Box springs and frames were deemed unnecessary and left behind. All the beds had been furnished with sheets, covers, and pillows, so those were kept too. In total, they got twelve mattresses of varying sizes, because some bedrooms had been furnished with two doubles. Most of the beds were king-sized, offering plenty of room for the twenty-one children to bunk together.

It was early afternoon when they finished. After that, they all went to Jack's cabin and sat in the comfortable chairs in front of a new fire.

"We're not done yet," Jack said around a mouthful of protein bar. He'd doled out the last of them to each of the leaders. The little ones had eaten rice and beans, prepared by Olivia after Lisa got the Skyline stove working.

Tony muttered under his breath.

Lisa said, "You got a problem? Spit it out."

He pointed at Jack. "Why we gotta do what he says?"

Jack said, "You don't have to. But this is my place. I found it, I brought us here, and I'm in charge. If you don't like it, we can drop you off somewhere cold."

"And what if I don't want to go?"

As tense as the room had gotten, Jack smiled easily. "Do you really want to take it there, Tony?"

The younger boy glanced from Jack to Lisa, her face hard as a stone, then to Greg, no less yielding, and then back again. "Nah, man. Just seeing what's what. It's cool."

Jack nodded and looked at each of them. "We have a number of pressing issues and not a whole lot of time. Chief of which is the bathroom situation. The cabins have toilets, but they were never hooked up to working plumbing. We definitely don't want the children using them, so we need to somehow keep them shut."

"How about that superglue Lisa fixed the safe with?" Greg said.

"Great idea," Jack said. "We're also going to need shovels. That pond gets fed from the hills behind us. In my opinion, it looked clean. A stream runs from the pond down through the valley. Fish swim upstream just as often as down, so we can't go dumping our waste there."

Brad smiled. "Fish? Really?"

"I saw some trout last time I was here," Jack said. "It'll be fun to go fishing, but only after we deal with the sanitation problem."

Olivia cleared her throat. "We should dig a ditch away from the water, down where the woods begin. At night, we can leave buckets outside the cabin. That way nobody has to walk in the dark and maybe get hurt or eaten by something."

Pete snorted, and Greg glared him into silence.

"That's a great idea," Jack said, trying not to smile. "But there's nothing up here that can hurt us." He thought it over. "Well, not anytime soon. A black bear, maybe, if you startle it. In time, I imagine the mountain lions will work their way back, but it won't be this season. Oh, Lisa, what time is it?"

She looked at her watch. "One thirty. You know, we should probably all get watches."

"Good idea. We also need more tools. Shovels for ditches, axes for chopping wood. Tony, Pete: if you continue past the turnoff, you'll come out of these hills into farmland. Around here, every house will have tools. Get them and Brad and I will do the work."

"Don't forget toilet paper," Olivia added.

Tony nodded. "If we find something else, can we bring it back?"

"Sure," he said. "Food, those watches she mentioned, ammo, guns, whatever. But don't take too long. In the hills like this, it gets dark earlier. And hey—if you see smoke from any houses, stay away from them."

Pete spoke up suddenly. "Is it okay if we bring Mandy?"

"Is she needed? She's kind of small."

"That's because she's nine," he said, snorting. "Take it from me: she's a good scavenger. She'll be fine, trust me."

The request hung in the air uncomfortably. Though Jack was inclined to say no, he didn't want to be a tyrant who made all the decisions for everyone. That and he was glad Pete was at least trying to help out now. He hoped to encourage the trend.

Slowly, he nodded. "All right. But you're responsible. Anything else?"

Both boys shook their heads—Pete impatiently, Tony as if he couldn't believe they were taking a nine-year-old girl with them.

After they left, Jack said to Olivia, "You were great with the children today. You don't have to be stuck with them if you don't want to, but right now ..."

She nodded. "Yeah, I know. I'm a toothpick."

"Your words, not mine," Jack said, embarrassed. "I'm just saying we need you stronger. Your main job is to eat. If you could keep watching the little ones for now, it'd help out a lot."

"I like children. It'll be fun."

"They're the future, as they say ... or used to say." He shook his head. "We need to teach them. And ourselves, too." He turned to Lisa and Greg, gathering his words. "I've been thinking—we need to loot a library, or a bookstore. Find stuff on raising animals, farming, medicine, math, that kind of thing. Whatever we can grab before some *cabbage* comes along and uses it for kindling."

Brad said, "Cabbage?"

"Don't ask," Greg said, rolling his eyes.

"What about history?" Lisa said. "Fiction?"

Jack frowned in thought. "History for sure, but maybe a later trip. Fiction, too. All work and no play and I'd be pretty dull, right?"

Olivia laughed and Greg joined her, grinning foolishly when she glanced at him.

"I guess that's it for now," Jack said, getting up. "Any questions?"

When nobody said anything, they filed out and got to work making the place livable.

FIFTEEN

While Tony, Pete, and Mandy were out scavenging, Greg discovered something amazing: a portable generator tucked inside a rain-protective hood, hooked up to a plug in the wall of the Saskatchewan. Jack had missed it because he hadn't been looking for one. None of the cabins had power lines connected to them, and Big Timber was too far off the beaten path for an underground connection to the grid.

In hindsight, when he'd come here with his parents, there were working lights and an instructional video on how to build log cabins. There had even been cold drinks and air-conditioning.

"Awesome job," Jack said and gave his smiling friend a high five.

"Too bad the tank's empty or we could try it now." He frowned in thought. "You know, we could always snag some gas from the bus. Just need a hose."

Jack shook his head. "First, I think the bus uses diesel, and it looks like this uses gas. Second, just because we have a generator, I'm not sure we should get too comfortable using it."

"Why not?"

"We shouldn't rely on our parents' technology." Seeing his friend's crestfallen expression he added, "Maybe for movies or something, once a week, or recharging batteries."

Greg snorted. "And that's not relying on technology?"

"You know what I mean: houselights, electric stoves, that kind of thing. We can't be constantly scrounging to feed it gas." Jack inspected the engine, not understanding any of it. "How big's that tank, anyway? Five gallons?"

"Looks like," Greg said dejectedly. "We could always stockpile some."

Jack nodded. "And we will. I'd rather have it and not need it than need it and not have it. Come on, let's go see if the Skyline has the same hookup."

There wasn't a generator connected to the Skyline, but it did have the special plug on the wall. Jack called in Lisa, who was helping Olivia rearrange the mattresses.

"Wow," Lisa said, admiring the generator. "Great job, brother mine."

It turned out the Skyline's hookup would work. The generator had wheels to assist moving it around, but it was heavy and clunky. Brad helped them wheel it over the uneven ground. The protective housing was detachable and fit easily over the unit once they had it and the tank in place.

Greg's find was a great moment for everyone, and Jack felt upbeat about their chances. There was still plenty to do, as well as the ever-present fear of someone getting hurt or seriously ill. Not to mention starvation. They still hadn't successfully acquired food that didn't come in a wrapper or can. But at least they didn't have to worry about maniacs like Blaze, or whichever gang attacked them at the Welcome Center, or freezing to death.

Jack laughed softly. *Or TV.*

***

The three scavengers returned later than Jack would have liked. Just as he wondered whether there'd be time to dig the sanitation ditch before dusk, Pete got out of the car and stormed toward him sporting a puffy eye.

"That jerk hit me!" he shouted, pointing back at Tony, who got out slowly with a wide smile on his still-chubby face.

Mandy jumped out too, frowning in anger. "Tony's a bully, that's what *he* is!"

"What the hell, Tony?" Jack said, checking Pete's eye to make sure it wasn't serious. They couldn't afford serious.

"He didn't wanna go in the house," Tony said, "so I made him."

"It had dead people in it!" Pete yelled.

Tony's smile fell away, replaced with an angry frown. "So? I went in. Everyone goes in. You gotta go in."

As much as Jack agreed with the sentiment, he couldn't condone the brutality.

"You two, in my cabin, now," he said, then turned around and entered the Paul Bunyan without looking back.

Wondering if they'd follow, he grew angry at the prospect of being ignored. He drew on that anger—he'd need it.

Pete came in first, followed by Tony, who shut the door behind him.

Like the other cabins, the Paul Bunyan had a vaulted ceiling with big windows to let in as much light as possible, so he could see them both clearly. Tony stood with that lazy smile still on his face. Pete settled for glowering, his hurt eye demanding justice.

Jack moved his hand casually to the butt of his gun. "Take out your pistol."

"Why?"

"Because I'm in charge. You want to sleep here tonight, not walk out of here in the cold with nothing, you'll do it. And you'll listen when I give an order. You're useless to anyone if you can't follow orders."

Tony opened his mouth to speak.

"*Quiet!*" Jack shouted. "Give me the damned gun!"

Both boys jerked like they'd been smacked. Tony took out his pistol and handed it barrel-first to Jack, who shook his head at the dangerousness of it. He should have put it down for Jack to pick up, but he'd deal with that later. It was about to get more dangerous.

"Is it loaded?"

"I think it—"

"All guns are loaded," Jack said. "That's your first

lesson. Here's another: in a world with no police, filled with people who don't have anything, you don't bully."

"But I was doing all the work! It's not fair!"

Ignoring that, Jack checked to see if the gun really was loaded—it was. He flicked the safety, then put it down.

To Pete, he said, "Now pick it up."

Tony breathed in sharply.

Pete swallowed, reached down, and picked it up. He stood stock-still, holding the weapon like it was slithery and poisonous.

"That button on the side is the safety," Jack said. "Just flick it forward so it shows red and it'll fire if you pull the trigger."

Pete stared at the switch, hands shaking in fear. His gaze moved from it to Tony, and then his expression edged back to angry. He flicked the safety off.

Tony reared back and sort of shrank in on himself.

"Finger off the trigger," Jack said quietly, then relaxed when Pete did so.

"Don't you touch me again!" Pete shouted, causing the other boy to flinch.

"Easy, Pete," Jack said, then turned to Tony. "Everyone carries guns except Pete and Olivia. So far. But there's guns everywhere. My rifle's upstairs, and I'm not watching it every minute. There's going to be more guns and more people, which means way more chances for tempers to flare. In the Old West, they called the gun the great equalizer. It didn't matter how strong you were. If you had one, you could take out the biggest bully in the world." He shifted his gaze to Pete. "Go ahead and put it on the table."

Pete held onto the pistol for perhaps five more seconds, still glaring at Tony, then put it down. When he did, the tension eased out of him like a spring uncoiled.

Tony sighed, visibly relieved. "Sorry for hitting you, man. *Real* sorry." He looked at Jack. "Can I have my gun back?"

"No, you can't. Tomorrow, you and Pete are going to get trained. Your gun safety sucks, and Pete needs to be able to defend himself from bullies. I would have liked to see about bagging a deer in the morning, but this is more important. Dismissed." When the two boys just stood there staring at him, he added, "That means get the hell out."

Nodding as one, they beat a hasty exit.

Jack went over to the door, locked it, then dropped down into a chair and exhaled loudly. He noted his heart was racing, and wondered if either of them had seen the tremor in his hands. Being a homeschooler didn't give him many opportunities for tense confrontations, armed or not. He wondered if he could have handled it differently.

Probably, he thought.

Still, he didn't think he'd done too badly. Nobody had died, and if it kept Tony from hitting people, and Pete from getting hit, that was a win.

Probably, he thought again, and went out to inspect the results from the scavenging expedition.

In addition to about ten watches and rolls of toilet paper, the two boys had returned with an assortment of picks, shovels, and axes. They'd also brought back several buckets, which Olivia set in a row outside the Skyline's front door. She told each child the rules: use the bucket and then leave it there for the next person. Every morning, a leader would take it and dispose of it.

Because of the lateness of the hour, Jack and Brad held off on any digging.

"I suppose we should think about building an outhouse," Jack said to him. "Unless you feel like dragging kiddie poop back and forth every day."

Brad made a face. "Is there more to outhouses than just digging a hole and putting a little house on top?"

"I'm sure there is. Just like everything else."

***

Before Jack had ever fired a handgun, his parents made him take a class on gun safety. They'd attended it with him, even though they were both trained already. That had been an early first lesson for him: "You're never too smart to learn more about safety."

Jack told Pete and Tony to meet him in the field behind the cabins, then found Olivia and took her aside.

"How you feeling these days?" he said cautiously.

"What do you mean?"

"Before we came here, you were sort of ..."

"Suicidal?" She shrugged, then smiled. "Maybe I was and maybe I wasn't. I don't know. I try not to think of my parents with people around because I get all leaky." As if proving a point, she wiped her eyes and laughed. "I'm okay. Knowing the children need me helps."

He told her how he wanted everyone old enough to carry a gun armed and trained in their use.

"That'd be cool, actually," she said. "I used to love action movies. But I'm not going to kill myself, Jack. Like you said—if I wanted to, I could have done it a hundred ways."

He nodded, patted her uncomfortably on the shoulder, and said, "Well good. That's just good."

He led her to where the others were waiting.

Thinking back to his safety course, he tried for the same air of competency the instructor had filled the room with that day.

"I'm going to be repeating myself a lot," Jack said, "because when it comes to safety, everything bears repeating. You'll be sick of it before we're done, and then you'll get to repeat it all back to me. If I've done my job properly, you'll probably mumble it in your sleep, too."

The basic rules for handling weapons were simple, and he wrote them out with a dry-erase marker on a whiteboard snagged from the sales trailer:

1) Finger off the trigger until ready to fire.

2) Never hand someone a gun. Put it down and let them pick it up.

3) Muzzle pointed in a safe direction at all times.

4) Treat every firearm as loaded.

5) Before handling a gun, understand how it works.

6) The safety switch is NOT to be relied upon.

7) Never goof off when handling weapons.

8) Address unsafe behavior immediately.

Jack turned to Tony. "Last night, I asked for your gun and you handed it to me, muzzle first. You also didn't check the chamber to see if it was empty." He turned to Pete. "I picked up the gun and chambered it, flicked the safety, and put it down. Then I told you to pick it up— someone untrained and obviously uncomfortable with guns, not to mention pissed off at the time. That was dumb of me. Can you think of the second thing I did wrong?"

The two boys looked at each other and shrugged.

Jack grinned. "*I* was pissed off, too."

That brought tentative smiles all around.

"Okay," Jack said. "Shooting rules."

He told them what not to shoot at, glass bottles being high on that list, as well as rocks, buildings, and bushes.

"And don't shoot up in the air like they do on TV," he said. "What goes up must come down."

After ensuring they were still listening—they were—he covered the proper care of weapons and ammunition, and demonstrated how to take apart his .40 caliber.

"Later on," Jack said, "I'll show you my cleaning kit, and we'll sit down together to clean and oil everything. We need more cleaner and gun oil. My kit isn't big enough for the whole group."

As he went on, Olivia peppered him with an endless number of hypothetical questions. Soon Tony, and even Pete, joined in.

Tony: "What if you have to run with a gun?"

Jack: "Never run with a gun."

Tony: "But what if I'm being chased by a bunch of people?"

Pete: "If I drop a gun, is it safe to pick up?"

Jack: "Yes. Pick it up by the grip, finger off the trigger, careful where you point it."

Pete: "But don't they sometimes go off when you drop them?"

Olivia: "You said we need to sleep near our guns in case we're attacked. What if someone sleepwalks?"

Jack: "Do you sleepwalk?"

She shook her head.

Eventually they got around to target practice, which everyone was geared up for after talking so long about guns and not using them. Even Pete looked excited.

Jack had brought a box from the trailer with him. When he asked Pete to set it up against a big rock in the middle of the field, he nodded in appreciation when Pete told him that was too dangerous.

When Jack handed back Tony's confiscated pistol, he felt warmed when the boy said, "Check to see if it's ready to shoot, then put it down. Then I'll take it."

When all the gotchas were out of the way, and after stuffing wads of toilet paper in their ears, they practiced with the various weapons in their arsenal, including Jack's AR-15. He hated losing the ammunition, but knew there was nothing better than shooting to drive home the training.

Two minutes into the shooting, Lisa rushed out to round up the children who'd come outside to watch. After thirty minutes of live firing, Jack called a halt.

To Pete, he said, "You sure you're a pacifist?"

"Yeah, why?"

Jack shook his head, openly impressed. "Because you're a crack shot with a .40 caliber, that's why."

Pete grinned happily, and everyone laughed. Even Tony.

SIXTEEN

In the days following the training, Pete and Tony gained a vigorous interest in shooting. It was pretty much the only thing to do for fun if they didn't like fishing, which they didn't. They returned from each outing with a wide assortment of shotguns, hunting rifles, pistols, and several more AR-15s, as well as ammunition. *Lots* of ammunition, clearly telegraphing their enthusiasm for more target practice.

"Have you run into anyone yet?" Jack said before their next outing. That was their other mission besides scavenging: report on possible additions to the group, regardless of age.

Tony said, "Sort of. We see cars sometimes. They pass us, stare us down so we know they're not scared. We detour around so they don't know where we're going or coming from. Other times, we see houses with smoke, but you said not to mess with those."

Jack nodded. He didn't want them knocking on a door and getting shot through a window. If they found someone outside walking around unarmed, they could go talk to him or her, see how they were doing, ask if they wanted to join.

"Well, keep looking. Meanwhile, I need you to shift gears a little. See if you can't find a small pickup truck that doesn't waste much gas. Nothing too big."

"We bring back gas every day," Pete said.

Because of their scavenging, the little community now had about fifty gallons of gasoline and thirty of diesel. Their biggest problem wasn't getting the stuff, it was storing it—most people, even farmers, didn't keep more than maybe one or two gas cans on hand, so they were always on the lookout for more.

"I know," Jack said, "and I appreciate that. But we still need to conserve. Get a truck with two tires up front, two in the back. If it has four in the back, just leave it."

They nodded.

"We gonna bring back something big?" Tony said.

Jack was concerned about the trench they'd been throwing their waste into. The buckets stank unless promptly washed, and you had to be careful not to slosh any foul water on your hands. Also, he'd caught Greg doing his business behind a tree rather than risk slipping and falling into the trench.

"Yep," Jack said. "Wood. Get as much lumber as you can. Two-by-fours, plywood, that kind of thing. Something that'll work for posts, too. And nails. We have like ten hammers and no nails."

Pete's eyes widened. He covered his mouth and made a series of weird, hiccupping sounds. "You're building the outhouse!"

It took Jack a moment, and then he realized: *Pete's laughing.*

He'd never heard the boy laugh before ... and yeah, it was strange, him covering his mouth and heaving around like that. But it was a refreshing change from the negativity he'd been displaying since they first met.

Mandy, who was listening quietly, covered her mouth and giggled.

Jack winked at her. "Stinky work, but someone's gotta do it. We're also building some other things, so make sure you get a lot."

Pete did the laugh thing again and shook his head. "We'll get plenty, don't worry. I know just the place. Right Tony?"

Tony glanced at him sideways and smirked. "No doubt."

The boys and Mandy got in the car and left, and Jack joined the rest of the group inside the Skyline cabin. Greg, Lisa, and Brad sat talking quietly just outside a ring of children lying down enjoying a rare event: television. Specifically, a DVD with friendly dinosaurs and kids getting along. Olivia sat with them, with a girl on her left named Pamela, a boy name Quinn on her right, and another boy named David next to him. Her little generals. Since taking the job, she'd augmented her power and influence by drafting the three most popular and passing instructions through them. Together, they were able to control even the most unruly behavior through a mix of peer pressure, positive reinforcement, and in the worst cases, the looming threat of being sent to Jack for punishment. For his part, Jack hoped it would never come to that, and didn't know what he'd do if it did.

"Hi, Jack," Brad whispered. He held his little brother, Tyler, rocking him gently while feeding him formula from a bottle. During their first week, the scavengers had managed to secure several more cans of the precious stuff.

"Heya," Jack said, then turned to Greg. "You think you can hold the fort?"

Greg's tone was confident. "With those new rifles, we should be fine."

Brad nodded. "Yep. What I wanna know is, when are we going for a deer?"

"Hopefully tomorrow," Jack said. "Provided today goes all right."

With winter fast approaching, Jack didn't want to waste any more time than he had to. They needed to bag as much game as they could, and possibly a cow. Then they needed to preserve the meat somehow. Neither Jack nor the twins, nor anyone else, knew exactly how to do that. They'd heard of smoking meat and salting it, and Jack knew how to turn it into jerky provided he had a gas stove, which he didn't. But everything else about food preservation was a mystery. A critical gap in his parents' lessons.

Lisa said, "I know where two libraries are, but those are back home."

"There's always downtown Front Royal," Jack said.

"Problem is, I've never been there, so we need a map. Easy enough."

Greg said, "What about GPS? Wouldn't take long to find one. Then you don't need a map."

Lisa shook her head. "I'm not sure. Doesn't that need the Internet or something?"

"To find shops and stuff, maybe," Greg said. "But the coordinates and all that come from satellites. I bet that part still works."

Jack thought about it, but ultimately rejected the idea. "We can't count on stuff like that. Not for the small amount of benefit we'd get. We'll always have maps. We need to keep those skills alive, and that means using them. Every town has a library. Just like every town has a school and a fire station. We'll just drive around until we find one. Honestly, I could use the time away."

Greg sighed. "Sort of wish I could go with you two. Guess I'm getting cabin fever. Get it?" He knocked on the exposed log wall. "Because of the cabins?"

Lisa rolled her eyes. Jack just smiled.

"I want one of you outside at all times," he said to Greg and Brad. "You can't just watch the entrance—you need to watch the perimeter as well. Everything up to the tree line. Anyone who shows up and isn't alone or at most two people, keep cover and tell them to scram. They reach for a gun—and they *will* be armed, don't doubt it—you shoot them and cry about it later. No warnings."

His voice had risen a little at the end of his speech, and a couple of the younger children looked back at him curiously.

"Say it, don't spray it, buddy," Greg said. "We got it, man, relax."

Jack stood up, chucked Greg on the shoulder, and nodded at Brad. "I know that. Ready, Lisa?"

***

Using an old road map plucked from one of the cars, Jack and Lisa left Big Timber, got on the highway, and found the exit for downtown Front Royal not ten miles away.

Much like Centreville, sporadic roadblocks made

traveling by car difficult. Many of the roadblocks had been nudged open, either by adults who'd tried to escape the Sickness, or by kids left behind. Wood smoke streamed from some of the houses they passed, and once or twice they ran into groups of little kids in the streets. Each time, he had to slow to a crawl and ease through because they just stood there staring at them. He wondered what would happen if he roared through without slowing. Would they scatter, or would they let themselves get hit?

"Jack, do these children seem healthy to you?"

He looked closely at a group of three throwing a ball. "They're skinny, but not as bad off as the ones back our way. Someone's been feeding them."

"Maybe we could live here instead of the cabins? Most of the houses have chimneys."

It was true—there *were* a lot of chimneys. The houses were packed close together with tiny yards in-between stretches of stores and other businesses. Everyone in the group could have his or her own house.

At one point, they passed a group of teenagers in a fast-looking car. Tied to the antenna was a big strip of black and white checkered cloth, like a racing flag. As a precaution, Jack edged his speed up a bit and took a random turn, then another, then another, hoping to put as much distance as possible between them and the other car. There were other cars they passed, each with those little strips tied to the antennas or off the side mirrors if they didn't have whip antennas. Each time, Jack took evasive measures while trying not to seem desperate or scared. Maybe they weren't hostile, but he wasn't willing to bet their lives on it.

After an hour of driving around in what seemed like circles, Lisa pointed at a little sign indicating a library somewhere ahead.

The library was a sprawling red-bricked building with white trim. None of the windows looked broken, and for that Jack was thankful.

"Samuels Public Library," Lisa read.

Jack found a spot out front and parked. When they got out, Lisa pulled her new AR-15 from the back seat and slung it over her shoulder. Jack grabbed his and did the same.

"You sure you're comfortable with that?" he said.

"Yeah," she said defensively. "You saw me shoot it, didn't you?"

He *had* seen her, during one of their popular target-practicing sessions. But target practicing and remembering how it operated during a tense situation were two different things. Particularly if it jammed.

Rather than risk irritating her further, he nodded, and they proceeded to the front doors.

By unsaid agreement, they went in with guns primed and ready to fire, aiming this way and that like a SWAT team. He felt safe and foolish, but it paid to be prepared.

"Seems clear," Lisa said.

"Yeah. So how do you want to do this?"

Lisa looked around. There was a desk laden with dead computer terminals. Beyond that were shelves of books on either side, stretching to the end of the building. "Hadn't thought that far. Can't really look anything up, can we?"

Jack shook his head. "I think in the old days they used catalogs with index cards. I guess we just sort of walk around looking."

Lisa nodded. "I'll do the stacks on the right. You do the left?"

"Sure."

Jack quickly learned the stacks on the left were mostly biographies, leading into fiction. Lisa started up near the front, so he went to the opposite end. There, he found collections of encyclopedias and big reference books on various subjects. Some of them were medical, and he grabbed those down. Then, realizing he didn't have anything to carry them in, he cursed quietly under his breath and grabbed a few more books on engineering and chemistry, and another medical book.

When he couldn't carry any more, he strode to the doors and called out, "Heading to the car."

Once outside, Jack popped the trunk and deposited the books in the back. A quick look around showed nobody there, which suited him fine. He passed Lisa on the way in. She had an even bigger stack than his—because she'd found a book return cart.

"I left the trunk open," he said, feeling faintly betrayed.

"Thanks," she said, smiling smugly and pushing the cart gently along with one hand.

And so it went for the next hour. Jack found as many books on science and math and engineering as he could, and Lisa snapped up everything she could find on animal husbandry, farming, and homesteading. He also broke down and snagged some interesting science fiction books and a bunch of age-appropriate stuff for the children.

"Hey, Jack, check this out," Lisa said at one point. When he came over to look, she showed him a book on raising rabbits.

"Rabbits," he said, smiling. "You're really going to eat cute little bunnies?"

"The cuter the tastier," she said innocently.

Later, as they were bringing out their last load of books, having filled up the trunk and the entire back seat, Lisa said, "Do you smell something?"

Jack sniffed the air and said, "Shit!"

He dropped his books, rushed to the front doors, and saw a big pile of books burning in the parking lot. Worse, their car was gone. Clearly someone other than Lisa had learned to hotwire cars.

Parked nearby were two sports cars with little checkered flags tied to the antennas. Sitting on the hoods or standing casually were several boys and girls in their early teens. All of them were armed. When they saw Jack, they waved for him to come out.

SEVENTEEN

"Now what?" Lisa said. "We going out to meet those gunslinging book burners?"

"Maybe they just want to talk?"

"Sure. Because they're sociable that way."

Jack grimaced. "Come on."

Without looking back, he delved deeper into the library, heading for the doors leading to the parking lot out back.

"If they're smart," she said, "they're guarding there, too."

"Don't count on it. My guess is they've never used the library even once in their dumb cabbage lives."

When he looked out the back doors, sure enough, there was a sports car out there, too.

Lisa smirked. "Cabbages, huh?"

Jack swore. "We're trapped. And we don't have a ride home."

"Sure we do," she said coldly. "There it is, right there." She was looking at the car the kids were using. There were three of them, all about twelve or older, two carrying pistols and one a hunting rifle. "I think we have the advantage. The sun's behind the building and the doors are shaded. They can't see us very easily, but we can see them. First shot breaks the glass, the rest break us out of here."

Quietly, Jack said, "Is that what we've come to? Killing

to steal a car?"

She shook her head. "More like killing to stay alive. See how healthy they look? I'm not trying to scare you, but what the heck are they eating? Not like the farmers brought in a bunch of crops over the summer. And I didn't see *that* many little kids on the way in ..."

Jack grinned. "What are you saying? Cannibalism? How's that not trying to scare me?"

A moment later, a car from the front joined the one in the back parking lot.

"So we take the one out front," she said, already moving.

He stopped her at the entrance. "I don't want to kill anyone else. Not if we can help it. Okay?"

"Fine," she said quietly. "But if they raise their guns or do anything threatening, we do what we have to. It sucks, but what choice do we have?"

"I agree," he said, then leaned in to kiss her. She tensed at first, then fell into it.

Since that first kiss on the bus, they'd been too busy to see what it meant. Half his reason for coming here together was to see if it might happen again. She was the smartest, prettiest girl he knew, and he wanted to protect her from every danger, up to and including herself. If she started thinking all her problems could be solved at the end of a gun, she was lost.

After pulling apart, they counted to three, then pushed through the glass front doors. Aiming as they went, they shouted things like, "Drop the guns!" and "Away from the car!" and "Don't even think about it!"

The three out front were completely taken by surprise. Jack felt a powerful surge of relief. These weren't steely-eyed commandos they were facing. They were just kids.

One said, "Don't shoot!" and dropped his gun. The others dropped theirs too, blubbering pathetically while backing up.

"Now run away!" Lisa shouted and shook her rifle.

They didn't hesitate—they dashed in all directions, sprinting as if they'd never stop. The two friends didn't wait to find out. They hopped in the sporty two door—still idling, wasting gas—and roared away without buckling in.

A sudden hiss of static sounded from a CB radio mounted under the dash, and a boy's voice said, "Kirby, you see them yet?"

Jack jerked the wheel in fright, nearly taking them into one of the quaint little streetlights decorating the town. Lisa screamed, raising her hands defensively and slamming her rifle hard against the side window, cracking it.

Jack steadied the car and kept going. "You may want to stow that."

She stashed her rifle on the back seat and pulled her pistol.

Static from the CB, then: "Dammit, what's happening? Pick up!"

Lisa moved to turn it off, but Jack stayed her hand. "Can't hurt to listen."

Doing his best to control his breathing and calm his jangling nerves, he wormed his way to one of the main roads leading back to the interstate. They didn't pass any other cars, but they did see more children out—little ones, none older than about ten. Again, he marveled at how well fed they looked, which made him think they had older brothers or sisters taking care of them. Despite the tenseness of the situation, he took comfort in that.

The CB crackled: "I know you can hear me! Bring back the car and we won't hurt you. If you keep running, you're dead!"

Jack snatched up the handset and looked at it, then pushed the side button. "You stole our car and tried to trap us. You do that to strangers, what do you expect?"

He waited for a reply, then realized he had to let go.

"—my city taking our stuff! You gotta give us something back."

Jack clicked the mic again. "First off, it's not a city, it's a town. Second, thanks for the car—full tank, too. And as for your dumb threats: my gang'll be back later to kill you all. We're pretty good at it, too. You won't even see us."

With an angry twist, he flicked off the power.

"Why did you say that?" Lisa said in a shocked tone.

Because I'm pissed.

A minute later he said, "The cabins aren't that far away. If we put them on alert, they'll spend more time defending the town than looking for us."

She didn't reply immediately.

"What?"

"We could do like you said. Hit them before they hit us."

He cast a worried glance her way.

She's just upset.

Shortly after finding the main road out, they passed another car with one of those checkered strips of cloth tied to it. The car stopped, half turned to follow them, but then just stayed there as if the driver were torn with indecision. Jack allowed a small sigh of satisfaction and kept going. A minute later, he pounded the steering wheel in frustration.

"What?" Lisa said.

"We needed those books."

"We'll get more," she said. "There's like a million libraries."

He nodded. "But I only know where my local one is, back home."

"Then we'll have to go back home," she said.

Shortly after getting on 66, Jack noticed they were being followed. Whoever it was kept their distance, pacing the two friends by the length of a city block.

"Are you sure they're the same ones?" Lisa said, peering through the side mirror.

He nodded. "They have one of those dumb flags. We can't let them follow us back to the cabins."

She turned in her seat and stared back at the car. "Looks like ... I think there's only two of them."

"Yeah, with a CB to tell their friends our exit and how to get to Big Timber." He swore. "Better get out that rifle. You were right after all. Sorry."

"Maybe not," she said. "They're flashing their lights."

Sure enough, the other car's lights were flashing on and off, repeatedly. Calmly, Lisa reached down and turned on the CB.

A boy's voice finished, "—you hear me? Over."

She picked up the handset.

"Hello? Uh ... um ... over."

She didn't forget to release the switch.

"Oh, thank goodness." The boy's voice was different than the one back in town. "Listen, can we come with you? It's just me and my girlfriend. We have food. We can help. Over."

Another voice broke in: "Steve, you're gonna pay if I see you again! Traitor! Thief!"

Jack said, "What do you think?"

"Could be a trap."

He nodded. "Doesn't change the fact that we still need people. Think we should stop and see?"

"I think we should. Just be careful."

"You'll have to cover me," he said.

Jack put on his right blinkers, pulled off to the side, and got out with his rifle drawn and ready to fire. Seconds later, the other car pulled up. The windows rolled down on both sides and two sets of hands popped out.

"Out of the car!" Jack shouted, muzzle forward but not actually pointing at them.

A boy in the older range stepped unsteadily from the driver's side, hands raised, face white with fear. He was skinny without being emaciated and had a mop of shaggy brown hair.

"You too!" Jack shouted at the girl in the front-side passenger seat. There didn't appear to be anyone else in the car, though he supposed someone could have been hiding in the back.

Carefully, the girl extricated herself and ambled over. Jack blinked and his mouth fell open. "What the ...?"

"She's pregnant," the boy said. "Can you please put the gun away? We're unarmed, see?" He turned around quickly, then motioned for the girl to do the same. She did so, too, though less quickly.

For some reason, Jack couldn't get his mind around what he was seeing. Couldn't she just be fat? How could she be pregnant? She was a teenager, sure, but she couldn't be *that* old. The news said nobody older than about fifteen ever recovered.

Maybe she never got sick.

"How old are you?" Jack said to her.

Her voice was soft and light, with a slight southern twang. "Sixteen. I just turned it. Didn't have no cake, though."

Sixteen.

She was the oldest survivor they'd found yet. Daring to hope, he turned to the boy and asked him, too.

Grinning goofily, the boy said, "I'm fourteen. She's robbing the cradle, hah hah." When Jack didn't grin back, the boy's manner switched to pleading. "I'm Steve, she's Molly. We can't go back. They'll kill us if we do. They were gonna kick her out. That's why we made our break. They said they didn't want pregnant girls in the gang. They wanted her to take a pill to, uh, kill it, and she didn't want to."

"Because I'm a Christian," she said defiantly.

Jack looked beyond their car and down the highway. Still no cars, but that didn't mean there wouldn't be.

"I don't get it," he said. "Why did you people steal our car? Burn our books?"

The boy grinned. "Carter, that's why. That was him on the CB. You were on his turf. We were supposed to beat you up, take your food, whatever. The gang has plenty of food, but it tastes like crap. Corn feed. Big, huge silo full of the stuff. Enough to last years, probably." He bit his lip. "Please, man, can we come with you? Like he said, we're dead if they catch us."

"Stay here," Jack said and went to talk to Lisa, who was covering him. Quietly, he explained the situation.

"Pregnant!" she said, eyes wide in wonder. "Of all the ... who gets pregnant at a time like this?"

He shook his head. "People like that, who knows why they do anything? Question is, do we take them in? The girl's sixteen. Just turned it."

She didn't hesitate. "I think we should. But we can't let them follow in that car. Just in case. You know?"

Jack nodded. "Totally."

He went back to the couple, who stood holding each other and shivering in the cold.

"You can come with us," he said, "but we have rules. Everyone chips in and works." He glanced briefly at Molly's stomach. "Within reason. Also, what I say goes. What *anyone* says goes, actually, until we're sure about you. Understand?"

"Oh yes, thank you," Molly said, eyes shining with happiness.

"Man, *thank* you," Steve said. "You won't regret it, I swear. I'll work hard, you'll see."

Jack told him his name and pointed back to their stolen car. "That's Lisa. Molly, you sit in the front. Steve, you're in the back with me. Wait a minute, turn around." They turned around and waited while Jack awkwardly frisked them. "Just being careful."

Steve nodded agreeably, pathetically eager to please.

"Hey, one thing though," the boy said. "We brought some food we were saving for when we split. Didn't think you'd take us unless we had something to give. That's how it is in my gang ... I mean my *old* gang. Nothing for free, and you gotta give something to get in or you're in debt and gotta pay it back. Usually guns and stuff, or sodas. Everyone wants sodas."

Molly snorted angrily. "Sodas? Yeah, right. If you're a *boy*, you mean."

Jack looked quickly at her, but didn't follow up. He wanted to get off the interstate as soon as possible. They seemed sincere, but he felt exposed. "Let's see this food."

He followed Steve to the back of their car and waited for him to pop the trunk. When he did, Jack's mouth fell open. The trunk was filled with heavy-duty contractor bags his dad had once used to throw away drywall after the basement flooded. If it really was food, there was a lot of it.

"What's in them?" he said.

Steve smiled proudly. "Like I said—corn feed. Tastes like cat shit, especially if you don't clean it first. But it eats fine after you grind it. Better if you put it in hot water and add salt, like grits. Some people add hot sauce."

Jack shook his head in wonder. "We're going to need a lot of hot sauce."

EIGHTEEN

As a precaution, Jack tied the black and white checkered flag around Molly's eyes. He made Steve pull his jacket over his head and lean forward over his shoes. Jack watched carefully in case he tried to peek out. When they hit the gravel road leading to Big Timber, Jack winced at the tiny reveal, then calmed himself with the fact that the county probably had dirt roads everywhere. Nobody could tell which was which by feel alone.

As they pulled into the meadow, Lisa gasped in alarm.

Greg and Brad were running toward them with rifles out, aiming at them. Their mouths moved, shouting instructions nobody could hear over the crunching tires, their faces tense with anger and fear.

Lisa slammed the brakes, sending their stolen car into a skid and bouncing Steve off the back seat.

Jack winced against the bite of the seatbelt. "Ooh ..."

"Molly, you okay?" Steve said.

"I'm fine," she groaned. "I think."

Outside, Greg and Brad stalked forward, still looking freaked out—then surprised when they saw the driver of the sports car was Lisa. Immediately upon recognition, they lowered their weapons.

Lisa rolled down her window. "It's us, you idiots!"

"We didn't know!" Greg shouted back angrily.

Jack snorted, shook his head, and opened his door. "You're gonna love it here, Steve."

Most of the children were near the pond when they arrived. They came running over with Olivia, who had her gun out. Pete came running too with his, as did Tony. He'd have to give his former students grief for running with firearms. For now, though, he felt proud of their quick response.

"This is Steve and Molly," Lisa said when everyone had gathered. "They're joining our team—and they brought food!"

Excited looks and chatter followed Lisa around to the trunk, which she sprang open like a pirate's treasure chest.

"Wow, what is it?" Greg said. "Beans? Rice?"

Steve grimaced. "Corn feed. Probably not enough for a big gang like yours."

Big gang? Jack thought. Then he remembered his threat on the radio.

Brad didn't wait to be told what to do—he grabbed a bag and carried it into the Skyline. Though Jack felt tired from yet another run-in with gun-toting cabbages, he nonetheless picked up a bag and followed suit.

"Greg!" he called back. "Seriously? Stop being a wimp and help out."

With a groan, Greg lifted a bag and shared the burden, then came back with Brad and Jack until the car was empty. In total, they had eleven bags of feed, each weighing between thirty and forty pounds. Easily enough to last the group through the winter and then some, provided they fortified it with protein, fat, and vitamin pills.

After the bags were loaded into the pantry, everyone except Jack gathered in the kitchen—the unofficial Skyline meeting room.

"Where you off to now?" Olivia said when he passed her on the way out.

"Be right back," he said.

He didn't like the sports car, figuring it used too much gas. He also didn't like the idea of knuckleheads like Pete and Tony speeding around and racing. Way too dangerous. To head that off, he parked it out in the grass on the other side of the Skyline. Then he crawled underneath the car and hid the keys in the undercarriage. When he got up, he dusted himself off and laughed as something occurred to him.

"Eureka," he said.

From now on, whenever the scavengers went out, he'd get them to bring an additional charged battery with them and find a car with a full tank of gas. Preferably older, so they could siphon more easily (Greg had discovered early on that new cars were protected against such tricks). Then they'd park it here in the grass. Each car would hold at least ten gallons, as well as provide a source of useful raw materials and parts. They could run them a little every few days to preserve the batteries, like Pete's parents had done. The meadow was so big they could stack them up a long time before running out of room.

When he entered the cabin—still grinning at his own cleverness—a quick glance around showed nobody was smiling but him, and no one was talking.

Greg bobbed his head at the newcomers. "They want to know where the rest of the *gang* is."

"You said on the radio," Steve said, just shy of accusingly. "You said you had a big gang. Threatened to come back and kill everyone. But all I see is a lot of little kids."

Jack nodded. "We were being chased by people with guns. I said what I had to." At the boy's confused look, he added, "Misinformation. If you fell for it, that means they did too."

Steve smiled halfheartedly. "Seems so, I guess."

"But all these children," Molly said, looking around. "How can you protect yourselves? Or my baby?"

Jack gazed levelly at her. "We'll start by not kicking you out with winter approaching, or making you take an abortion pill. We'll finish by keeping this place secret and killing anyone who tries to harm us."

Steve held up his hands. "No need to get mad, man, she was just asking. So how many you got? Teenagers, I mean."

"Seven before you came, so nine now. We don't turn anyone away." He nodded at Brad. "He's got a baby brother. Would your old gang take in a baby?"

"Not in a million years," Steve said.

"You said they had a bunch of grain. What's their plan if it spoils? Or gets eaten by rats? Are they planning to grow their own crops?"

Molly snorted. "Those idiots? They'll just take it from someone else. Probably starve to death."

Jack said, "We plan to grow our own food. We'll do a lot of other things too, like continue our educations and see if we can't make something out of what's left. These children, us, your baby—we're the future. But if you want to go back, we can blindfold you and take you to your car, no problem. We'll even give you a few gallons of gas, guns, and some of your food."

No way was he giving back all of it, not with so many mouths to feed. They hadn't even bagged a deer yet, and they'd only caught four fish.

Molly took Steve's hand, looked in his eyes, and nodded.

Steve said, "We want to stay. Please. The Dragsters— that's what they call themselves, 'cause of the checkered flags—they only got about fifty people. Mostly wimps. About eight are pretty mean, though. Carter played football with some of them." He smiled, then laughed. "We were about to leave anyway. But we wouldn't have found anything this nice." He looked around, really taking it in. "This place is cool. Back in town, we had to stay in dead people houses. Even if you get the bodies out, the stink stays around. Gave me nightmares."

Jack paused in consideration, dragging it out like he had to think about it, though he was quietly pleased. The CB in the car had been an eye-opener, and he wished he'd thought of getting some earlier—to keep tabs on the scavengers when they made their runs, if nothing else. Steve and Molly offered more than just two additional people to the group. They added their own unique knowledge and experiences.

"All right," he said. "I'll come up with work assignments. And when we finally get new books, you'll study along with the rest of us."

Steve bobbed his head up and down, eager to please.

"You got it, man. Never liked school, but might like it more now seeing how there's nothing to do." He stuck out his hand and Jack shook it.

"Brad," Jack said with a sideways glance at his friend, "how's the hole coming along?"

"Haven't started it yet. We got some of the wood today. No nails, though. I'm sure we can dig the hole, if you want."

Jack nodded. "Awesome. How about we start Steve there?" He thought for a second. "We got any gloves?"

"You never asked us to get gloves," Pete said grumpily.

"Right. Well, next time then." He turned to Steve. "Just work until you can't dig without getting blisters. We can't risk infection, not anymore."

Smiling, Steve said, "Absolutely. I love digging. My dad used to make me dig stuff all the time. Trees, fence posts, rocks, stumps—all kinds of stuff."

"Ready when you are," Brad said.

As the two filed out, Jack leaned over and said to Brad, "Thanks, man."

"What about me?" Molly said after they'd left.

He looked her over with a considering eye. "How long have you been ...?"

She placed her hands on her belly and gazed down lovingly. "Six months."

Jack hated the idea of making only girls deal with the children, but he worried about her condition. He had no idea what pregnant people could and couldn't do.

"For now, work with Olivia," he said. "She's doing really good with the kids, but there's too many of them. I'm sure she could use the help." He paused as something occurred to him. "I'm thinking they can help, too—the children. We could use more branches and kindling. It's a pain to gather, and we need to get it in now, before it snows."

Olivia grinned. "Finally, something for the little roaches to do. You'll have so much kindling you won't know what to do with it."

Jack had a mattress brought into Lisa and Olivia's room for Molly to sleep on. He brought another into Greg's room for Steve. That way, his friends could keep an eye on both of them. Again, he didn't think they were spies, not the way they were acting, but he also worried they might get cold feet and make a break for it in the middle of the night. If they tried, he'd have to stop them before they got to the road. Thus the hidden keys.

He wasn't sure what bothered him more. That he might have to kill them both—one of them pregnant—to protect the secret of their location, or that he'd be too weak to go through with it.

***

The next week passed in a whirlwind of activity.

Greg and Steve got the outhouse hole dug to four feet deep and erected a little structure over it. For the seat, they used a hand drill and a keyhole saw to cut a hole in the middle of a kitchen chair, then secured it to the floor with hammered-in blocks. Sheets of plastic were tacked up inside to keep out the wind, and they added an overhead shelf stocked with packs of toilet paper still in the packaging.

When it was finally completed, Olivia spray painted "POOP SHACK" on the door in brown paint. Everyone thought it was funny because she'd made it look like the letters were smeared there.

At Brad's insistence, the scavengers brought back an assortment of chainsaws for cutting firewood. They also collected a bunch of CB radios and various antennas, and Lisa puzzled through hooking up the best one inside. At her insistence, Brad hammered a ladder made from two-by-fours up along the side of the Skyline, then attached the longest antenna to the roof. Afterward, she drilled a hole through the wall and connected the antenna to the CB using a length of coaxial cable. When she turned it on, it worked perfectly.

Steve didn't know much more about CB radios than Jack did, so they spent some time experimenting. Despite the height of the antenna, when they keyed in the frequency used by the Dragsters, they never heard more than hissing whispers of conversation.

Lisa convinced Jack to let her, Greg, and Tony go back to Centreville to hit the library just off the interstate. He didn't like staying behind, not with that maniac Blaze in control, but he didn't have much choice. He needed to keep an eye on Steve and Molly. They seemed all right, but he didn't want to leave and spend the whole time worrying if they were running off to rejoin their old friends.

The second library mission was launched at night, this time with an added element: they needed to test the range of their CB setup heading east.

It was Greg's job to call back every mile until he stopped getting replies. They did it on one of the channels not used by the Dragsters, and managed to go fifteen miles before the transmissions failed.

Jack hoped the gang hadn't set out a fan of scouts to monitor all stations—a sensible move if they were serious about revenge.

"No way those guys did anything like that," Steve said with a smirk. "They ain't much for planning."

The four hours waiting by the radio were the longest he'd ever experienced. Regrettably, his nervousness transmitted to Brad and the others, who kept creeping over to see if he was all right.

Sometime after 3 a.m., Greg's voice came faintly over the radio. "Anyone there? Over."

With mingled feelings of relief and anxiety, Jack said, "Yeah, how'd it go?"

"Jeez, Jack, you're supposed to say *over*. But we're fine. Wait till you see what we got. Over."

Even over the radio, Greg could be a real pest.

"Well what did you find?"

"Sorry—*chhhh!*—you're breaking up," Greg said, making the radio static noises himself. A few seconds later, he added, "Over!"

Jack was outside shivering in the cold when they arrived. Lisa got out of the car, then Greg, then Tony. A second later, a fourth person popped out, followed by a fifth.

Lisa's wide smile was infectious. "Come meet Miguel and Paul. They're brothers."

NINETEEN

Miguel was thirteen and his brother was twelve. Definitely leadership age, though Paul seemed a bit ... well, it wasn't a crime to be happy, but did he have to be so chipper about it?

The younger brother blinked and looked around, smiling so wide Jack's face hurt in sympathy.

"Wow, this is a really cool place!" Paul said. "Look at all these cabins! Are they made of real logs? Does everyone have one or just some of you? Oh, it's just four. Still cool, though. Who sleeps in the trailer? What's with that school bus? You guys have a boat to go in that pond? You should totally get a boat. That's what I'd do if I had a pond."

"Paul," Miguel said with suffering patience, "for the love of everything, would you please shut up? They're not used to your noise the way I am."

"Sure, yeah I know, sorry," he said, pausing briefly for a breath. "Miguel, why do you think I talk so much? Sometimes I'm quiet for hours at a time, but nobody knows unless I tell them. Hey, Miguel, why's Tony staring at me like that?"

Tony was staring at Paul with a familiar look, reminiscent of when he and Pete were going at it all the time back at the Welcome Center.

"Man," Tony said, "tell this fool to shut the h—"

Jack said, "Quiet, Tony." He turned to the newcomers. "Go on in and get warm. Pete, take Paul with you. Get him settled on one of the empty mattresses. If you can't find an empty one, move someone. And keep your voices low."

"Sure, sure," Pete said, glaring at Paul. "Another job for me tonight. Come on, you. And stop talking so much. You're driving everyone crazy."

Lisa raised a hand and said, "I'm going to bed. It's been a long night. I'll show you the books in the morning. Better than the first time."

Moments later, it was just Jack, Miguel, and Greg standing outside. Beautiful night, lots of stars. Jack had seen satellites up there while waiting for them to return. It broke his heart that humans wouldn't go back to the Moon or visit Mars or far off solar systems like in the books he'd grown up with. They'd lost so much.

"Sorry about Paul," Miguel said sheepishly, pulling him from his musings. "He's a good guy, not a bad bone in his body, but he goes on and on. He used to be on Ritalin, but it didn't help." He coughed a quiet laugh. "Because of him, we spent one day in the Pyros before they kicked us out."

Greg said, "He's talking about Blaze, Jack. The guy you told us about. They call themselves that. *Pyros*. Everyone's got a gang name now. We should totally get one, too. My vote? Lava Demons. Nobody messes with lava demons."

Miguel seemed unsure whether to laugh or nod. "Uh, yeah. That's a good name."

"Horrible name," Jack said. "So, tell me about Blaze—what did he look like?"

Jack knew, but felt a certain degree of caution made sense.

"Red hair, tall, lots of zits. Asked us right off if we had pills, then threw us out as soon as Paul started up. I hope my brother's not gonna be a problem here—he'll be fine once he calms down."

Jack smiled. "Your brother seems nice. How'd you run into Blaze?"

"We were heading south from Herndon, passing through Centreville in my parents' car. They came up behind us honking, so we pulled over. Probably a dumb move, but I didn't want them ramming us or whatever. Next thing you know they're saying we need to join or get out of the area. They said they had food and a warm place to sleep." He shrugged helplessly. "That guy, Blaze—he made me swear an oath never to betray him."

"What'd you do?"

Miguel laughed. "I swore the oath! It was funny—he didn't have anything memorized. He just made it up as he went along. Stuff like, *You will always be loyal to me and my sister, no matter what, or you'll burn in Hell forever. Now say it!*" Miguel shook his head. "That's what he said after every line. *Now say it!*"

Jack smiled because it was expected, but he didn't feel happy. "You and your brother have any guns? It's sort of a gun world now."

Miguel shook his head. "Would have been nice, but my parents didn't have one. Because of Paul, you know? My bro's in a different world half the time."

"So how did you meet my friends?"

Jack didn't feel any sort of concern about the two new recruits. Totally different situation than with Steve and Molly. Being kicked out of Blaze's group may have had something to do with it—a mark in their favor. And they hadn't come calling on the promise of a bigger gang.

Greg said, "Lisa found them outside the library. They seemed cool, so we invited them back."

"Let's go inside," Jack said. "My place. It's freezing out here."

The three boys went in and Jack got the fire going. They talked a little more, mostly about the organization of Blaze's gang, the Pyros. Despite only being there a day, Miguel had a lot of information about them: who the key members were, their personalities. Bullies, mostly. The only thing troubling was they were in contact with some of the other gangs in the area, trading things they had too much of for stuff they didn't.

Greg grinned at his friend's troubled frown. "He's just a bully with red hair, man, stop worrying."

With more heat than he'd shown all night, Miguel said, "Bunch of morons."

They talked a little more about this and that. When Miguel started yawning, Jack told him to sleep on the couch and wished Greg a good night. Then he went to bed.

***

The scavengers were hauling in new stuff every day, not all of it practical. They brought fun stuff like board games, remote control cars, and art supplies. Jack wasn't very popular when he told them to get rid of the fireworks they found, but that was fine. Someone had to be the adult.

At Jack's instruction, they also brought cars full of fuel to stack up in the meadow near the Skyline. With so many different vehicles coming in, Jack established a signal where they beeped their horn upon entering: two long blasts followed by two short ones.

They seemed to like the work, taking to it so enthusiastically Jack was actually jealous he couldn't tag along.

Everyone had requests.

Molly wanted maternity outfits and baby stuff.

Brad needed work boots and socks—size twelve—and toys for his brother.

Paul wanted a boat for the trout pond, but nobody listened to him.

Greg asked for more wood and some wire mesh to build rabbit hutches. On the second library trip, Lisa had found another book about rabbits. Her brother was sure he could raise them—even hares, if he had to—figuring modern food rabbits had to have been domesticated from wild stock thousands of years ago.

Olivia wanted compasses for the children, and white paint for marking trees. During one of their kindling expeditions, a little boy named Teddy had gotten lost. Everyone had to stop what they were doing to search for him, risking yet more lost people. It took over an hour before they found the boy curled up next to a log, shivering in the cold.

Jack was growing to hate their reliance on the technology of their parents. He wanted them getting used to doing stuff themselves, like Greg and his rabbits. To that end, following a diagram in a hunting book, he and Brad quickly built a rudimentary smoker and used it to smoke their first deer, which Brad had taken early one morning.

The older boy hadn't enjoyed shooting it, and his disgust was quickly multiplied when Jack showed him how to field dress it.

"Ugh ... how can we live like this?" Brad said, staring at the spilled mess of blood and guts after Jack slit it open with a specially hooked knife.

Jack grinned at Brad's expression when he said they'd also be preserving—and eating—the liver, kidneys, and lungs.

"They're tasty, once you get used to them," he said. "A hundred years ago, we'd eat the brains, too. These days, it's supposedly not safe anymore. I don't know if that's true, but why take the chance?"

Brad nodded, his face a sweaty shade of green. "Yeah. Good call."

The smoker worked great. Basically, a wooden lattice with a tarp over it and a hole at the top. After slicing the meat, they hung it in strips while burning a slow, smoky fire beneath it using hardwood collected from deadfalls. The point of smoking wasn't simply to get smoke onto the meat, but rather to mildly cook it while sucking out as much moisture as possible in order to halt the growth of bacteria. Or so the book said. The book also recommended salt for preservation—same principal.

When Jack tried it, the meat tasted okay, but there was an odd plastic taste at the end. He blamed the plastic tarp. He didn't think it was dangerous, though, so they kept using it.

For the next few days, Brad took down deer after deer in that field behind the cabins.

"Eventually they'll stop coming around," Jack said while dressing Brad's latest buck for him. "Kind of like staying away from a wolf's den."

"So what do we do? Drive somewhere?"

"We could do that. But I'm thinking of something bigger. And tastier."

Later on, he caught up with Tony and Miguel, who were hauling down an old-fashioned bathtub from the back of the new truck.

"Hey, guys."

"Hey, man," Tony said. "What's up?"

"You said you found a farm with live cattle. How close is it?"

"I can't bring you back no cow," he said laughing. "And I ain't gonna shoot one and bring it back in pieces, neither. That's just gross."

Jack smiled indulgently. "We need more meat to get through the winter. I think we can all agree the grain's pretty nasty. Now that we can smoke our food, we don't need to carry it back uncooked. We'll slaughter it where we find it, smoke it there, then hang it up in the Abe Lincoln to keep cold."

"Problem is bringing it back. We could find some trash bags," Tony said. "Real big ones. Cows are pretty big."

Jack nodded. "Good idea. Make sure they're unscented. How long will that take?"

Tony paused, scratching his chin slowly, as if enjoying his sudden importance. "I dunno. Maybe tomorrow if we hold off looking for them rubber sheets the girls keep asking about. Some of them little ones keep peeing the bed. Where we supposed to find sheets made of rubber? That's a lot of driving. Closest stores are in that crazy town."

"I'll talk to Olivia," Jack said. "Maybe we can rig something with trash bags for now. Two birds, one stone." He patted him soundly on the back. "Thanks, Tony."

He turned around without waiting for a reply. A leader had to do that. If everything was constantly up for a vote or waiting on opinions, nothing would get done, and it'd undermine his authority. He needed to maintain the illusion that he actually *had* authority, or everything would fly apart.

With nothing else that needed attending, Jack returned to the Paul Bunyan and got his backpack out of the closet. At the bottom, wedged beneath an unused roll of toilet paper, his camping stove, and his mess kit, was a copy of Winston Churchill's *Memoirs Of The Second World War*. His dad had bought it for him more than a year ago, but Jack hadn't read it. The huge book had sat on his desk with a bookmark strategically placed so his dad would think he was making progress. Every day, then every week, the bookmark moved a little farther along. Now, looking back at what he'd considered a pretty clever ruse, he felt ashamed.

His dad had said, "You want to know about leadership? Shackleton's fine, but he only had about twenty people to keep alive. Try dealing with forty-six million starving countrymen, with bombs dropping out of the sky night and day."

Feeling like they were finally making some progress, and concerned about his leadership skills, Jack retired for the evening and continued reading the book.

TWENTY

The next morning was so cold a puddle in front of the Skyline had skimmed over with ice. Also, it had started to snow. Not much, but enough to get the youngest kids' hopes up. Everyone else was worried.

With the onset of snow, the group's scavenging took on a sudden urgency. So much so that Jack sent out a second team—Greg, Steve, Miguel, and Olivia—to see what they could dig up in Gainesville, to the east, while Pete, Tony, and Mandy scouted Warrenton, to the south. Priorities included: trash bags, soap, brand-new AGM car batteries (Steve's tip), more flashlights, more candles, air mattresses for the bed wetters, spices for Lisa, ammunition (as always), blankets and sheets, more vitamins, and iodized salt.

Olivia had freaked everyone out, saying they needed iodine or risk growing something horrible on their necks called a *goiter*.

Jack hoped they could eventually get their vitamins from plants and animals. Before the Sickness, his mom told him prehistoric humans got almost all their nutrients from organ meat, with the occasional infusion of seasonal berries and tubers. It wasn't just academic theorizing, at least not for her—the Ferris household had organ meat several times a week. They never got scurvy, and they passed their physicals with no signs of vitamin deficiency. The downside was Greg and Lisa had always declined their invitations to dinner.

With deep winter almost upon them, the group had no choice but to rely on the old world and its abandoned stuff. He reminded himself with every shake of salt or DVD on movie night that, as a matter of policy, it was all just temporary. That said, he hoped to keep the movies going as long as possible. The children had surprised everyone by mostly ignoring the cartoons and puppet shows in favor of films with adults in them. They'd sit wide-eyed, excitedly pointing out which ones looked most like their mommies, daddies, grandparents, or whoever they used to know.

The children weren't the only ones affected this way. Everyone showed up for movie night, regardless of what was playing.

***

Warrenton was free of gangs, and a spooky sight by Pete's account, with only the occasional whiff of wood smoke in the air. There were no cars or survivors of any age on the mostly blocked-off streets.

Jack had no problem with spooky. With just a little work clearing the barricades, the town was ripe for the picking.

Though the adults in their final days had eaten through whatever food they'd had, the boys and Mandy found a small hoard of canned goods in the basement of a church, making them the heroes that night at dinner. Everyone was already sick of grain and plastic-flavored venison, and were overjoyed with anything different.

Gainesville *did* have gangs, it turned out, but they didn't do more than drive by and stare. As a precaution, Jack nonetheless added Lisa to the Gainesville group and reassigned Miguel to Big Timber's security rotation, after checking him out on guns. This left Big Timber guarded by four leaders during the day, one of whom was pregnant. Five, if you counted Paul, which nobody did.

While the others were out on their daily runs, Brad took on the brunt of the hard work, and Jack helped whenever possible. Over dinner one night, the older boy had admitted to clearing all the deadwood in a twenty yard ring around the property starting at the tree line. Though they now had three cords stacked away—enough to last them all winter—he was busily hunting for living trees to fell.

"That green stuff we tried made too much smoke and soot," Brad said. "It's also harder to light. I think when people build furniture, they use something called *seasoned wood*." He grinned. "I guess it means they leave it out a season to dry. Anyway, if we don't want to keep cleaning the stove all the time, we gotta prepare some for next winter."

And so it went, day after day, with supplies coming in and nothing more troubling from other gangs than hard stares. Perhaps they preferred the warmth of their cars to the chilly weather, which had plummeted into the low teens. Or maybe Lisa's policy of leaving two armed guards outside each store they looted kept them at bay. Whatever it was, it was a relief.

One day, Jack took a ride with Tony and Brad in one of the trucks. Loaded in the back was a bunch of lumber they'd snagged from a hardware store, a box of nails, a toolbox, a gallon of vegetable oil found in a fast food place, rolls of twine, and a painter's drop cloth. Everyone hated the way the plastic tarp had made the deer meat taste. His solution was to soak the drop cloth in vegetable oil to prevent too much smoke from escaping out the sides. Then they'd hang the meat in strips beneath it from twine.

Unlike most of the farms in the area, the one Tony brought them to didn't grow crops. It was a cattle farm. Black Angus cattle, Jack assumed, because the cows were black. Other than that, he didn't know much about cows.

The cows weren't fat, but they weren't skinny, either. What grass he could see through the snowmelt was meager in comparison to the growth outside the fence. The pastureland seemed to go on forever, disappearing behind a hill at the farthest reaches, with lots of little fences sectioning it off throughout and keeping the animals together.

"So what do you think?" Jack said, alternating staring between the cattle and the two-story white house with the plume of blue smoke billowing from the chimney.

"Could be anyone in there," Tony said.

"How'd you find this place?" Brad said. "I'm totally lost."

Brad hadn't ventured out since their arrival at the cabins. He was only there now because Molly had agreed to watch Tyler.

"Just driving around," Tony said.

Jack kept staring at the house. Tony was right—anyone could be in there. Then he saw something that brought an instant smile to his face.

"Is that a chicken?" he said.

"Look at that!" Tony said. "Man, I'm getting hungry."

Brad said, "Think maybe we could raise some chickens?"

That would be amazing, Jack thought.

"Sure, if we play our cards right," he said. "You two cover me. Beep first so we don't surprise whoever's there. I'll go up with my hands raised."

Tony pressed the horn down and held it for five seconds. Jack wished he'd done a peppy little *beep-beep-beep*, but didn't say anything. Tony would just brush it off, eroding his authority a little bit more.

"Be careful," Brad said.

Tony smiled arrogantly. "Man, go on. We got you."

Jack nodded, got out, and approached the front gate unarmed, hands in the air. He paused there a moment, as if admiring the house: two stories, old-fashioned gables, decorative white columns, and a wraparound porch. A few seconds later, he couldn't believe it when a big dog came running around the side barking at him and scattering chickens in its wake. Jack leapt back automatically. He hated dogs ... well, he hated big, angry, slobbering dogs that could rip him to shreds. Thank goodness the gate was latched.

His first instinct was to run back to the truck, but worried his friends—his *subordinates*—would see that as cowardice and lose respect for him. Then he wondered if that really mattered if it meant keeping his face from being torn off.

"That's far enough!" a girl shouted from the porch.

Jack looked up and saw a tough-looking girl pointing a rifle at him. She was in that general age range of teenager he'd hoped to find more of. She moved aside and another girl came out, a little younger, wielding a meat cleaver.

He shook his head. Not a year ago, the sight of two girls brandishing guns and meat cleavers would have prompted a call to the police. These days, it was the definition of sanity.

"I'm unarmed!" Jack shouted, hands raised. "No guns, see?" He turned in a circle so they could get a good look.

"You best get back in your truck and leave, unless you wanna die!" the first girl shouted, pointing over his head. Then she fired.

BANG!

Though his instinct was to flee—stumbling and falling and blubbering as he went—Jack controlled himself and took a step back. The girl hadn't shot him, which meant she still retained some basic respect for the dignity of human—

She worked the bolt and fired again: *BANG!*

Ditching all worries about his subordinates—both visibly laughing at him from the front seat—Jack ran stumbling and blubbering back to the truck, opened the door, and shoved in beside Brad.

Tony—still laughing, really laying it on—edged the truck into a turn and took them back to the cabins.

***

The next day, shortly after dawn, Tony and Jack returned without Brad to the house with the homicidal girls and their mutant dog.

"Man, all you gonna do is get shot," Tony said for the tenth time. He even sounded bothered by the prospect.

"We'll see," Jack said, tired of his constant needling.

Tony was only slightly less irritating than Pete—half the reason he'd given them the bulk of the scavenger duties, so they'd be out of his hair. Despite that, there was truth in his words. He *could* get shot. He would have done this alone, but if something happened, he wanted Lisa and Greg to know. For some reason, this was vitally important, his friends knowing how he lived and how he died. He didn't want to be forgotten like so many others who'd wasted away on their death beds, or starved to death in the city streets, alone and unmourned.

Jack turned the lumpy rock over in his hand, studying it. About as big as a baseball, he'd sealed it in a freezer bag with a neatly folded note inside proclaiming their intentions. Namely, to trade food and other supplies in exchange for one of their cows. Lisa had written out the note the night after they'd gotten back. He and Brad agreed she was a natural diplomat and praised her sparkling penmanship. Lisa—nobody's fool—called them out for being lazy and foisting more work on her after a long day in Gainesville.

"Here goes," Jack said as they approached the house. "Hit it."

Tony pressed the horn as they passed, loud and long (despite being told to make it sound peppier), and waited for the front door to open. Jack threw the rock onto the lawn, then ducked down as they sped away. Nobody shot at them, and a minute later they were far enough that they could stop and turn.

"Now what?" Tony said, breathing heavily for some reason.

"Now we wait. The note said we'd be back in an hour to talk. Why don't you put on some music?"

The younger boy snorted. "Thought you hated that stuff?"

Anything's better than listening to you right now, Jack thought glumly.

"It's growing on me," was all he said.

Tony laughed and turned on his pop music, then leaned back and closed his eyes. Jack leaned back, too. Instead of closing his eyes, he took Churchill's memoire from under his seat and continued reading. It was pretty good. He admired how the man had pulled the country together during their national crisis. He'd organized supply-lines from the United States, an island-wide communication network, an underground command center, and rallied the civic defense against day and night air raids by German bombers—all while launching attacks and counterattacks in Africa and plotting with FDR and Stalin on how best to defeat Hitler.

As awful as the war had been, the events had been made more tragic by the Sickness. All those lives lost, all that struggle, and so many accomplishments and inventions— all of it swept away like it had never happened.

"Tony," he said after closing the book. "Ever hear of Erwin Rommel?"

"Nope."

"Churchill? Stalin?"

"Still nope."

"The battle of Stalingrad?"

Tony looked at him sideways, frowning as if sensing he was being talked down to. "No, and don't care, neither. We doing this or what?"

Jack nodded. "Sure, man. Do what I said and drive off a ways. We don't need you getting shot, too."

Putting it in drive, Tony said, "First smart thing you said today."

A minute later, they were at the house.

TWENTY-ONE

Tony dropped him off and tore away like someone was shooting at him. The girls from the day before were out on the porch. The shorter of the two had replaced her meat clever with a rifle. Both were aiming steadily at him.

The dog wasn't in the yard this time. Jack could hear it inside barking nonstop.

"Don't shoot!" he said, throwing his hands in the air.

"We read your note, boy." This from the girl who'd spoken the first day. "You ain't touching our stock. They're all we got left."

The animals stood off in a field to the left of the house, nibbling on the meager pasture. About thirty of them.

"But you have so many," he said, trying not to sound as defeated as he felt. "Oh, and by the way, my name's Jack."

The girl spit. "Your name's what I say it is until I feel like changing it. That okay with you, Boy?"

Nodding—smiling his best don't-shoot-me smile—he said, "Sure, absolutely. But please, if you wouldn't mind aiming that gun away, I'd really appreciate it. I've got this nutty fear of my head exploding like a water balloon. Everyone ribs me for it, but I'm basically immune to ribbing. Bullets, not so much."

The shorter girl put her hand over her mouth and giggled.

"Shut up, Carla," the taller one said. "Don't be fooled. He's trying to steal our cows like them others, and there you are mooning after him? Just like sixth grade. Boys on the brain. That's all you are."

Others? What others?

Carla's voice was high and sweet, with even more country twang than her friend. "Why can't we bring him in? It's cold out. He ain't got no friends with him, and he *is* cute. We never have no one over now, and I miss company."

Jack said, "My arms are getting tired. Can I at least lower them? Or lie down flat and hold them out like Superman?"

Carla giggled again. "Oh, Freida, he's funny. Let him go, come on." As if proving a point, she lowered her gun.

Jack risked a slight bow, hoping to further endear himself to the friendlier one. "So, like the note said, we don't want to *take* your cows. That's why we're *asking*. All the herds we've found have been killed or are too far away." He smiled. "You two have the best cows we've seen yet."

It was true. Tony said these were the healthiest-looking and most abundant cows in the area. If the girls decided to pass on a deal, they'd look elsewhere. Disappointing, because the farm was so close to Big Timber.

"I helped my daddy sometimes," Freida said, her tone softening a little. "And I got a good memory. Most of the work's just common sense. The reason they're not skinny is because we got land, and after you know ... the disease ... we opened the gates so they could spread around." She chewed her bottom lip in thought. "Truth is, we still got too many. No feed, no hay, just what's growing, and that's about gone." She went quiet for a bit, seeming to think it over. "So what kinda stuff you trading?"

She pointed her gun away, and Jack tentatively lowered his hands.

"Plenty," he said, trying not to crack a tooth from grinning too widely. "Mind if I come in?"

Freida stared at him a moment more, her face alternating between hope and stubbornness. Then she nodded. "Carla, put Max out back so he don't kill him."

***

The girls' home was spacious and nicely furnished, with antique-looking tables and chairs, and wallpaper patterned in intricate silver, blue, and green filigree. Golden light glinted off the polished furniture under the radiance of old-fashioned lanterns. Everything looked beautiful except for the ornate rug, now dull from months of use with no vacuum to clean it.

There were four other survivors in the house, all much younger, ranging between three and maybe six or seven years old. They stared fearfully at Jack, and two of them started crying, forcing the girls to take a few minutes to calm them down before sending them upstairs to play.

"Wow," Jack said. "Big family."

Freida glared at him. "They ain't family. And don't act like you don't know how many of us there are after your friends pushed in here, taking what's ours. *Now* you wanna trade." She snorted. "You tell them buttholes we'll be ready next time—with this." She shook her rifle in case he hadn't seen it already.

Carla stepped between them. "Dang it, Freida, can't you see he's not with them? He came in a truck, not a slick car with flags on it." She turned to Jack. "She's still smarting from last time. They killed two of our nicest cows—cut off the legs and left the rest. We cooked as much as we could, but it didn't last long."

Noting she'd used the word *our* in reference to the cows, he said, "So you two are sisters?"

Carla smiled. "I got the boobs in the family. Can't you tell?" She thrust out her small chest for him to see.

Jack swallowed and glanced nervously at Freida.

Sighing, she said, "Leave the boy alone, you rat. Okay, Jack, what do you got that we don't?"

"We have plenty to trade, don't worry. But first, what's this about flags on cars?"

The two girls looked at each other, then back at him.

Carla said, "They call themselves *Dragsters*. So stupid. What they gonna do when they run out of gas, hmm? Walk around going vroom-vroom-vroom? If they had any brains they'd save every drop, but they don't. I went to town one time to look in on a friend. My friend ..." Briefly, she looked like she might cry. Then she took a deep breath and forced a smile. "Well ... he didn't make it. Anyway, when I went there, they was tearing up and down the street bumping into each other and raising hell."

"You've met them, haven't you?" Freida said. She held up a hand at his rising protest. "I know now you're not with them, don't worry. How'd it happen?"

Quickly, Jack recounted his trip to the library with Lisa. He didn't leave anything out.

Carla frowned. "Who's this *Lisa?* Your sister?"

Freida threw her a disgusted look and shook her head. To Jack, she said, "You sure showed those fools. Sorry about your books, though."

Jack shrugged. "We replaced them. So what kind of stuff do you need?"

For the next half hour, Freida and Jack went back and forth on everything the girls needed. Soap, shampoo, and stuff for cooking were high on the list. The biggest item was feed for the cows and chickens. The chickens were free ranging at this point, but she worried about the winter. The cows had run out of grazable pasture and were living mostly off their fat. Jack said he had some feed, but not enough for twenty cows.

At their crestfallen looks, he added, "But there's someone in our group who knows where we can get more. Not sure how much, just that it's a lot. If we can get you some, you think you might be able to offer up two cows? Maybe some eggs?"

Freida smiled. "If you can feed our herd through the winter, you got a deal. Now, how do you feel about potatoes?"

Jack shook his head. "We can't get anything like that. Just—"

"Not you," she said. "*Us.* We have plenty. They grew wild at a neighbor's farm over the summer."

With this latest development, the negotiations launched anew. Potatoes, it turned out, didn't come cheap anymore. The going rate was five rolls of toilet paper per potato, or two rolls and a tube of toothpaste, or possibly one roll and a box of laundry soap.

At one point, honking sounded from outside, causing both girls to seize up in sudden terror. Jack looked out the window and said, "It's only my ride. You mind if he comes in?"

Carla came around and looked out. "Oh, Freida, he's black!"

Jack looked at her strangely. "Is that a problem?"

She looked faintly embarrassed. "I was just letting her know is all."

If she had a problem with Tony being black, her head would explode when Brad came down to help build the smoker.

Freida threw him an apologetic glance, then went to the door to wave in Tony. "Come on in. It's cold out, huh?"

Tony stared wild-eyed between Carla, Jack, and Freida.

"Yeah," he said, looking pointedly at Jack. "When we leaving?"

"In a minute. Go and sit down with Carla. Get to know each other."

Carla smiled shyly and led him over to the couch.

Freida stepped into the kitchen and motioned for Jack to follow.

"Don't mind my sister," she said. "She's no racist. She just don't know too many folks that ain't white."

Jack nodded politely. "So here's the thing: we have a place a few miles from here. It's secret. Lots of children and some teenagers. Normally I'd beg you and Carla to come out and join us, but you have something we don't: *cows*, and a place to keep them. But you also have a problem."

She snorted. "The Dragsters, no feed, not enough wood for winter, a leaky roof ..."

"Okay, lots of problems," he said. "I want to help you because I think you'd make good allies. We need beef for today, but we also need to ensure more for the future. Slaughtering them without a plan makes no sense at all."

"You going somewhere with this?"

"Yep. With your permission, I'd like to station a couple of our people here with a CB. I'd also like to better arm you two and train you a little. We'll set up the smoker outside and share whatever we preserve with you. And we'll get you enough wood for the winter. How's that sound?"

Freida went quiet for a time, and Jack wondered if maybe he'd been too forward. It had to have been traumatic, the Dragsters barging in and shooting their livestock like that.

Just as he was about to tone down his suggestion for fear of messing up their original deal, she said, "I think God must have sent you down to us, Jack." Her eyes turned glossy with tears and she wiped them. "Yes. A thousand times, *yes*."

They spent a few more minutes going over logistics. During that time, she told him more about their root cellar. In addition to potatoes, they'd managed to store preserves over the summer, and she offered to send some back with him. When he accepted, she also asked if she could send back the children upstairs.

Jack's eyes widened. "I thought they were family."

Freida snorted. "Heck no. Neighbors' kids, all of them. The older ones cry a lot at night. The younger ones take it better."

Lisa had mentioned the same thing, how the younger ones seemed mostly to have recovered, whereas she, Molly, and Olivia still cried themselves to sleep sometimes. When she'd asked if he sometimes cried, Jack categorically assured her he did *not*.

"There's plenty of room," he said. "We'll unload the wood we brought and put them in the back with blankets when we leave. They'll fit right in. We're setting up a school. We want everyone reading and learning as quickly as possible."

"Could I get some of those books you picked up?" Freida said. "I used to love reading. Must have read everything in the house a thousand times already and I'm going crazy."

Jack laughed. "Sure, if you don't mind nonfiction. We can get different books on a future run. Right now, there's too much to do."

She nodded. "That'd be great. Something on farming would be nice. I can get seeds from Jesse's farm—that's one of the boys upstairs."

Smiling ear to ear, he said, "I think we'll make great partners, Freida. Now I'm doubly happy you didn't blow my head off out there."

They shared a quick laugh, then Jack said he and Tony had to get back.

When they returned to the living room, the new friends were halted by an alarming sight: Tony and Carla lip-locked on the couch, eyes closed, oblivious to anyone and anything.

That is, until Jack—barely concealing his laughter—cupped his hands around his mouth and yelled, *"BOOO!"*

TWENTY-TWO

The next day, Jack, Steve, and Lisa approached a farmhouse a few miles north of the 66-81 split. It was here, Steve said, where the Dragsters had their stash of grain, and it was always guarded.

"You there, Greg?" Jack whispered into his new walkie-talkie, recently scavenged from a Radio Shack in Gainesville.

"You gotta say *over*, Jack, I keep telling you," Greg said. "*Over*. See? That's how you know someone's done talking."

"*You* didn't say over," Jack said, still not tired of the joke. He turned to the others squatting behind him in the dark. "Looks pretty clear, doesn't it?"

The farmhouse was at least a hundred yards from the silo and tractors and other farm equipment. But to get into and out of the property, Greg would need to come up the road, through a gate, then circle around behind the house. In the front were several cars and trucks, one of which looked speedy and impractical. Dark as it was, Jack couldn't see a flag, but knew it had one.

"You sure there's only two people inside?" he said, eyeing the candlelit side window.

"Pretty sure, yeah," Steve whispered. "Least that's how it was before."

They'd parked down the road, then crept in on foot and

crossed a barbed-wire fence about twenty yards down. A precaution in case someone was watching out the front window. The field was barren in parts and overgrown with dried cornstalks in others. Jack figured the farmer had gotten about half the yield in before the Sickness took him.

Lisa looked worried. "Run this plan by me again?"

"One second," he said and looked at Steve. "We shouldn't expect anyone else tonight, right? Just who's already there?"

Steve nodded. "When I was out here, we were pretty much on our own. During the day, others would come to get feed or just to hang out. The town's pretty much screwed for good food, and all the nearby places with cattle have already been ... well you know. Picked over. There's another group out in Winchester, and they sometimes come by and trade for stuff we kill. Pretty sure they don't kill anything out there, because one time they showed up with jugs of milk."

Not for the first time, Jack questioned the wisdom of bringing someone into the group who'd participated in such abject stupidity and waste. He was curious about this Winchester group, though. Sounded like they had their act together.

"Right," he said in a neutral tone. "Okay, I'll approach from this side and peek through the window, see where everyone is. You two cover me while I bang on the front door and say hello. If they don't want to come out, that'll suck a little, but it's still doable—we'll just be here longer while we get the bags loaded. A little more risk, but not too much. Cold as it is, I doubt anyone will come out here at night."

Steve snorted. "Totally."

Lisa said, "I don't like it. What if they shoot through the door?"

"I'll stand off to the side," Jack said. "Then I'll reason with them. I'm very reassuring sometimes. Charming, even."

She didn't smile the way he wanted her to, but she didn't raise any more objections, either.

"Go on," he said. "I'll be around in a minute. Get to your

spots."

Lisa and Steve crossed the field ahead of him, heading for positions in the front yard facing the entrance. Jack crept to the window.

As he approached, a sense of dread stole over him. It was one thing to risk himself like this. Quite another to endanger Lisa. Then again, he didn't have much choice if they wanted to eat. Not unless he stooped to stealing. And no, he didn't consider what he was doing here stealing—it was taking back. They'd stolen his car and burned his books. Bunch of Nazis, if you asked him.

When he was under the window, he raised his head up for a look, but didn't see anyone inside. A kitchen window, as it turned out, and there was a lit candle on the counter. More light came from another room. Maybe whoever was there had gone to sleep without blowing out the candles.

Typical, he thought. But it posed a problem. Waking up from a sound sleep, they'd be shocked and afraid if someone came pounding on the door in the night.

Just as he was about to head around to let Lisa and Steve know, someone walked through his field of vision—a girl about Jack's age, and she was *naked*.

Until that night, Jack had never seen an in-person naked girl before. He'd seen breasts in an R-rated movie about the Holocaust with his parents, but that was it.

Greg had told him some interesting facts about sex from one of his rogue trips onto the Internet at a friend's house. Greg's family had the Internet, but it was locked down tightly. Jack's family locked it down, too, but not because of nudity. His parents wanted him learning the old-fashioned way—through books, trial and error, and thinking through his problems. Not by Googling. They'd told him about sex once, but not with near enough detail as Greg had. His parents' description had been mechanical and bland, delivered quickly and—now that he thought back—nervously. Greg's tale had been drawn out and deliciously lurid.

The girl in the kitchen paused briefly. She folded her arms and hugged herself. Then her shoulders shook quietly, making him think she was laughing about something. A second later he changed his mind. She wasn't laughing—she was crying.

Through the closed window, Jack heard a male voice yell something in anger, but couldn't make out the words. A second later, a boy about the same age walked in, also naked.

Jack couldn't believe it. Naked people everywhere.

He left the window and went to the front door, looking for and finding the shapes of his friends crouched in the dark. Carefully, he reached down and tried the doorknob. Locked, of course. He wasn't supposed to just barge in, but nothing could be simpler and safer than getting the drop on them with their pants down. Literally.

Hoping Lisa would roll with it, he raised his rifle to the door knob, looked away, and fired a round—then nearly dropped his gun when the knob flew off and banged painfully against his shin. Desperately, he checked to see if he'd been hit by anything else, but felt fine. He still remembered the fate of the kid who'd shot the safe at the Welcome Center. They hadn't found a body, but they'd seen the blood trail.

He tried the door, but it didn't budge. Wincing, worried he might hit an artery, but committed to the entry, he angled his gun so the bullet would ricochet into the jamb and fired another round. Again, he was fine, and his kick to the door sent it flying inward.

Without stopping to see if the others were following, Jack entered with his gun raised. There was an ascending flight of stairs on his left, a short hall in front of him, a rustic-looking living room just across from the kitchen, and his Peeping Tom window over on the left.

"Down on the ground!" he shouted unnecessarily at the boy and girl lying terrified on a sleeping bag.

"Don't shoot!" the boy cried, covering his head.

The girl was content to scream and cover herself. A detached part of Jack's awareness noted that both her eyes were red and puffy.

The boy found his spine a second later. "What the ... Who the hell are you? Do you know who I am?"

Jack smirked. "You must be Mr. and Ms. naked. Any

more of the Naked family upstairs?"

The boy glared at him and pulled more of the sleeping bag from the girl, who tugged it back angrily.

"Leave her some, would you?" Jack said, angling his gun at him.

"Man, you got no idea who you're messing with."

"Whew, huh?"

A second later, Lisa and Steve burst through the door—her aiming, him with fists raised. They stopped abruptly when they saw Jack's prisoners.

"What the hell were you thinking?" Lisa said. "You were supposed to knock. Not shoot the stupid door! You trying to get killed?"

Jack opened his mouth to respond, then felt himself shoved aside when Steve launched himself at the boy.

"I'll kill you!" Steve shouted.

The girl shrieked, leapt up—still naked, Jack noted—and ran deeper into the house.

"Stay here," Lisa said, and tore after her.

"Dude, back off!" Jack shouted at Steve, reaching for him.

"I'm gonna kill him!"

Steve was the only one in the group who'd come unarmed—because Jack hadn't yet put him through a safety course. He was here as a guide only. That didn't stop him, though. He punched and kicked and swore at the boy, who was doing his best not to get hit.

Jack broke his own safety rule, aimed at the couch, and pulled the trigger. The sound in the enclosed space was shockingly loud, and he wished he'd thought to cover his ears. The results, however, were successful—the boys separated, eyes widened in terror.

"Knock it off!" Jack roared, pressing his psychological advantage.

"Jack?" Lisa shouted from the other room.

"Just a warning shot!" He looked at Steve. "You two know each other?"

Steve spit. Not to the side, like they did in movies, but directly onto the naked boy. "I know he's a snake and a rapist. If I had a gun I'd shoot him dead, after what he did to Molly."

Jack's eyes narrowed. "You knew he'd be up here, didn't you?"

Steve shrugged. "Thought he might. He comes here a lot to ..." He shook his head. "Doesn't matter. Still doesn't change the fact we need the grain out back. Shouldn't matter, me knowing."

"What I do is my business, traitor," Carter said.

Jack shifted his aim. "You shut up."

The boy just glowered.

Lisa came in pushing the runaway girl in front of her. The girl now had on pants and a shirt, and was carrying more clothes in her arms. She tossed them at Carter—none too gently—and then sat when Lisa told her to.

"Easy," Jack said when the boy looked like he might try to hit her. "Dress yourself. Don't stand up."

Carter pulled the sleeping bag over him and scooted around under it as he got dressed.

"So you're Carter, huh?"

"Yeah," he said.

"You really a snake and a rapist like Steve says?"

"He is!" Steve said, fists clenched. "He raped Molly! Look at Trisha's face!"

"No I didn't! I didn't do anything!"

Jack considered the girl, now crying quietly on the couch. "What did he do to you?"

Trisha shrugged. "N-nothing. I let him."

"What about your face?"

"We were just playing," Carter said. "She hurt herself. Tell him, Trisha."

In response, Trisha cried harder and didn't say anything else. Steve swore.

Lisa said, "What happened to her eyes? Did you hit her?"

He snorted like it was obvious. "She came here on her own, like they all do. Trisha just falls down a lot."

"Carter's the head of the Dragsters," Steve said. "Stupid name, by the way. Everyone says so." He paused, panting, gritting his teeth. "Molly didn't wanna take the pill or screw him anymore so he threw her out."

"See? I didn't rape anybody. Just gave her a choice."

"Some choice—have sex with your ugly ass or starve."

Carter smirked. "How's my baby doing?"

Steve roared and tried to kick him, only to be held back by Lisa, shouting at him to calm down.

She threw Jack a look that said, *Do something, will you?*

Carter said, "You're kidding me. You actually told them it was *yours?* You're still a virgin!"

When Steve redoubled his efforts to murder him, Jack shouted, "Steve, enough! Carter, open your mouth again and I'm beating the shit out of you. Now get up." When Trisha started to rise, he added, "Just him. Lisa, you all right here?"

She nodded wearily, her face a wash of concern and outrage.

Jack pulled out his walkie-talkie and said, "Greg, come on down."

"Copy that. Over."

When Greg arrived, he didn't stop out front—he backed his pickup to the silo, per the plan, then took out several big boxes of contractor bags. Jack and Steve—prodding Carter—joined him a minute later.

"Start loading," Jack told Carter. "Don't make them too heavy. About halfway per bag. Fill up the truck."

"You gotta be kidding me," Carter said. Then he laughed. "That's what this is about?" He looked at Steve. "You just can't stop stealing from me, can you?"

"This is for those books you burned and the car you stole," Jack said. "And the cattle you took from Carla and Freida. They're under my protection, by the way. Anyone messes with them gets dead pretty quick."

Much as he hated saying so, he meant it. He'd kill to protect the sisters and their farm.

"Oh yeah? Who the hell are you?"

Greg grinned, enjoying the show. "He is the one they call *Jack*, and he is the Chosen One. We're Jack's Rippers—the biggest, baddest, deadliest gang this side of the Sickness."

Jack stared at Greg in shock. *Jack's Rippers?*

"Just start loading," he said, shaking his head. "Do a good job and I won't sic Steve on you. Or that girl you beat up."

Still glowering, Steve said, "Do a bad job. *Please.* I'm begging you."

Carter looked from Steve to Greg and then to Jack, not finding any mercy in their eyes. Then he nodded, took the bag they gave him, walked over to an upturned plastic bin, and wrapped the bag around the nozzle. When he released a catch, the bag began filling with grain. He stopped it a little more than halfway and said, "Here?"

Greg went over and hefted it. "Could probably go a little more."

Scowling, Carter filled it a little more, tied it off, and started on the next one.

TWENTY-THREE

At Lisa's urging, Trisha returned with them in the truck, now crowded with five people jammed together.

The whole way back to the cabins, Jack endured the stony silence of both Lisa and Steve. Steve, absurdly, because Jack hadn't executed Carter before they left—something he couldn't and would never do, not in cold blood. Lisa was mad because he'd changed plans and scared her by barging in like that. He'd talk to her about it later, apologize as best he could, and explain the situation.

Greg, for his part, acted like nothing in the world was wrong.

"That dude, Carter, sure was mad, huh?" he whispered loudly across the front seat. "So your name's Trisha? Nice to meet you."

"Greg, not now," Lisa said.

"Yeah," Steve said. "Butt out."

Lisa whipped around. "Don't talk to my brother that way! All of you, just shut up!"

After that, nobody said anything to anyone for the rest of the ride home. When they got inside, everyone was awake except the children.

Quietly, Lisa introduced Trisha to Olivia. She apparently knew Molly, because the two girls hugged and smiled and talked quietly for a bit.

"She can have my spot tonight," Molly said.

Lisa shook her head. "I'm sleeping on the couch. We'll figure out something more permanent tomorrow."

"Uh, you can sleep in my bed, if ..." Jack said, then quieted when Lisa glared at him. Too late, he realized how that sounded. He'd only meant Lisa could have his bed, and that *he'd* sleep on the couch. But whatever. She obviously wanted to fight tonight, and he was too tired for that.

"Night everyone," he said and went to his cabin. Along the way, he tried to shake the feeling he was running away from her. Which was crazy, really. Nobody could run away from her. If they tried, she'd beat them up.

***

The next day, Jack brought Brad, Miguel, Paul, and Steve with him to the farm, in two trucks. One was filled with grain, the other with wood and other materials. He also brought five more AR-style weapons with him and trained both girls, Steve, and Miguel's younger brother how to shoot them safely and accurately.

Pete had come up with a great way of finding the military-style weapons: look for cars with NRA or pro-gun stickers on the bumpers, then search the houses they were parked in front of.

Jack wasn't concerned about the lost ammo because he figured it was better spent on targets than fatal accidents. It helped that the bumper sticker trick had turned up so much ammo he didn't know what to do with it all.

After the verbal lesson on rules and safety, Jack halted the live training at three thousand rounds and made them clean their guns with the new cleaning kits. After a thorough inspection of their work, he pronounced them officially fit to run around with deadly weapons.

Fit enough, he thought resignedly.

Just like back at the cabins, the joy of shooting seemed to lift everyone's morale. So much so that Steve made an effort at joking conversation. For his part, Jack joked back, happy to forget the bad blood of the previous night. Looked at in the light of the new day, he could even empathize with the former Dragster. If that bully had exploited Lisa the way he'd done Molly, he might not be alive today.

"Okay," Jack said after a short break. "For the record, I don't like killing animals. That said, we need to eat to survive, and I for one am *not* eating corn grain for the rest of my life. It's bad for our teeth, and you just get hungry again after a few hours. You're all still brushing your teeth every day, after every meal, right?"

Heads nodded—some guiltily, some with impatience.

"Good," he said, gazing at the pasture stretching beyond the house. "Anyone have a problem with what we're doing today?" He looked from Brad to Paul and Miguel, from Steve to the two girls, and when nobody objected, he nodded. "Brad and I are going to build a smoker big enough to preserve a whole cow. Much bigger than the one back at the cabins. After that ..." He took a breath and let it out slowly. "I'll be the one that does it. And I'll try not to waste anything, I promise. We're not like the Dragsters."

Freida smiled at him. "We know, Jack. We trust you. You saved my daddy's herd."

After the smoker frame was built—an hour's work—Brad, the tallest, wrapped it in oiled painter's cloth with a hole in the top like a chimney. Then he and Jack stacked a big pile of hardwood next to it, as well as four logs and kindling underneath it in a shallow pit.

When everything was done to their best ability, Jack found one of the smaller cows and brought it down with a 5.56 round between the eyes, which seemed like the best place to do it.

As awful an experience as it was—way different than shooting a deer from two hundred yards—he didn't mess up. Somehow, in a way he couldn't explain, shooting that poor, defenseless cow felt even worse than shooting those kids back at the Welcome Center.

Though he felt rotten, he took comfort in the fact that he hadn't embarrassed himself by throwing up or crying.

Chatter-mouthed Paul felt no such restraint. After demanding to watch, when it was done, he bawled like a baby with no sign of letting up. The girls did their best to comfort him, with many a "there, there" and "that ol' cow didn't feel a thing" and other reassurances as they led him into the house. Even Brad was affected, coming over to pat Jack on the shoulder and offer a brave smile.

"I'm fine," Jack said, then set about getting his knives ready.

Unlike a deer, cows had a tremendous amount of fat, and thick muscles and bones. After cutting its throat to drain the blood into the cold ground, sudden and violent retching sent Steve to join Paul in the house, leaving only Miguel and Brad to help position and hold the big animal. Because they couldn't hoist it up over a tree to gut it like a deer, they balanced it on its back.

It was all a learning experience, which was why Jack had picked the smallest one. The less meat wasted on mistakes, the better.

The hide was much thicker than deerskin, and tugging and cutting with a knife sized for deer was a great way to slice open a finger. His one lucky break was the additional fur provided useful grab-holds to stretch the skin taut for safe, clean slices. Sawing through the tendons around the hooves was a chore. The back hooves were especially trying, and he ended up scoring them with his knife and then breaking them off with a hammer.

"Sorry, man," Brad said, his face an unhealthy shade of green. "Call me if you get uh, stuck or something. I just ... I gotta go, man." Then he fled to the safety of the house.

When he was gone, Miguel offered a sickly grin. "Bunch of wimps, huh?" He looked around, as if checking whether they were really alone. "You know, I've been thinking. You and me make a good team. We do the things we gotta do and we don't look back. People don't understand us because we're different. With all them grownups dead, *we* gotta be the parents. Like I am with Paul."

"Yeah," Jack said, wondering where he was going with this.

"The Pyros didn't understand me. That's why I left."

Jack paused and looked at him. "I thought you said you and your brother were kicked out."

Miguel glanced quickly at him and then laughed. A bit too loudly, Jack thought.

"Well yeah," he said. "But, you know, it was sort of um

... you know ... *mutual*. Screw those guys. Bunch of freaks, if you ask me."

Jack nodded and wiped his brow. Cutting up cows wasn't just tricky, it was physically taxing. And standing around talking wouldn't get it done any sooner.

"Let's get this over with," he said, and pushed ahead, determined not to squander the animal's sacrifice by doing a less than thorough job.

After they'd skinned it, he learned very quickly he couldn't get through the breastbone without something more serious than his knives. A quick check in the house yielded an axe and a hacksaw. Jack chose the saw, and soon he opened the chest for easy access to the lungs, heart, and liver. These he placed in clean buckets and set aside—disregarding the carefully extracted intestines, anus, and gal bladder, which he'd separated first to keep from spoiling the meat. Another bucket was used to hold the hard, white fat surrounding the organs, which Freida had said could be cooked down, stored at room temperature, and used as cooking oil.

He would have liked to hang the carcass to drain, but couldn't think of anything big enough to hoist it onto, even if they'd had the strength.

"I don't think we can do two of them," Miguel said, looking between the carcass on the ground to the sky. "Time to go chill out for a while. Maybe get Freida to make us some of them eggs."

"That'd be nice," Jack said, wondering if he'd ever feel comfortable saying things like *chill out*. "We still have to smoke it."

The skin was valuable, or would be one day as they became more self-reliant. For now, he was only concerned with saving the meat, fat, and organs. One day, when they had a bigger herd, there'd be room for experimentation. He was particularly looking forward to making *pemmican*—a Native American food Lisa had dredged up from a book on homesteading, and which could last months and even years without refrigeration, or so the book had said. For now, though—with so many mouths to feed—he sliced the animal into manageable pieces.

"We're gonna need another smoker," Miguel said while they were hanging the meat in thick strips. "There's just too much cow, man."

Jack sighed. "Yeah, I know. Wait here while I talk to Brad."

So long as he didn't have to see the cow, Brad was more than happy to quit the house and help out. He used the remaining wood and some lampposts from inside to build a separate, smaller scaffolding. They didn't have another drop cloth, so they draped it in old, wet blankets. This smoker, they reserved for the organs and extra meat. They barely got it all in before running out of room.

A half hour later, Jack said, "I'm worried about our wood supply. Think we'll run out?"

Brad shrugged. "Hard to say. I can probably get more." He eyed the bloody remains of the carcass dubiously, clearly wanting to get as far away from it as possible.

"No need. I'll call back for more."

Thanks to Lisa's research, the farm was easily in range of the cabins through use of a handy feature called *sideband*. Very useful, and he maintained a rule that someone had to be next to a radio at all times. In this case, that person was Lisa.

"Heya, Lisa," Jack said, making it sound casual. In truth, he worried she was still mad at him. "How's it going?"

"How's it going *over*," she said. "I'm telling Greg."

Jack smiled. If she could joke around, he was off the hook. "You know me. How is everyone?"

"Better, now that steak's on the menu. Is the smoker working okay?"

Jack filled her in, glossing over the slaughterhouse scene, then asked how Olivia and Molly were doing with the children. Lisa confirmed today's lesson was science, with an emphasis on plants. At the end of every lesson, each child had to stand up and say what he or she learned that day, reinforcing the new knowledge and spreading it to those who may have missed something. The next day, they'd go over it again quickly before moving on.

"That's awesome," Jack said. "So hey: we need more

wood."

Lisa just laughed at him.

"Very funny," he said, blushing a little. "Can you see if Tony can bring some out? Actually, wait, send Pete." He remembered the scene with Tony and Carla on the couch. The last thing he wanted was more babies on the way.

"Sure," she said.

Jack said goodbye, then went to check on the smokers.

The meat and organs seemed to be coming along fine, in that they didn't look burnt. Beyond that, he didn't know what constituted a proper smoking other than general dryness. With the deer, he'd managed to keep the meat edible for two weeks before they'd eaten it. In theory, smoking the meat should make it last the whole winter. Come February, if they were still alive and not dead from food poisoning, he'd know how he did.

Two hours later, when Pete still hadn't arrived with the wood, Jack got back on the radio.

"You there, Lisa?"

He had to try a few more times, but eventually she picked up. "Go ahead."

"Has Pete left yet? We're running really low on wood and I'm about to start raiding the house for furniture."

Lisa didn't reply immediately. When she did, her voice sounded troubled. "Um ... Pete left over an hour ago. With Mandy. She wanted to see the chickens."

Could just be a flat.

He forced a laugh he didn't feel. "I'll see if I can find them. Probably just car trouble. Remember about his driving."

Lisa sounded concerned. "Be careful, Jack. Just in case. You know?"

"Will do. Thanks."

He left Brad in charge of the smokers, with instructions not to let the fires die down even if he had to pull apart the patio railing, then left with Steve to find Pete and Mandy.

They followed the likeliest route the boy would have taken. Halfway there, they found Pete's car in the middle of the road. Beside it on the ground was a dark shape, lying flat.

Jack parked and rushed from the car.

"Oh, no," Steve said behind him.

Jack bit off an angry retort, refusing to believe what his eyes were telling him. His arms felt fat and light, like balloons, and a terrible pressure was building in his head and chest as the awful realization came crashing down around him. Pete had been shot multiple times and left in the road. Someone had poured corn grain into his mouth and sprinkled it around his body.

Mandy, only nine years old—so fun and full of life—had managed to run a short ways before being gunned down from behind.

On closer inspection, Jack found a rolled-up piece of notebook paper sticking out of Pete's shirt pocket.

He opened it and read the words: *EAT THIS RIPPER FAGS!!!*

TWENTY-FOUR

Jack read the note again, digesting the awful truth of the word *Ripper* and what it implied.

All he wanted was to grab his rifle and go after Carter and his gang. Anything was better than enduring the dead, accusing stares of Pete and Mandy. Their eyes could see what the others had missed. That he was a failure. That his parents' dream of raising some kind of leader or super boy or whatever was in their heads had been a misguided hobby.

How could he be so arrogant to think he could lead these boys and girls through the biggest calamity in human history? Why the hell had they trusted him? He felt like a fraud.

"Man, oh man," Steve said looking back and forth between the bodies.

Jack squeezed his temples and focused on breathing. He couldn't get enough air.

"What do we do, Jack?" Steve said, voice edging toward panic. "Do you think they'll come back?"

Jack looked around, but all he saw was empty road forward and back, and a pull-off ahead with a big metal gate wide enough for tractors, or perhaps to stage an ambush.

None of this should have been surprising after he'd told

Carter to stay away from Freida and Carla's farm. He'd never felt so stupid or guilty in his life. He'd *humiliated* that guy. Caught him naked, held him at gunpoint, and forced him to work under threat of violence. Of course he'd want revenge. Probably spent the day near the farm scanning radio channels, obsessing over the opportunity to strike back.

The farm.

Jack ran to the car and snatched up the mic. "Lisa? Brad?" His voice emerged as a harsh croak. A moment later when nobody answered, he added, "Carter?"

Still nobody answered. Either Carter was too close and didn't want to give himself away, or he'd fled far enough that he was out of range.

Jack tried again. "Lisa? Anyone?"

"I'm here, Jack," Lisa said sounding out of breath. "What's wrong?"

"Here, boss," Brad said a second later.

Now that he had them on, he couldn't get the words out. He clicked the button and squeezed his eyes shut. Willing himself to say it. The truth. All of it.

He held the mic close and spoke quietly. "We've been attacked. Red alert. Red alert."

Crosstalk rendered their frantic replies unintelligible, though the emotions carried clear: confusion and fear, and worry for Pete and Mandy.

"Later," he said, light headed, trying to breathe. "I think they might be listening. Watch what you say. Double the patrols. No driving." He glanced at Mandy and Pete again and closed his eyes. It didn't help—they were still there, waiting for him. "Just be safe."

Steve was standing over Pete, staring down at him, shaking his head. "I can't believe it."

Jack turned off the radio and swore, wanting to cry, to kill ... wanting for all the world to get out and throttle Steve, the former Dragster. How dare he stand there looking at his dead friends? How *dare* he?

He approached the boy with clenched fists.

Still shaking his head, Steve said, "I just can't believe it. You should have let me kill Carter when I could of. He was right there. We had him."

"*Shut up!*" Jack yelled and punched him in the face as hard as he could.

Steve screamed and went down. Jack followed, landing blow after blow while Steve scrabbled to get away.

"Jack, I didn't—"

He hit him again and climbed on top. Then they were rolling around, Jack trying to pummel him and Steve trying not to get pummeled. With tears streaming down his face, the hate in his chest burst forth in a wordless roar of impotent sorrow as he struck the boy again and again. Then Jack's whole being flashed in an eruption of pain, and he was suddenly staring up at the sky.

Curiously, he noted his ears were ringing, as if someone had bashed him with a hastily grabbed rock from the side of the road. Also curiously, the right side of his neck felt colder than his left, as if said rock had cut his scalp.

"*Jesus*, Jack, what the hell?" Steve said from a million miles away.

Jack's view of the careening sky was crowded out by Steve, staring down at him, panting and wild-eyed.

"Steve ...?"

"I didn't do anything! Why'd you hit me for? They were my friends too!"

He felt suddenly afraid. What would Steve do if he thought Jack wanted to hurt him? Would he stupidly show mercy, as Jack had done with Carter? Or would he follow his own advice from the previous night and finish him off?

Laughter sounded from nearby, joyful and familiar. Desperate hope welled within him and he struggled to get up, but his body couldn't do that anymore.

"Steve ... she's all alone ... have to find her ..."

"What, Jack? You're mumbling."

After that, he must have blacked out, because the next thing he remembered was waking up in the car outside the cattle farm. Gentle hands pulled him from the back and brought him inside. Then came raised voices and accusations from another room as Steve related the events up to and including the fight.

"Wake up!" Freida said loudly, snapping her fingers.

"Just leave me," Jack whispered.

"You can't sleep if you have a concussion," she said patiently. "I heard that somewhere."

Do something, you stupid cabbage. You're supposed to do something.

"Where's Brad?" he said tiredly.

"Right here, dude."

Jack moved his head to see him, then yelped at the pain, prompting everyone in the room to shout advice all at the same time.

"You need to finish the work," Jack said. "We need that meat. Whatever you do, finish the work."

"Already done. Don't worry about it."

"Both of them?" he said.

"What? Oh. Uh ... we only did the one. The wood ran out."

With an effort, Jack said, "You ... we need to ... everyone ... I'm sorry."

Then, whether from stress or the blow to the head or a combination of both, he blacked out again.

***

He woke with a splitting headache and a stiff neck. He didn't recognize the bed, but the lack of exposed logs told him he was still at the farm. There was nobody in the room with him and the house was quiet. A quick glance out the window showed it was either dusk or dawn, depending on how long he'd been incapacitated. When he tried to get up, pain flared from the side of his head down along his neck, hurting so bad he felt nauseous.

He pondered what was wrong with him. Then he remembered the struggle with Steve. The fight he'd *started* with Steve.

You idiot. How was that supposed to help?

Tentatively, he reached up to touch his head and found it wrapped in bandages. Beside him on the table next to a lamp was a full glass of water and a bottle of prescription medicine. He looked at the label and saw it was for pain. Hoping it still worked, he took two like the instructions said and swallowed it down with water. Then he lay back and considered the situation.

The group—his *Rippers*, for lack of a better name—was spread out over two locations. One of them, the bad guys clearly knew about. The other was hidden back in the woods, accessible by an unremarkable dirt road. Short of someone following them home in secret, the place was safe.

The farm, however, was definitely *not* safe. Freida and Carla's herd was here—something that could grow to help the group for years. The Dragsters could use it like a leash around their necks, knowing they couldn't abandon it, and thus knowing how to find them whenever they wanted to.

A sudden flash of anger sent his head throbbing. He needed to relax. Steve had really walloped him good.

Thirty minutes later, his pain had dipped to the tolerable regions. When he felt ready, he sat up. The room seemed a little wobblier than he'd come to expect from most houses, but it settled down after he got a few breaths into him.

He still had his clothing on and found his shoes beside the nightstand. To avoid leaning over, he twisted into them like slippers, not worrying about socks, then made his way to the door. A short flight down and he was in the living room.

Tony sat staring intently out the window. His rifle leaned against the wall beside him.

"What time is it?" Jack said.

Tony turned in sudden fright, then sighed with relief. "Morning time. You feeling okay?"

"Well enough," he said, not wanting to get into it.

"Everyone got real worried after Steve popped you. Lisa made him come back to the cabins. He's afraid you're gonna kick him out. She said you'd never do that."

His words hung in the air like a question.

"No one's getting kicked out. He didn't start it."

Tony nodded. "I still can't believe what happened. Killing them two like that. Why they do that for? It's just ... just *stupid*."

Not wanting to think about it right now, Jack said, "Any news from Lisa?"

"She's got everyone on alert. Nobody's allowed to use the radio except for really basic stuff. Every hour, I gotta get on and say we're fine and ask if they're fine. Olivia's over there right now watching outside, just like me."

Remembering how he'd snuck up on Carter and Trisha, Jack said, "We need to be outside. It sucks, but—"

"We *are* going outside, just not my turn yet." He looked at his watch. "Freida be along in a minute."

Sure enough, a minute later, Freida came through the back door in a puffy winter coat, pullover cap, and scarf. She blinked in surprise at Jack, then gave him hell for being out of bed.

Minutes later, he could barely make it back upstairs before the narcotics took full effect.

***

The next few days passed in a drug-induced haze, with watches Jack couldn't participate in, chores he couldn't help with and—thanks to Lisa—planning he was mostly left out of. His head hurt all the time, though luckily nothing was broken. Apparently there'd been a jagged edge on that rock. Freida had sewn up his scalp with some thread, after first boiling it and the needle.

Christmas was a cheerless occasion with no gifts, punctuated by a double funeral service for Pete and Mandy, who were buried near the farmhouse under a grove of apple trees. Jack checked with Lisa for the best way to hook up a battery to one of the CBs. Pretty easy, it turned out. Brad, the tallest, held the mic open during the final respects so those at the cabins could hear and share.

People had a lot to say about Mandy: her enthusiasm for exploring, her constant cheer, her fondness for profanity. When they got to Pete, it was Jack who spoke.

"The day before Pete joined me, he'd taken a car for a ride, crashed into a tree, and then stumbled off."

Some of them laughed nervously at that.

"But he was the first person to join me when I was chased from my house by the same types who killed him. We owe a lot to Pete and Mandy for what they brought us every day, and not just the stuff they found in houses and stores. We'll miss Mandy's energy and beautiful smile. We'll miss Pete's weird laugh and his willingness to say what he felt. They were with me from the beginning, and

I'll remember them both for the rest of my life."

A sob broke from Tony. "They killed my best friend! We need to kill them all!"

Carla and Freida took him in their arms and hugged him.

Brad's eyes were shining with rage, and he nodded his agreement.

Miguel watched everyone, his face devoid of any emotion. His brother, Paul, cried openly.

"My first concern is keeping the rest of us safe," Jack said carefully. "There are things we still need to do to survive. For now, let survival be your revenge."

"They're gonna do it again as long as we're out here," Miguel said. "Look, I have a plan. The only reason they came after us is because we went after them first. If you think about it ... look, I don't wanna say we got what's coming to us, but in a way we did. After what you stole."

Jack's jaw clenched and unclenched in anger. "We didn't kill their people. And if you have a problem with the grain we took, you don't have to eat the meat we got for it."

Miguel held up his hands for calm. "I know, *I know*. I'm just *saying*. I told you, I got a plan. You might not want hear it right now, but still. We need to join the Dragsters. It's the only way we'll be safe." At Jack's glower, his tone turned placating. "I can go there if you don't want to. They don't know me. I can tell them *I'm* the new leader. Once we join them, this guy Carter will be the boss anyway, so it's not like it matters."

The room fell quiet as everyone considered his words. Jack considered them too. He considered them incredibly stupid, and the white-hot anger he'd felt for Steve the other day came crashing over him. Just barely, he held it in check.

Miguel took advantage of the silence. "We should have a vote—all those who want to join the Dragsters, raise your hands." He immediately raised his hand, then nudged his brother, who half-heartedly raised his, too.

Carla raised hers.

"You take that hand down right now, Carla," Freida said in a low growl, and the younger girl lowered it. "We ain't joining them animals. Not ever."

Jack let his eyes sweep the rest of the group, taking their measure.

"I won't join them, especially under these conditions," he said. "What the Dragsters did was designed to push us into acting dumb. Fortunately for us, I intend to do the smart thing. I'm asking you to trust me. One more time."

Miguel looked around for more supporters. When he didn't find them, he and his brother lowered their hands.

TWENTY-FIVE

Jack asked Freida if they could slaughter five more cows, explaining that if they had to retreat from the farm under Carter's larger force, it was better to have the meat in storage than doing without and feeding the enemy.

"You really think he'd do that?" she said.

"I didn't think they'd come after us. I was dumb, and two people paid for my mistake. He knows you're under our protection. But they're your animals. If you don't want to, we'll be fine." He shrugged. "Or we won't. Guess we'll find out, huh?"

Laughing, she said, "Don't be so negative. I like you being nice about it, but from now on, what's mine is yours, so long as what's yours is mine. Deal?"

Hardly believing she was serious, he held out his hand and said, "Deal."

Freida shook it firmly. "But I'm the only one who gets to boss my sister around."

"Definitely," he said, smiling.

A few days after the murders, Lisa and Steve came to the farm in a truck filled with wood. Jack showed her the meat they'd smoked from the first and only cow slaughtered so far. They'd stored it in trash bags with as much air pressed out as possible.

"What do you think?" he said, taking out a stringy piece

and handing it to her.

Lisa put it in her mouth and chewed slowly.

"It's good," she said. "For now. But I'm worried it's not dry enough, or that it'll suck up moisture every time you open the bag. The books all say the best way to do this is a combination of salt *and* smoke. They say if you do that, you can keep it for years. Doing it this way"—she gestured at the bags—"I'm worried you'll only get a few weeks."

Lisa was a stickler in the truest sense—a perfectionist who found fault in other perfectionists. In contrast, Jack was more likely to do the best he could and make adjustments on the fly. But not when it came to food safety.

"If you want salt," he said, "we'll get salt."

Miguel and his brother joined Tony, replacing the two lost friends as the group's newest scavengers. Not wanting to tangle with any more gangs, Jack had them focus their hunt for salt in Warrenton.

The first day out brought in boxes of salt from supermarkets. Lisa said some of it was okay to use, but the rest was iodized table salt. The books all said sea salt or rock salt was the best. She didn't know if you could use table salt or whether it would mess up the meat, and she didn't want to chance it.

While that was going on, Brad constructed the biggest smoke rack yet—fifteen feet long and five feet high. When he was satisfied with it, he returned to Big Timber in the middle of the night, which they all agreed was the safest time to travel alone.

It quickly became apparent the scavengers wouldn't find enough salt in stores and houses to meet their needs. In the end, it was Steve who solved their problem.

"My dad used to de-ice the roads every winter," he said. "Had to use lots of salt to do it. They store them in those big cone things near the roads. If we can find one of those, maybe that'd work."

Jack knew what he was talking about, having seen the curious structures himself countless times. He'd always thought they had sand in them, or maybe gravel if he thought about them at all. "But where would we get it for this winter?"

Steve smiled slyly. "When did the Sickness first start?"

Jack looked at him blankly, then his eyes widened. "*Last* winter. And people stopped going to work around that time, too."

Carla, who was always there so long as Tony was around, said in a mock-complaining tone, "Last year's fashions for the rest of my life. I'm cursed."

Jack forced a laugh, happy others were here to act as a buffer between him and Steve. Jack had been the first to apologize after the former Dragster returned, and Steve had graciously accepted it. Still, it felt weird hanging around the guy who'd nearly killed him.

Tony said, "I know where one is, but it's way over on the Dragsters' turf. Seen it one time when I was out, up by the main exit."

Jack wanted to yell at him for venturing so close to the hostile town, but held off. One, it wouldn't do any good. Tony would just smirk and act cool, the way he always did. Two, if he wanted to get himself killed, that was his problem. It was hard enough protecting people who listened and used their heads.

"I say go at night, when they're sleeping," Steve said. "I'll even go with you."

He sounded enthusiastic about it—almost like he wanted to make up for the fight Jack started. And though Jack knew it was unfair to let him risk his life for crimes he wasn't guilty of, he also couldn't pass up the help.

"We'll go in with our lights off," Jack said. "No radios. The four of us should be enough."

What Steve said about the Dragsters sleeping rang true. No one at the farm liked keeping a night watch, or doing patrols out in the cold. Jack had almost relented on that, but images of Mandy and Pete's broken bodies stayed him. He couldn't let something like that happen again. Really, he was just counting down the time until he made another mistake. Someone had to lead, though—and not Miguel, however much he was angling for the job.

After turning down for the night and taking another two painkillers—which he'd come to look forward to, adding to his worry—Jack awoke to the sharp crack of pistols.

Following that was more gunfire, this from a carbine. Then came what sounded like a muffled crash.

Though sluggish from the medication, he stumbled from bed, dressed hastily, and hurried down the stairs. Too late, he remembered his pistol on the nightstand. Returning for it, he ran into Freida.

"What's happening?" she said. "Who the heck's shooting?"

"Don't know."

He continued past her, collected his pistol, then joined her in the living room.

More rifle shots boomed from outside.

"It's Tony!" she shouted, pointing out the window. "He's shooting at some car!"

Tony and Miguel were on watch that night.

"Stay here," he said, then left through the front entrance with his weapon ready.

Out in the road was a black four-door sedan with the windshield shot up and shining white in the moonlight. The car had dipped into the drainage ditch in front of the house where the fence began. The back window was either blown out or rolled down. Two boys were lying slumped in the front.

Miguel was crouched behind the truck with his rifle raised, a look of horror on his face.

Tony fired into the car. Then he fired again, and again, and *again*. When he stopped, the only sound was of cows mooing loudly in terror.

"I think you got them," Jack said, flicking on the flashlight he'd snagged on the way out.

Tony jerked his head around and aimed at him. Gone was his usual swagger and bluster. Here was a frightened child in a demented world.

"Jack!" he said, eyes widened. "I think I killed them. They drove up and I was making my rounds, just like Lisa said to, and then they come up and started shooting. I didn't think—I just shot back."

"First, lower the gun," Jack said, staring at the steaming hot muzzle.

"Huh?" he said, then looked down. A second later, he

nodded. "Oh yeah. Safety rules. Gotta remember. My head's all foggy." As if punctuating the point, he dropped his rifle with a clatter and stumbled toward Carla and Freida, who were standing outside with weapons of their own.

Jack looked between the rifle on the ground and the motionless car and tightened his grip on the pistol. Cautiously, he approached the vehicle. The headlights were on, but it wasn't running. Both boys in the front were in the useful age range. They were also clearly dead.

Freida yelled something in alarm, and he flinched at the crack of gunfire from the car.

"I'll shoot you, you come any closer!" someone shouted from inside it.

Jack dropped back, his body low. "Hey, stop shooting!"

"No, *you* stop shooting! We was just trying to scare you!"

Jack stashed his pistol in his back pocket and raised his hands in the air. "How about you toss that gun out? We'll talk about it inside, where it's warm."

"I don't trust you!"

Jack seethed quietly. "You gotta do something, kid. All we want is to talk. We're not letting you go until we find out what this is about, so you may as well come in now."

Several moments passed where he worried the boy was trying to get a bead on him, or possibly make a break for it. Then he shouted, "You better not shoot me! I'm coming out, okay? I'm unarmed. None of this was my idea. We was just scaring you is all."

"I know that," Jack said calmly. "You're perfectly safe."

Over behind the truck, Miguel stirred from his spot and said, "Dude, what are you doing?"

Freida, who'd come down into the yard, said, "Be careful, Jack."

Hands came out of the window and then a head popped out. The expression on the kid's face was one of misery and fear. "You said you weren't going to shoot me!"

"We won't," Jack said. "They're just being cautious. Now hurry up."

The boy crawled out like a bug from a hole and fell over

in a heap into the ditch. He scrambled unsteadily to his feet and threw his hands in the air.

"Come closer," Jack said.

The boy crawled out of the ditch and stopped about five feet away.

"You can lower your hands," Jack said. "What's your name?"

"Ray," he said. "They made me come with them to scare you, that's the truth a hundred percent. I swear on my folks. I swear."

"Who made you come? Who's idea was it?"

"Carter and his friends. All of them. They're real pissed at you guys."

Jack nodded toward the car. "Is one of them Carter?"

Ray snorted. "No way—he's back in town. He's still not sure how many you are. He figures not many, but ain't sure on account of what you said that time on the radio. That was you, right? On the radio that day?"

"Yeah."

"Carter's mad as hell about how ... uh, what happened the other day. With Trisha and all. So he made us come."

"To scare us," Jack said.

The boy nodded. "Yeah."

"You killed my friends. Was that also to scare us?"

Ray said, "That wasn't me! That was Tucker, in the car." His eyes grew desperate. "Oh, man, can I stay with you? Here in your gang? He's gonna be so mad. We need to run. Get as far away as we can."

"I'll think about it," Jack said. "Who's the other kid in the car?"

"Bill. He's like me, just following orders."

"To scare us," Jack said again.

"Yeah. I swear."

Lisa had been right all along. Steve, too. The Dragsters would keep coming, and there was nothing he could do to stop them if he didn't adjust. Society was gone. Laws were just how you felt that day. The world had fallen on dark times, and it craved dark solutions.

Jack pulled his pistol and shot Ray in the chest.

"I know, man," he said. "It worked."

TWENTY-SIX

Jack turned around to the shocked stares of Miguel, Freida, and Carla. A few seconds later, Tony stumbled back outside, his face a mask of fear.

The farm was silent. Even the cows had quieted.

Steve said, "Why'd you shoot Ray for? He didn't have a gun. Ray was okay, man. I can't believe it."

Tony got in the boy's face. "They killed our friends! They shot at the house! What if someone else died? Huh? Hell with him. Got what he deserved, you ask me."

Steve backed away, cringing under the other boy's menacing rage.

Jack said, "He came here to hurt us, plain and simple. Carter picked him because he wouldn't have problems shooting up houses in the middle of the night, or gunning down helpless people who'd never hurt him." He looked down, saw he was still holding the pistol, and stuck it back in his pocket. "I know some of these guys are your old friends. But you're either with us or you're not—you and Molly and anyone else who joins. We don't have a jail or police or any of that. One day, maybe. For now, the punishment for attacking our people is death. It has to be."

Not waiting for a reply, he pushed past, heading for the front door. Before entering, he turned back and said, "Be ready to move in five minutes. We're going for the salt tonight."

After Jack got his rifle and jacket, Tony helped him stack the three bodies in the trunk of one of the cars. Every time Tony touched skin and not clothing, he grimaced and wiped his hand. They didn't talk. They just did the work.

Jack wanted to thank him for his support, because he was beginning to regret Ray's summary execution. Ray had said the driver—Tucker—had killed Pete and Mandy. If that was true, did that mean Ray really was an *okay guy*, like Steve said? Was the bar really that low?

A darker part of him saw a political angle to his violence: to instill fear in the enemy. If he'd spared Ray, Carter would have seen it as weakness. Not just him, either. Miguel was already challenging his decisions, and Tony had never been completely on board with him as leader.

"Hey, man, you okay?" Tony said after they closed the trunk.

"Not even a little bit," Jack said tightly. "We need to do something about them. The Dragsters."

Tony nodded. "Like what? I ain't joining them, and I don't wanna kill no more people, if that's what you mean. Tonight was self-defense. What you did?" He shook his head. "I mean, I get it. But I dunno ... maybe we should just get the hell out of here like Steve said. Sounds like a whole lotta them and not many of *us*. You feel me?"

Jack had nothing to say to that. It was the truth.

***

Inside the salt thing, as Jack thought of it, there was indeed a tremendous amount of salt piled up. So much so that Miguel and Tony had to take several short breaks as they filled up the truck bed. Outside the salt thing was a big mound of sand, but they left that alone, not knowing what to do with sand even if they had another truck to take it.

Jack heard about all this after the boys returned to the farm with Steve around three in the morning—because he wasn't with them. They parted ways just after the first exit into town. His mission was more grim, more ruthless, and he'd already lost enough of their respect.

He peered across the big bridge into town. A sign said

the river was the south fork of the Shenandoah.

The dumb cabbages hadn't placed a watch on the bridge. In a way, this offended him. Kill his friends, shoot up the house he was sleeping in, and not set a watch? Carter and his gang needed to experience the same sort of fear they'd been dishing out.

"You think they have guards posted in town?" Jack said.

Steve said, "Even if he tried to, people would just sneak off after he left. It ain't like the army."

Jack nodded.

The bridge had a double-lane road going in and one coming out. The right lane was blocked by cars. The left lane offered a narrow entrance that nobody had plugged since the last time he was here.

He looked off to the side. The bridge would have been a beautiful way to enter the town, up high with the river shining below. Hard to believe how mighty humans had gotten, that they could defy geography so effortlessly. If someone asked him to build such a bridge, he wouldn't know where to begin. In fact, there probably wasn't a single person left in the world who knew how to make concrete.

From his studies, he knew the Dark Ages had been the same way. The Romans knew about concrete. That's how they'd made the domes on their temples. Then Europe forgot the secret when the empire fell.

"Quit stalling," Jack said quietly.

"What?"

"Nothing."

He pulled through and into town with his lights off, driving slowly. Steve told him where to turn and he did, following his instructions past lightless shops and houses stacked like monuments to forgotten kings. The world had become a museum, or more accurately a cemetery. He knew if he opened the windows or turned on the fan, the sickly smell of death would invade the car.

They came to a section of neighborhoods with colorful, fanciful old homes interspersed amongst regular houses. Along the street, the parked cars changed from boring and sensible to fast-looking and flashy, each of them sporting little checkered flags tied to the mirrors and antennas.

"Slow up, man," Steve said. "It's down there, see? The big one."

Down on the right was the biggest house in the area, trendy-looking and out of place. Jack couldn't understand why anyone would put something like that next to the colorful houses with their rounded spires and wraparound porches.

Every house had a chimney here, but Carter had taken the biggest, ugliest one. Probably took a constant supply of wood to heat it.

"What are you doing?" Steve said when Jack pulled into a driveway.

"Turning around."

"But I thought you wanted to—"

"I am, shush."

Jack backed into the street, turned on the headlights, and reversed down to where the big house was. When nobody came out to challenge him, he popped the trunk and got out. One by one, he dragged each corpse over and stacked them face-up to the sky. Nobody coming outside could miss it. And just so there was no doubt who'd done it, he slipped a folded note into Ray's front pocket:

Carter,

Before the Sickness, littering was a crime. So keep your trash off my property. Also, why don't you come yourself next time? Our snipers need the practice.

He signed the note "Jack."

"That ought to do it," Steve said, staring down at the dead face of Ray.

"Not even close," Jack said.

He unslung his rifle, pulled and released the charging handle with a snap, then began firing at Carter's house, aiming for the windows.

"Dude, what are you doing?" Steve said, holding his ears, eyes widened in shock. "We need to go!'

There were six windows in the front, all easy targets even in the dark. When he ran out of bullets, he loaded another magazine and stowed the spent one in his belt. Then he resumed shooting. He liked the idea of Carter trying to heat his big house with busted-up windows. He wasn't worried about hurting someone innocent because Steve said Carter didn't like children hanging around, and the gang was guilty as hell.

"Over there!" Steve yelled, pointing across the street at another house.

Someone with a flashlight came out, shining it at them.

Jack aimed at the flashlight and hit whoever was carrying it. A girl, it turned out, now screaming on the ground in agony. He'd feel bad later. Not as bad as he'd felt burying Mandy, but bad.

Another flashlight, this one from Carter's house. Another shot, and more screaming from the boy carrying it.

"Jack, stop! Let's *go!*"

More were coming out, some with flashlights, others were shooting at them with pistols. These cabbages loved their pistols. No long-range accuracy at all, even if they'd had training.

Steve got in the driver's seat and screamed back a final time, threatening to leave him.

At the last second, Jack jumped in. Bullets whacked into the back of the car as they tore out of there. When they were clear, Steve chose a back way out of town he knew about.

Nobody followed them.

***

By the time Jack returned to the farm, Lisa and Greg had arrived. Molly, Olivia, and Brad had stayed behind to watch the children.

As requested, his friends came in two of the vans, which they used to block the western approach. Anyone trying to slip around it would get trapped in the ditch running along both sides of the road, making an easy target.

Even a small force could be devastating on the defense. He remembered seeing WWI footage with his parents during the "folly of man" phase of his education. Now he wished his group had machine guns.

Tony and Miguel had filled the truck bed high with salt. It sloped on one side like a snowdrift.

Lisa said, "Oh, Tone, this is perfect, thank you."

Jack cocked his head at that, wondering when she'd started calling him *Tone*.

"There was a whole lot of it," Tony said, smiling bashfully. "Not too heavy, neither. Figured better having too much than not enough."

To Lisa, Jack said, "Did you bring everything I asked for?"

"Sure. What the heck do you want that crap for?"

Jack mustered a halfhearted smile. "Since you asked so nicely."

He told them.

"Are you out of your stupid mind?" Lisa said when he was done. "That guy's crazy! He's not gonna help us. What are you thinking?"

"Blaze isn't crazy. He's something better."

"Yeah what?" she said.

"He's a bully, like Carter, which makes him predictable. We can use that. Or we can pack up and run somewhere else to hide. But guaranteed, everywhere we go has a different set of bullies in charge."

Greg said, "Maybe not. It's a big country."

He was right about that. It made sense that places existed with nobody left alive at all, or places so remote they never had many people to begin with. But he hated the idea of starting again, especially this late in the season. He wouldn't force anyone to stay, though. That was definitely no way to lead.

Miguel sighed loudly. "I'm not sure about this crazy plan, bro. Why don't we just make peace with them? All this meat we're getting, they'd have to take us in. We can't defend this place forever. You know we can't."

By mutual agreement, neither Jack nor Steve had told anyone about the shooting outside Carter's house. All it would do was serve to worry them further. There was no way to join Carter now, even if he wanted to, which he didn't.

Freida marched over and poked Miguel hard in the chest. "This is my property and my stock, and I ain't giving it to them murdering criminals. You keep talking like that, you won't be welcome. You hear me?"

Miguel backed up. "I'm sorry, I'm just saying ... we gotta use our heads. I mean ... I like Jack and all, but ..."

Now it was Greg's turn. "But what? We took you in, fed you, taught you to shoot. You're as safe with us as with them. Safer, because we actually plan things out. You should have stayed with Blaze, you like killing and stealing so much."

After that, Miguel stayed quiet, his face blank while the others fleshed out the plan.

The next day was spent butchering and preserving. If Jack's plan worked, they wouldn't have to find somewhere new. Then they could grow their own food one day, consuming less beef while they built up the herd—add more deer and other game animals, like squirrels and turkeys. Maybe those rabbits they'd talked about raising. Lots of possibilities.

"Before you leave on your dumb stunt," Lisa said, "who's going to finish the butchering?"

There were still three cows to go, and Jack's head was killing him. He wouldn't be able to help.

Jack said, "Miguel. He knows what to do. We need people to step in for these types of things. Steve bashing me in the head proved that." He smiled to show he wasn't mad.

Steve's guilty expression cracked into a nervous smile.

"It's too hard for one person," Miguel said. "Or even two people."

Greg said, "I'll help. But I'm not good around blood."

Jack shook his head. "I have plans for you, Greg. You're off the hook."

His friend frowned at that, but didn't reply.

Freida said, "I'll help you, Miguel. I got a strong stomach."

"Me too," Lisa said.

"Just be extra careful about the gall bladder," Jack said. Then, blushing a little, he added, "And, the uh ... *poop* area."

Carla snorted.

"You and Tony defend the road. One of you watches from the vans, the other sits in a car looking the other way.

No sleeping."

Steve said, "What about me?"

Greg patted his arm calmly. "Question not the Chosen One, young warrior. Even the smallest among us play a part in *His* plan."

"That's the spirit," Jack said, and told them both what he wanted.

TWENTY-SEVEN

Jack's head still hurt, and he felt achy and sore from resting all day back at the cabins. In retrospect, he'd pushed himself too hard with the attack on Carter. Still, he felt guilty, knowing Lisa and the others were at the farm finishing the job he'd started. These days, it seemed guilt was his constant companion. Now he felt it for risking his life on what had seemed like such a good idea the night before.

Somewhere near the Centreville exit, Jack slowed his car to a crawl. The way ahead was blocked with vehicles on both sides of the highway. The roadblock hadn't been there when they'd first left for Big Timber in the school bus. And it wasn't there when Lisa and Greg had taken that second trip to the library, or they would have told him.

On the eastbound approach, there was a fire going. The flames flickered off chrome and glass, casting huge shadows on the noise barrier along the side of the road. With his lights out and driving as slow as he was, Jack figured whoever had started it couldn't see him.

He turned on the CB and flipped through various channels listening for chatter and not finding any. Either the Pyros weren't using CBs or it was too late and everyone sane was in bed already.

If he backed up, he could take the Gainesville exit and

maneuver his way down side roads back to 28, and from there, down into Centreville. Unless they'd blocked that way, too. Could be, but he doubted it. Much smarter to concentrate their attention on the main arteries. If this was Blaze's doing, he probably didn't have enough control over his people to plug every hole.

Jack turned the car around, went back to the last exit, and found the ramp blocked by an unmanned roadblock. He pulled up to the jumble of vehicles and parked close to the others, effectively hiding the car in plain sight.

After a quick look around, he popped the trunk and hid the keys in the undercarriage like they did with the fuel cars back at the cabins. This way, if his plan didn't work— and he lived to tell the tale—he could get home with everything he'd brought with him.

Jack examined the contents of the trunk using his LED flashlight. Thanks to Lisa, it was piled high with bags of potato chips, candy bars, cookies, pastries, and other junk—all the foods they'd decided only to eat on special occasions for fear of tooth decay.

It was Miguel who'd spawned the idea. Their cowardly new friend hadn't been in the Pyros for very long, but during his time, he'd learned Blaze had a sweet tooth. Jack was hoping the murderous redhead would love the hoard they'd gathered. Lisa had thrown in some of their precious canned food, too, to round it out. That and one other thing: *pain medication.*

Without the drugs, he didn't know how he would have gotten through those first few days after getting smashed in the head. While on them, he'd never felt better in his life. Not just physically, but emotionally. Maybe his dosage had been too high, but for the first time since the Sickness, he'd felt truly happy—giddy, even.

Miguel had said Blaze asked about pills when they'd first met. If candy and canned food wasn't enough to entice the murderous leader and his gang, pills might be just the nudge he needed.

The question was: how much to carry in? A dilemma, really. Too much and someone might try to take it. Too little and he wouldn't merit an audience with Blaze.

Ultimately, he brought half the drugs, ten chocolate bars, six packages of cookies, three boxes of individually wrapped brownies, five cans of chili, and five cans of corn. Then, after double-checking his pack and ensuring the .40 caliber was loaded and ready, he set off walking back toward the new roadblock.

***

It was just after ten o'clock in the evening when Jack fell in sight of the wall of cars. The car on the left shoulder was parked in front of the others, forming a gate that could be rolled in and out. There was nobody around, and the fire from earlier had died down to dull embers, flaring sporadically with each frigid gust of wind. As he got closer, he noticed the rollaway car's windows were steamed up.

After a moment's hesitation, he approached it.

Tap, tap, tap.

The car shook as whoever was inside began moving about. Then the side door flew open and a boy stumbled out clutching something shiny in his hand that could only be a gun.

As a precaution, Jack pulled his own, but kept it lowered.

"Easy there," he said. "Just calm down."

The boy—about nine or ten—found his feet, then swung around in Jack's direction and fired.

Jack yelped and dove for the cover of the blockade. "Stop shooting, you idiot!"

In response, the boy fired two more shots—somewhere—and shouted back, "You better leave me alone, kid! I'll kill you! I'll do it, too!"

He didn't know what to say that would calm the boy down, and wondered if he could slip away from the roadblock. If he ducked down low enough, maybe he could slink off in the shadow of the gully and the noise barrier. Then he'd get back in his car and figure out what to do next.

On the other side of the roadblock, another boy's voice said, "Joey, what are you shooting at? Who's there?"

"Some weirdo with a gun! He tried to kill me!"

"What weirdo?"

"I think he means me," Jack called back. "I'm not a weirdo, and all I did was wake him up. Then he started shooting. What kind of roadblock is this, anyway?"

A tense moment passed where no one said anything. Jack was about to suggest they all put their guns away when the new kid said, "Come out so I can see you."

"No," Jack said. "*You* come out where I can see *you*."

"Fine. Joey, you started this. Put down your gun and go say hi."

"But Tom ..."

"Just do it."

Another moment passed, then the trigger-happy kid climbed over the hood of the rollaway car. He had long hair and a dirty face, and his hands were empty. Jack saw a big holster on his side with a pistol in it.

"You shoot me, you're dead," Joey said.

"Understood."

"How come I gotta put my gun away but you still got yours?"

"You're right," he said, holstering it. "I'm Jack. You know, you really shouldn't go around shooting at people."

"And *you* shouldn't sneak up on people you don't know!"

Jack wondered if maybe the boy was unhinged. A second later, another boy scooted cautiously over the hood, hands in the air. A few years older than Joey, Tom seemed less jumpy and more intelligent.

"So as you can see," Tom said, "this is our roadblock. You have to pay us or you can't go past."

"*Your* roadblock?"

"Well, not mine. It belongs to the Pyros. That's my gang. So the roadblock's ours a little. And like I said, you gotta pay. Like I said."

"Like you said."

"Yeah. So, um ... what do you got to pay with?"

Before he could answer, Joey said, "Make him give you that gun, first of all. He ain't allowed to have one past here anyways. Blaze said."

Tom grimaced and rolled his eyes. "Not like he can't get himself another one super fast." He looked at Jack. "Just hide it in your pack till you get down near Fairfax—that's a city. It's like four more exits. You should totally get a car and drive. It's too cold out. But you need a good battery. We can trade you one if you want. Driving's easy, just go slow at first until you learn how."

Joey said, "You got any food in that backpack?"

"I do," Jack said. "That's actually why I'm here. Have a look."

Cautiously, Jack shrugged out of his backpack and tossed it across, causing Joey to flinch.

"Would you calm down?" Tom said and snatched up the pack. Then he opened it. "Holy mother of Christmas—look at that! Pills, too. Everyone wants pills, now."

Jack didn't miss the gleam in Tom's eye at the sight of the little brown bottles. That's why his hand was resting casually on his .40 caliber, ready to pull it if needed. He hoped he wouldn't have to. Other than being desperate and greedy, Tom seemed okay.

"So how much is the toll?"

"You gotta give us everything," Joey said. Then he giggled. "That's the rules. Man, you sure screwed up today."

Tom frowned at Joey and shook his head. "Why don't you shut up for once?" His gaze swung to Jack, who was watching them with a patient smile. "So here's the thing, uh ... Jack?"

He nodded.

"Okay ... so here's the thing. Blaze is sort of, uh ... *strict*. Normally he wants everything, then he dishes it out later to whoever he likes most. Kind of like an allowance. And normally we just take a few things on our own and let people go by. Otherwise people like you would just starve or whatever. But *man*." He shook his head in amazement. "This is some great stuff here. If we bring in all this, we won't have to sit out here in the cold no more. That's how it works. The more you bring in, the higher up in the gang you get. You should totally join up."

Jack nodded. That was pretty much what Miguel had said. Well, that and one more thing.

"How much credit do you get for bringing in new

people? Ones that know how to shoot?"

Tom laughed. "Everyone knows how to shoot." He waved it away, a nonissue. "But all this great stuff ..."

"What if you bring in someone who knows where there's a whole house filled to the ceiling with stuff like this? Not just a little sack?"

"For serious?" Joey said.

Just barely, Jack kept from laughing as Tom and Joey's eyes widened in awe. Then he nodded. "For serious."

***

The three boys got in the car together and set out, with Jack in the back seat. They'd tried to put him in the front. He'd just smiled and shook his head, and they hadn't pressed the issue. As they drove, he asked whether it was safe to leave without finding a replacement at the roadblock.

"We're fine," Tom said. Another nonissue.

"You sure about that?" Jack said. "I've heard that troops who leave a post unguarded get in a lot of trouble. Like in the Army."

In truth, he was worried the two would get killed. He still remembered the fate of the boy who'd tried to cut a side deal the day he'd met Pete and Mandy. Blaze had seemed to relish the opportunity to deliver capital punishment—personally, with Jack's sword, no less.

Joey snorted. "What's he gonna do, kill all of us? Then what? He can kiss my ass if—"

Tom smacked him in the face with a quick backhand, bringing a startled yelp from the boy.

"Shut your mouth! Quit acting like you're safe. 'Cause you're not. Blaze'll skin you so fast you won't even *know* what." A minute later, he relented. "You gotta know how far you can push and when to shut up and take it. Right now, until you're mature, you shut up and take it." He glanced in the mirror at Jack, who sat quietly listening, fascinated.

Pretty soon, they were on 29 heading toward Fairfax, away from Centreville.

"I thought Blaze was over at the high school," Jack said.

"How'd you know that?" Tom said suspiciously.

"Oh, I just heard about it."

"Well he's not there no more. Got his headquarters in a big house in Clifton. That's a *place*. It's got fireplaces and woods everywhere outside. The high school got too cold, so we moved."

Jack thought for a second. "He lives there alone, or with other people?"

"His friends are there sometimes. Everyone mostly sleeps at the hotel down in the town area, or in other houses. Nobody can have a bigger house than Blaze. That's one of the rules in case nobody tells you. There's lots of rules, by the way." He said this matter-of-factly. "Truth is, Blaze gives me the creeps. Him and his sister."

"That girl's stupid and ugly, like a toad," Joey said, snorting.

"I said shut up," Tom said.

"*You* say she's ugly," Joey said in a pouty tone. "All the time."

Tom raised his hand and the younger boy flinched.

A few minutes later, he turned and followed a long road with big houses on either side. They passed through a touristy area with kids outside sitting around campfires. Cold as it was, there were cars with music blaring and people chasing each other and having fun. Some of the boys had what looked like liquor bottles in their hands.

They drove through quickly. Then more trees, then up and down hills along a winding road. Soon, the trees got bigger—much bigger. Had to have been hundreds of years old. The houses turned into mansions. At the bottom of one of the hills, they turned left and proceeded up a curving drive that led to a huge, white house. Jack counted five RV trailers parked out front. There was also a big fire with teenagers sitting around it.

Jack's mouth fell open at the lights gleaming from every window of the mansion.

"Electricity?"

"This one's got a generator hooked up," Tom said. "Lucky him, huh? So listen: these guys are real mean sometimes. Just smile and nod and say *yes* to everything, okay?"

Jack nodded obediently. "Yes."

"And leave your gun in the car. Nobody's supposed to have a gun but us Pyros. Cool?"

After a brief hesitation, he said, "Cool." Then he pretended to put his gun under the driver's seat.

"Crap, here they come," Tom said.

From the direction of the mansion, several boys were coming their way, all of them pushing fifteen. Each carried the military-style weapons Jack and his Rippers preferred. Unlike almost every other survivor Jack had seen, they appeared plump in the face, not scrawny and half-starved like Tom and Joey and the ones around the fires.

Tom rolled down his window and whispered back, "Remember what I said."

TWENTY-EIGHT

One of the pudgier boys looked in with a flashlight. "What are *you* doing here? You're supposed to be watching the highway." He shined the beam in the back seat. "Who the hell is he?"

"I'm, Jack. I'm here to—"

In a loud, official voice, Tom said, "We're here to see Blaze—super important."

"About what?"

"Super important stuff," Jack said, smiling.

"Was I talking to you?" the boy said. "Get out of the car. All of you!"

Grimacing, Tom and Joey got out, followed by Jack on the far side, carrying his pack. The boy came around and got in his face.

"What'chu say to me, punk? Say it to my face, punk."

He had his rifle pointed down, and he was pushing up against Jack and doing this weird thing with his shoulder, bumping it against Jack again and again. It was such an odd thing to do, Jack couldn't help himself. He laughed.

"Think I'm funny?" the boy said, faking a bump and taking a swing.

Jack, who'd anticipated the punch, dropped his pack and stepped into it, locking the boy up in a tangle of arms so that neither of them could move. Well, Jack could, a little—not bogged down with a rifle and having years of martial arts experience behind him.

The boy's ear was very close to Jack's mouth.

"Listen here, you pudgy little cabbage," Jack said quietly over the grunting. "If I want, I can snap you in two. If you try for that gun of yours, I'll kill you where you stand. Got it?"

The boy swore and tried to break loose, but couldn't.

Jack reached up and squeezed the soft spot behind his ear, bringing a loud yelp. "*Got it?*"

"Yeah, get off!"

Jack gave a final squeeze, earning another yelp, and pushed him away. Casually, he hooked his thumb near where his shirt covered the .40 caliber. Just in case.

The crowd watched excitedly, happy for any kind of entertainment in a world without game consoles and social media. They shouted at the boy to keep fighting, to do something. His face grew madder and madder as he worked himself up to a fatal decision for one of them. It wouldn't be long.

From the direction of the house, a large boy with flaming red hair pushed through in a cloud of cigarette smoke.

"What the hell's going on?" Blaze said. "Who's this asshole?"

***

Blaze was big like Brad, easily fifteen or sixteen, and his red hair was cut flat on top and gelled in a spiky landing pad. His acne, coupled with the evil gleam in his eyes, made him look almost demonic. The effect was added to with every puff of his foul-smelling cigarette.

The one Jack had been fighting shoved him from behind as they made their way to the front door. Boys and girls Jack's age and some younger crowded around as they came in. There was a sense of excitement in the air. As if any moment something interesting or violent or both might happen.

Everyone gathered in the large living room, which had a single fireplace in it and no stove. Despite that, the room was warm. Looking around, Jack couldn't believe his eyes.

There were space heaters in the corners of the room, as well as a king-size bed pushed up against a window-free wall. The windows had been packed with fiberglass insulation that looked ripped from an attic, and there was a big screen TV in the room showing some kind of monster movie.

Jack couldn't help but disapprove of all that gasoline wasting away for no good reason. Especially with everyone shivering outside in the RVs. If he were in charge, they'd be inside the house, where it was warm.

"The new kid's a tard! The new kid's a tard!" shouted the boy he'd been fighting, trying to get the others to sing along.

Nobody sang along with him. If anything, they looked like they didn't think much of their obnoxious companion.

Blaze flopped down onto a big black couch next to a scantily-clad girl. Her expression looked permanently bored, verging on annoyed.

"You're messing up the show," she said.

"Tom, right?" Blaze said, ignoring her.

Tom nodded. "And he's Joey. My cousin."

"Shut up a minute, Tom," Blaze said absently, stroking his hairless chin. He took a puff from his cigarette and exhaled loudly. "You left your post to bring me this kid here—the tard. What for?"

The boy who'd started the name-calling laughed overly loud at this, and one or two others joined in. If Blaze thought it was funny, they did too. The girl rolled her eyes and waited with suffering patience.

"He's got a lot of great stuff," Tom said, swallowing nervously.

"Blaze, seriously, you need to see this," Joey said, turning to Jack. "Show him what you got. Show him."

With an indulgent smirk plastered across his pimply face, Blaze turned to Jack and said, "Well, tard? *Show* me."

Jack hoisted his pack toward Blaze and said, "Have a look for yourself."

Some of the others made *woooah* sounds, as if Jack had somehow challenged the big leader—insulted him, even. Which he hadn't, of course, but that didn't matter.

Blaze rolled his eyes, refusing to bite. "Shut up while I look at this." He opened the pack and rooted around, then dumped out the pills, cookies, cans, and candies onto the table in front of him. The pack was big, thanks to Jack's Mom, who'd wanted something large enough to stuff the whole world into. Fully packed with junk, it weighed about thirty-five pounds.

Blaze whistled appreciatively, then looked at him sideways. "Why haven't you eaten it yet?"

Jack shrugged nonchalantly. "Eh, you get tired of the sugar after a while. Too much gives me heartburn." He'd never had heartburn in his life, at least he didn't think so, but nobody knew that.

"What about the pills? Those *definitely* don't get old."

Jack shrugged. "I hurt my head the other day, see?" He showed them Freida's stitches. "I'm better now, though. You can have the rest. Plenty more where those came from."

A look of greed stole over the pimply redhead. He gestured impatiently at the crowd. "Everyone, out. Except you, Eddie. We're gonna talk with the tard, here." When nobody moved right away, he raised his voice. "*I said get out!*"

They jumped as one and scrambled out the front door. Tom and Joey, too. The girl seemed to know she could stay and didn't get up. One other person stayed behind—a slender, mean-faced boy with a striped cap and a pistol on his side.

The boy smirked, his expression full of contempt. "What you looking at, freak-tard?"

Miguel had mentioned Eddie—one of the higher-ups in the gang, and not particularly friendly.

Jack was considering how best to answer when Blaze said, "Leave him alone. Actually no, come here. Take a look at our new friend here. What's your name, dude?"

"Jack."

"Have a look at Jack, Eddie. Is he ... does he look familiar?"

Eddie came over and made a big show of looking him up and down. Apparently he wasn't impressed. "Looks like a wimpy freak-tard. All freak-tards look the same to me."

Blaze was shaking his head, staring at Jack with a weird look in his eye. "Something about you, man ..."

Jack smiled innocently and bided his time. They'd never met before, though Jack of course recognized him from the two occasions he'd seen him. The first time, before fleeing his house, and later that night when Blaze murdered one of his own gang members. He was obviously trying to psych him out—probably did it to everyone he met.

A moment more and Blaze said, "Eh, it'll come to me. Always does. So come on, where'd you get all this? What's this about a stash? And don't lie, 'cause I'll know."

Jack had seen people like Eddie and Blaze before. Usually at the mall where his dad took him people watching, but sometimes when he made his rounds through neighborhoods leaving flyers on doors for his knife-sharpening business. He'd observed them with an analytical eye, sizing up their strengths and weaknesses automatically as his dad had trained him.

Blaze said, "Well, Jack? You gonna say something? I'm starting to get pissed off."

He'd thought he could handle people like this when it finally came to it. In Carter's case, he'd gotten the drop on him, and he'd had the backing of Greg and Lisa. On trips to the mall with his dad, he'd been safely protected by the customs of civilization, where nobody carried a gun except police or soldiers. Now here he was, no parents, no police officers, a half-dressed girl smiling at him like she wanted him to smile back, and guns everywhere he looked. He'd never been so far out of his element before.

Eddie said, "Answer him, dummy. He asked you a question! Don't you got sense enough to answer a question?"

But he *trusted* his parents. In all their field trips and all their lessons, everything came back to one thing: motivations. People always wanted something, even if it wasn't real, like money or cupcakes. Greg and Lisa wanted his friendship, and all the benefits of that. Tony wanted a strong leader, and Steve wanted safety for himself, Molly, and her baby. And every day, people wanted food and a place to sleep and protection from the cold. The wild bunch outside wanted the security offered by brutes like Blaze more than the uncertainty of striking out on their own.

"Dammit, kid," Blaze said through clenched teeth, "speak up or Eddie's gonna beat the shit out of you. That's what Eddie does."

So it didn't matter that he was a total fish out of water on this one, because everything was exactly the same. The rules of the game hadn't changed, only the pieces. Eddie could look as tough and mean as he wanted and nothing would change that. Blaze could be huge and spiky-haired, smoking cigarettes and acting scary as all hell, and that girl could keep freaking him out staring at him like that. None of that mattered, because his compass had found true north at last, and it wasn't moving.

"That's it," Eddie said, smacking his fist. "I'll make him talk."

The boy approached languidly from behind, not bothering at guile or speed, secure in his superiority, at home in his environment. Which is why it was easy to duck his slow, ponderous haymaker and jab him hard under the ribs, dropping him gasping to his knees. Jack's old karate instructor would have been proud. He probably wouldn't have approved of the follow-up kick to the ribs—bad sportsmanship—but some things couldn't be helped.

"Oh, wow!" Blaze said, laughing, clapping his hands. The girl's eyes widened slightly, but that was it. "Eddie got the crap kicked outta' him by the new guy."

Eddie struggled to his feet, gasping for breath and holding his side, eyes raging.

Calmly, Jack indicated the contents of his pack, now strewn on the table. "There's a whole room full of this kind of stuff, all the way to the ceiling, with almost nobody guarding it. Just a few kids with hunting rifles they can barely use. I'd hoped to enlist the world-famous Blaze and his so-called *Pyros* to score more food and drugs than they've ever seen. But if this guy's the best you have"—he looked derisively at Eddie, throwing back the same scorn he'd received since showing up—"then maybe I made a mistake."

Eddie launched himself forward, arms outstretched. Jack sidestepped toward the table, hooked it with his foot, and tugged it in front of him. Eddie slammed into it shin-first and toppled over. Jack kicked him in the same side as last time, causing his breath to whoosh out in an involuntary scream.

To Jack, Eddie's motivations were clear: regain whatever reputation he'd lost after squirming around on the floor like that. It wouldn't be long until he pulled that pistol on his side. To head that off, Jack kneeled on his back, popped the clasp on the holster, and pulled it free.

Sure, he could have shot Blaze if he'd wanted to. He could have done that with his .40 caliber, still hidden under his shirt. But it wouldn't serve any purpose. Also, he was tired of killing, even though he'd learned he could do it without throwing up. He felt guilty about what he'd done to Ray—and later, at the Dragsters' headquarters. A little worried, too. That wasn't who his parents had raised, or the person he wanted to be. For now, though, it was who he needed to be if he wanted to help his friends.

Blaze's eyes had gone very wide at the sight of the stranger he'd been pushing around brandishing a pistol and nobody there to protect him.

Jack smiled innocently, placed the gun next to a package of peanut butter cookies, and said, "What do you say we stack this place high with canned food and happy pills?"

TWENTY-NINE

At first, Blaze seemed excited by the possibility of a house full of junk food and drugs. Then a strange girl showed up who could only be his sister, and everything got derailed.

Jack wouldn't call her ugly—or anyone ugly, really—but she was definitely odd to look at. She had wild eyes, tangled red hair, and a perpetual scowl. She stormed in howling at the top of her lungs because of some insult, real or imagined, from someone outside.

At one point, she noticed Jack standing there and screamed, "Who the hell is he?" Not waiting for an answer, she ran at him with hands hooked into claws, slashing the air and spitting when her brother grabbed her around the middle and dumped her onto the couch. The girl sitting there leapt out of the way and cursed at her, further adding to the drama.

"Dude, get out of here," Blaze said to Jack, his face a mask of annoyance and embarrassment.

When Jack started toward the front door, Blaze said something to the first girl. She nodded and stopped him just as he reached for the knob.

"You're sleeping upstairs tonight," she said simply. "Stay here. I'll get you a heater."

He nodded and tried to ignore the shouts from the living room. The girl left and stayed gone a few minutes.

Just when he thought he'd been abandoned, she came back with a small space heater.

"Come on," she said and led him up a wide, sweeping staircase.

Jack cleared his throat. "That's his sister?"

The girl laughed. "Alice, yeah. She's out of her mind. They had her on schizo meds before the Sickness. Now there's no meds, least not the kind she needs. Does the dirty with every boy around, too." She looked back at him and smirked. "But I wouldn't if I were you. She'll freak on you and try to stab you or something. Killed one person already. I'm Amber, by the way."

Blinking in surprise, he held out his hand. "Jack. Nice to meet you."

Amber glanced at his hand, snorted, and escorted him down a hall to an open door.

"This okay?" she said.

Before he could reply, she walked in with the heater and plugged it in near a big bed covered thickly in blankets and comforters.

"This used to be Ron's room. Alice stabbed him in the throat. Right on this bed, as a matter of fact. Just snuck in and did it. Don't worry, the blood's all dried. I don't think the lock works, but maybe you can block the door with something."

Jack just stared at her, desperately trying to process everything he'd seen and heard. "Should I get a different room?"

Amber stepped in closer than he was used to anyone standing. Her head was tilted down, and the effect when their eyes met took his breath away. "I saw the way you handled Eddie. He's a mean little dickhead. Likes to punch people. You need to watch out for him, now that you beat him up. He lives outside, but comes in when he wants to. Just so happens I have a lock on my door." She leaned in and kissed him on the lips too quickly for him to react. "After Alice settles, Blaze's gonna be on those pills you brought. So what do you say? I mean, unless you're a fag or something."

Adrenaline-spiked blood rushed to his recently bashed-in head, causing him to wince in pain. When he rubbed his head, she shoved him away.

"Don't flatter yourself!" she snapped, then stalked from the room. Over her shoulder she added, "Oh, and *you're welcome*, by the way. Didn't have to get you that heater. Only did because *he* said to! Stupid fag!"

Seconds later, stunned by what had happened ... wondering what *could* have happened ... he called after her. "Goodnight!"

Down the hall, Amber slammed her door in answer.

"Well, that was different," he said, and turned to examine his suddenly very important door.

He pushed the little brass button, gave the outside knob a twist, and it turned easily. Clearly broken, just like the strange, homophobic girl had said. He looked around for something to jam against it, like a chair, but all he found was a big dresser on the far side of the room. He considered dragging it over, but didn't. Too big, too noisy. Also, it would send the wrong message.

One thing he'd learned growing up camping and hiking was never show fear in front of a wild animal. It only encouraged them to attack. By blocking it so obviously, they'd know he was afraid. Instead, he took out the smaller top drawers and stacked them in the way. If anyone came in, the clatter would wake him up and scare the intruder, possibly sending him or her fleeing.

"Awesome," he said, admiring the ingenious little structure.

The room was cold, though not freezing, thanks to the space heater. The thick mound of covers helped, too. Despite that, he couldn't sleep. Occasional snatches of manic yelling from downstairs jolted him each time he started to nod off. Also, his mind kept turning back to the half-dressed girl, her kiss, and her taboo invitation. He wondered about that, what it meant. He thought about Lisa, and pondered how he felt about her. They'd had no real time together alone since their second kiss. What time they'd had, nothing much happened except a few lingering looks and secret smiles. Hardly the stuff of epic romance.

Public schoolers seemed to mature earlier in these

things. Not for the first time, he found himself envying these so-called cabbages. Maybe he'd been wrong to let his dad's prejudices influence him.

He must have fallen asleep because he suddenly found there was someone sitting next to him on the bed. He tensed and tried to get up.

Blaze grabbed his shoulders and said, "Relax, man, I just came to talk."

Jack struggled briefly against him, then stopped when the message sank in. *Blaze. In his room. Wanting to talk.*

"Sorry about Alice. She's been sick for a long time. Way worse now than before."

Alice? Oh ...

"Uh ... yeah," he said, voice raspy with sleep. "Sure, man. No biggie." When he didn't leave, Jack added, "Totally understand."

The older boy still didn't leave, but he relaxed his grip and let go.

"So what's up?" Jack said.

Blaze didn't speak. He just sat there.

Jack was content to wait him out. Maybe Blaze was doing the same thing, waiting *him* out, because a good five minutes went by in silence like that, just the two of them. And because he was still drowsy, Jack began to fade.

"Dude, you asleep?" Blaze said quietly, shaking him. "I can come back later if you are."

"Huh?" Jack said, startled back awake. "Um. No, I'm fine. What's up?"

"I noticed you're not with Amber," he said. "Don't worry, I told her she could. She's cool like that." He smiled suddenly. "Bet she didn't like it when you said no, did she?"

"Uh, yeah."

"She's got a big heart, that's why." The silence between them grew again. "Alice ... she killed someone last week. Everyone expects me to do something about it, but she's my sister. They keep it up, I'm gonna shoot someone, and it won't be her." He went quiet a moment, then sighed. "Still, I can't go shooting everyone. Eddie won't lay off me about it. And after what you did today ..." He shrugged.

"Any other time, I'd have loved it. But it's a real bad time for you to be here if you're gonna beat up my best men." He turned his head this way and that, peering intently at Jack's face. "I swear there's something about you. You sure we never met?"

Jack nodded carefully, unsure where this was going. "I've never met you. Sorry about Eddie. I had a right to defend myself, didn't I?"

Blaze shook his head. "Doesn't matter." He reached down to Jack's belt and tugged, causing him to tense up in a shock of understanding. Then he pulled the .40 caliber from Jack's holster and held it up.

"Would you calm down?" Blaze said, laughing and waving the gun. "I've been thinking about this really hard. I've changed my mind a few times, just so you know. I want you to keep it." He handed him back the gun. "I'm trusting you, see?"

Jack took the gun and stared at it, sensing a trap. "I can keep it?"

"Sure, to defend yourself. If Eddie tries anything again, you need to shoot him." He shook his head. "House full of food, huh? I sure hope it ain't a pack of lies. Where's this place at, anyway?"

This was the part in the plan that worried him—that he'd be forced to provide a location for something that didn't exist.

Back at the cabins, the idea had seemed so simple. Show up, say Carter had a bunch of great stuff, then sit back and watch the show. Except now there was a problem—the plan had been based on the belief that Blaze was a homicidal maniac. The Pyros' leader was aggressive, sure, but nothing in his manner struck Jack as insane. He didn't seem dumb, either. Jack's cabbage-based theory of society had taken a serious beating.

"I have more proof if you want it—more food and stuff," he said. "But the house has a couple of kids in it, and they shoot at anyone who comes near. The food's in the basement."

"The basement," Blaze said flatly.

Jack nodded. "Yeah. The leader's a guy named Carter,

and he wears the key around his neck. A friend of mine picked the lock and snuck in a few days ago. When I was loading up the car, Carter shot and killed him. I barely got away. I can show you the car tomorrow, but I'm not going near that house without an army. The car's still got the food in it and a bunch of bullet holes, too."

Blaze's eyes grew hard in the moonlight through the windows. "And this is all true?"

"Yep. I meant to tell you that earlier, but then your sister—"

"Don't talk about my sister," he said and stood up. His voice took on a dangerous huskiness. "Just so you know, you don't ever want to lie to me. So if you're lying, maybe you need to get out of here before morning. That's all I'm saying. If you're still here, we're gonna go look at this car of yours. And it better be something, man, that's all I can say."

With that, he stalked from the room.

For the next few minutes, Jack considered the older boy's offer: get out now and save himself. He'd even let him keep his gun.

In the end, Jack rejected the idea. It could be a test. There could be people outside waiting to shoot him down if he tried.

More and more, he regretted his decision to come here. It wasn't so much that the operation was likely to fail, but rather that it might actually work.

Back at the farm, it seemed like the kind of plan Churchill might love because it pitted two aggressive powers against each other. Even if one side didn't annihilate the other, Carter and his gang would be far more worried about Blaze than Jack's little group. And Blaze would forever dream about the mythical house filled with food—like El Dorado to the Conquistadors. The problem was there were real people involved here. Kids like Tom and Joey. And Amber. Heck, even Blaze seemed sort of human, up close. Less like a maniac, more like someone in need of a few years of community service. The redheaded leader was stuck with his sick sister and guys like Eddie constantly pushing him. Jack could empathize, having felt the same sort of pressure from Tony, Pete, and now Miguel.

For now, he decided to stick with the plan. At the end of the day, his own people came first, and his conscience second. With luck, Carter'd be killed with little or no collateral damage, and the Dragsters maybe changed into something better.

Before nodding off, his eyes snapped open with a jolt and he looked over at the door. The two drawers he'd stacked had scooted a few feet and not scattered from Blaze walking in—as if he'd slowly pushed open the door. After that, Blaze had sat down quietly on the bed so as not to wake him. He could have been sitting there for two seconds or twenty minutes.

Sleep was a while in coming. And despite how incredibly unsafe it was, Jack made sure his gun was chambered, and he slept with it under his pillow.

THIRTY

Jack stumbled from bed in terror at the sound of a machine gun blasting away outside. He ran to the window and saw Blaze standing in the back yard spraying rounds from an M4 carbine—the same one he'd carried that day back at Jack's old neighborhood. Wood chips flew everywhere with each short burst. Moments later he ejected the magazine, loaded another, and the shower of chips resumed. He switched magazines several more times while Jack watched in fascination. Soon, the table cracked and fell in two pieces.

With the target now dead, Blaze fired the remainder of the ammo into the air, picked up his spent magazines, and started back to the house. He glanced up and saw Jack in the window, nodded in greeting, and went inside.

When Jack turned around, Amber was standing in the door eyeing the stack of wooden drawers on the ground with a wry grin.

"He sure loves that gun," she said.

Jack nodded. "Where did he get it?"

"The CIA."

That was odd. "He drove all the way to Langley?"

She looked at him funny. "What the heck's a *Langley*?"

"It's a where, not a what. You don't know where Langley is?"

Her expression grew angry. "You didn't know there was a CIA building around here, did you? So don't act all smart."

She's got you there.

"Sorry."

"Yeah, I guess," she said and tugged a few stray hairs away from her face. "Sorry I called you a fag. I totally know you're not one. I was just angry."

He wanted to ask her why she kept using that word. But the day was young, she wasn't yelling at him anymore, and he wanted to keep it that way.

"So, what's up?" he said.

"Seeing if you wanted breakfast."

Jack smiled at the enticing prospect. If Blaze could tote around military weaponry, who knew what sort of table he set?

No smells of bacon and eggs carried to him as he followed Amber downstairs. And the sight that greeted him as he entered the dining room was both strange and disheartening. Strange because Blaze was sitting with his feet on the table messing with his M4, an unlit cigarette dangling from his lips. Disheartening because breakfast was none other than the junk food Jack had brought with him the day before.

"Go ahead, man," Blaze said, nodding at it. "I already ate."

"Sure ... uh, thanks."

Jack scooted a package of cookies out of the way and snagged a can of baked beans. He looked around for a can opener.

"Want me to shoot it open?" Blaze said and shifted his grip on the rifle.

Jack flinched and Blaze laughed. Then, despite how crazy it was for someone to joke around with a gun, Jack laughed too. Briefly, they seemed like a couple of friends having fun and not people who'd chosen to kill.

In that moment, he knew he couldn't march him or anyone else into a confrontation with Carter, not based on a lie. It may have made military sense, but it wasn't right. The question was: how to do the right thing without getting his head blown off?

Blaze said, "I finally figured out where I know you from. You're gonna laugh when you see this."

Sudden terror seized him. "How? I mean, what do you mean?"

"See for yourself." He picked something off the chair next to him, winked at Amber, and then handed it to him. It was a photograph of Jack and his parents. They'd taken it last year on their last trip to the mountains. He had a smaller version back at his cabin.

Jack tensed up and instinctively raised back his can of beans.

"Hah! Oh my God, look at you," Blaze said, laughing and clutching his stomach. Amber was laughing, too. "Man, I ain't gonna do nothing. Only reason I took it is because of that trick you pulled. Drilling through all those roofs to get out? Totally awesome. I said to myself, I ever find this guy, he's joining my gang." He pointed at him. "And here you are. It's fate, that's what it is."

"Total karma," Amber said, nodding her head.

Jack took a few breaths—beans still raised for battle— before deciding maybe he wouldn't be held against the wall and executed. Then he smiled weakly, still not entirely convinced.

"Yeah, well," he said, "you were sort of scary. Told me to come out or you'd kill me."

Blaze looked offended. "I *never* said that. We don't do that kind of thing. We were just gonna rob you, that's all. Tell you to join up or get going, like we do everyone. That's the rules."

"You burned my house down."

He shook his head. "Not me—that was Alice. She likes burning stuff." He indicated the space around him. "This is the third place we've stayed after leaving the school. She burned all the others."

"So why do they call you Blaze? Shouldn't that be her?"

Amber laughed. "His real name's Shane. Alice started the whole *Blaze* thing. She tried calling herself Dragon for a while, but nobody else did, so she stopped."

Jack felt a rogue smile creeping across his face at the

image of the tough boy's sister giving him a nickname. He was about to ask about his sword, then held off at the last second. For whatever reason, Blaze was doing his best to show what a normal, rational human he was. Mentioning the sword would let him know Jack had seen him execute that kid in the street that night.

"Do you still want me to call you Blaze? Or do you like Shane?"

"Nah, I hate Shane. Know what? You should get a nickname."

Amber suggested a nickname using her favorite word, then said she was just kidding. Blaze joked back and forth with her. They each came up with increasingly insulting nicknames, making Jack blush and feel weirdly included at the same time.

Then Alice walked in.

"Morning everyone," she said, smiling wide for all to see. Gone was the scowling, scratching, spitting horror from the night before. In its place was someone so happy it was frightening. "Oh, look at all the snacks! I'm gonna try each one!"

She sat down and started scooping up the various packages and putting them in front of her.

Blaze's voice became artificially soft and friendly. "Jeez, Alice, those are my favorites."

"Hah!" she said triumphantly and opened a package of cookies. She took a big bite and giggled around a mouthful of oatmeal raisin.

Amber, for her part, looked like she could barely contain her disgust, her face almost insultingly neutral through the exchange. A minute later, she stood up and said, "I'll find you a can opener, Jack."

"Thanks," he said.

After breakfast, Amber disappeared. Blaze led Alice off somewhere for about ten minutes, then returned alone.

"She's doing good this morning," he said, sitting back down. "But anything can set her off. So long as she gets her way—thinks everyone loves her—she's fine."

Jack nodded agreeably. "When do you want to see the stuff?"

"I would say we go now, but I have to meet someone at the airport about taking more little kids. We'll go when I get back."

Jack blinked in confusion, thinking he'd misheard him. "Uh, what kids? What do you mean the airport?"

"There's a group living at the airport," he said, then laughed. "They don't fly planes or nothing. They just live there. They're taking in all the brats around here—from everywhere, I think. I say, why not? Someone's got to, and I sure as hell ain't." He shrugged. "They also give us cool stuff sometimes. One time was a box of tasers." He lowered his voice. "There's other groups out there you don't wanna know about, trust me."

Jack couldn't believe it. All this time, he'd thought Blaze was a brute who got off on stealing and killing. Now he'd learned he also helped children. Well, sure, there was an exchange going on, but Jack sensed a layer of concern under the surface.

An hour later and Blaze was gone, leaving Jack to roam the grounds. There wasn't much to see.

Feeling bored, wondering how his friends were doing—Greg, specifically—he sat down on the couch in the living room and picked through Blaze's extensive DVD collection. Then he watched a movie.

***

Late that afternoon, after Jack had watched several R-rated movies his parents would have disapproved of, Blaze returned.

"You ready?" he said.

"Sure," Jack said, hitting pause on the remote and trying to stay calm in the face of his looming deception. He'd spent the entire day feeling like a condemned man.

"I'll grab Eddie and the guys. We'll take the Humvee."

Jack had seen the vehicle during a walk outside. Big, yellow, and gas guzzling. He couldn't imagine anyone wanting one unless they had access to a refinery or something.

When Eddie appeared, he laughed at Jack's wary expression. "Hey man, no hard feelings. I can be a real asshole sometimes. We cool?" He held out his hand.

Jack took it, expecting a trap, then blinked in surprise when Eddie didn't squeeze it to death or try to throw him. His apology seemed genuine.

"Sure," Jack said. "We're cool."

Eddie smiled broadly and clapped him on the shoulder, then got in the back with two other boys, both armed. The three of them were quiet, content to let Blaze fill up the space talking about the various sports cars and weapons he wanted to get one day. And poisonous snakes. He was convinced they could find cobras and Gaboon vipers still alive at the National Zoo.

"Snakes only need to eat like twice a year," he said. "The zookeepers probably would have fed them before going home to die, right?"

"What about the cold?" Jack said, trying to talk him out of the horrible idea. "Don't they live in tropical forests?"

From the back, Eddie said, "He's got you there, Shane."

The two other Pyros laughed as if on cue.

Blaze cast an irritated glance back. "I'll get *something* from the zoo, dammit. Can't everything be dead in there. Maybe one of them big turtles."

After that, they traveled in relative silence, broken once for directions from Jack to take 66. Despite there being no traffic at all, it felt weird and a little scary when he said to drive in the opposite lane.

Upon reaching the exit with his car, Jack said, "It's up on the ramp."

"At the roadblock?" Blaze said, frowning.

"I hid the car there. See that blue one?"

They pulled up behind Jack's car and everyone got out.

Eddie looked inside. "I don't see nothing."

"It's in the trunk," Jack said. "Hold on."

He crawled underneath the car and searched around in the fading light, grabbed the keys, then crawled out and popped the trunk. Smiling in relief at the delicious sight before him, he felt convinced it would soften the reveal to come. It was a good thing Blaze didn't have his M4 with him. He did have a sidearm, though—a big one.

Blaze stepped around the front of the car to relieve himself. When he finished, Jack approached from behind and said, "Sorry to bug you while you're ..."

Blaze glanced back and snorted. "What's up?"

"Can we talk a minute?"

"Why not?"

Jack walked past him. "Just up here."

Blaze followed along, a bemused smile on his face. When they were out of earshot, Jack said, "I can get you more food than you'll ever eat, but ..."

"But what?"

"It's all corn grain, and some beef. Not cookies and cakes and canned food like I brought with me." He nodded back at the car. "You can have all of that. But you gotta listen to me and stay calm, okay? I'm only telling you because you're—"

"Because I'm what?" he said, a steely hardness edging into his voice.

Jack was about to say how Blaze wasn't the drooling maniac he'd assumed, and how he didn't want people like Tom and Joey and Amber—or Blaze and his sister—getting hurt. He didn't actually *like* the big leader, or Eddie or the others, but decided that shouldn't matter. Also, Blaze was helping out the children in Centreville. That had to count for something.

"You seem cool," Jack said at last.

In the end, he opted for simple honesty: he told him everything. The whole plan. All of it.

By the end, Blaze was shaking his head in quiet fury. "You lied to me? I *told* you not to lie—what would happen. Everyone expects—"

"Food, right? Well, I have that. But I need your help against Carter. He and his gang killed two of my friends and attacked another friend's farm. If we work together, we can get rid of him, split them up, and then see about building something lasting. Be honest: how long do you think you can live off cookies and cake?"

After the initial shock, Blaze seemed to have calmed down somewhat. He looked back once at Eddie and the two others, all of whom were watching them.

"All right," he said. "Don't say anything to anyone. I'll handle it when we get back. I need to make some changes.

You lied to me once, so I shouldn't believe you, but for some reason I do. I mean ... the stuff you brought came from somewhere. Actually, where *did* you get it?"

"For the last couple months," Jack said, "my group's been out scrounging, just like yours. We only eat the healthy stuff. There's no doctors or dentists anymore."

Blaze snorted. "You sound like a bunch of adults or something."

"That's sort of the point."

"All right," he said, shaking his head. "Let's head back. Remember: not a word."

As they approached Eddie and the other two, Jack noticed several things at once: the trunk was closed, each boy clutched a pistol, and Eddie wore a vicious smile on his face.

Blaze began to say something, then Eddie raised his pistol and shot him in the chest and head. Jack flinched and covered himself automatically, then remembered he had a gun and grabbed for it.

"Don't make me shoot you," Eddie said, aiming at him. He had a mean smile on his face and his eyes sparkled with glee. "If you're cool, you live. Got it?"

Jack glanced down at Blaze while they disarmed him, mourning what was and what could have been.

Glumly, he nodded.

THIRTY-ONE

Lisa swore quietly, lest she wake anyone still sleeping upstairs.

It was well and good for Jack to go off on foolish adventures, but someone had to be the full time adult, and she was that person. *Again.* His view of adulthood was limited to giving orders and risking his life. She knew what real leadership meant: soothing tempers, listening to problems, and making sure nobody killed themselves on stunts like this. It didn't help that Greg had jumped right on the bandwagon.

She'd given her brother an earful. Fat lot of good it did. Ever since arriving at the cabins, he'd been itching for excitement—because he was a boy, and boys were stupid. Especially *that* boy. And that's why early that morning after the salt run, Greg and Steve had snuck into town to execute their part of the plan.

Jack—no less stupid—had gone back to the cabins to rest before his trip later into Blaze's territory. She'd tried to talk him out of it but he hadn't listened. Kept going on about Winston Churchill and Shackleton. Maybe that rock Steve hit him with had done permanent damage.

At 8 a.m., she got on the radio. "Farm here. Checking in."

Almost immediately, Olivia's voice came back, "Big T,

all clear."

They didn't talk after that, preferring to keep the airwaves free of unnecessary chatter. As a precaution, they now referred to Big Timber as *Big T,* for fear of eavesdroppers. Maybe someone in the Dragsters had heard of it, or maybe there were brochures out there someone might have seen.

While the boys were gone, Lisa, Freida, and Miguel slaughtered three more cows. Because of all the blood, she worried the meat from the first two was still too wet inside for proper preservation. A fully-grown cow weighed a ton, making it impossible for anyone to hoist and drain. Lisa's solution was to bring in Freida's tractor, tie a cable around the animal's knees in a slipknot, and hoist it onto the sawed-off branches of the big tree out front. After they were up, they rubbed each carcass down with salt, drying the shiny fascia and sealing it further from decay.

They didn't stop there. Skunks, rats, and other nocturnal predators and scavengers were a worry, so they kept Freida's dog, Max, next to it in his doghouse, dragged from out back and packed with blankets. There had been a brief discussion about whether he'd go for the meat himself. In the end, they fed him some of Jack's dried meat and an extra portion of gourmet kibble, which Tony had scavenged at Carla's request.

Carla took the big dog's face in her hands and said, "Now, Max, don't you go eating these big ol' cows. It's people food, not puppy food. Okay, Max? You listening, boy?"

Lisa covered her mouth to keep from laughing. The dog was fit to bursting on dried beef and the girl was telling him beef was people food.

Just after dark, she got on the radio to see if Jack had left yet.

"Howdy, cowgirl," he said, his voice coming back faint and grainy. "One second, I'll pull over."

"You left already?"

"A few minutes ago. How'd the work go?"

She told him in general terms what they'd done.

"Wow," he said. "That's brilliant. Never would have

thought to use a tractor."

Also in vague terms, Jack assured her again how fine he would be, and again she voiced her disapproval.

They didn't say much after that, and ended the transmission with mutual wishes for the other to be safe.

In the morning, Lisa checked the carcasses and found them untouched by dog or critter, and they smelled fresh and healthy. She would have liked to hang them longer, but didn't want to risk the meat freezing and thawing repeatedly.

For the rest of the day, she and the sisters butchered, smoked, and then packed the meat in trash bags. They did this without Miguel. He and his chatty brother had disappeared in one of the cars without telling anyone. The work was brutal, bloody, and exhausting, and now she had to worry about them, too.

A call to the cabins turned up nothing. A few hours later, Brad and Olivia went out armed, taking the preferred route to the farm and meeting Tony halfway. Thankfully, there were no grisly discoveries along the way.

Tony said he'd stay out and keep looking for them, and she relented, provided he got back before dark.

She tried not to let her worry for the two brothers add to her fears, and instead concentrated on the work, telling herself they were most likely out scavenging—something they weren't supposed to be doing after the drive-by attack. In a way, she was happy they were gone. If she couldn't make them work, at least they were out of her hair.

Around 5 p.m., she got on the radio for the hourly check-in. It took ten minutes before someone answered, and that someone was Miguel.

"Hey, Lisa, how are you?"

"Good," she said. "Uh ... where'd you go to?"

"Eh, you know ... Just had to go."

She wanted to yell at him for worrying everyone, but kept it in check. "Where's Olivia?"

"Helping Greg. Um ... hey, listen. Some bad news. Greg got shot. In the leg. He's gonna be fine, but you should definitely come back."

Lisa felt the world drop out from under her, and she

held onto the dinner table for support. "*What do you mean he got shot?* Put him on right now!"

"I would, but he's asleep," Miguel said, his voice almost pleading. "He's got bandages on. He's gonna be fine ... I mean, you really ought to get back here. I'd hurry, if I were you."

"*Hurry?* Is he okay or isn't he?"

Miguel didn't reply immediately. Then he said, "Um ... I gotta go help, uh ... Olivia. See you soon, all right?"

After that, no amount of pleading would get him or anyone to come back on.

Tony called in after that, saying he'd heard the whole thing. Lisa told him to get back right away to watch the farm.

"You want me to go with you?" Freida said after hearing the news.

"No, we need you here. Stay armed, watch the road." She paused, struggling against a desire to protect the farm and a need to keep everyone safe. "If you have to, it's fine to run."

Freida's eyes narrowed and she patted her new rifle— one of the high-capacity AR-15s they were all carrying. "I'll blow their damn heads off, they try anything here."

Lisa hugged her and Carla and then left, heading for the cabins. At the last minute, she turned off and took a road to 66, hoping to arrive at Big Timber that way rather than the usual route.

Her eyes swept the interstate for signs of Jack coming back with an army of greedy Pyros in tow, but didn't see them. Either they hadn't attacked yet or he was still spinning tales about the Dragsters' supposed hoard of food. She tried to have faith that he could pull it off and get out before they discovered the truth.

Greg's part in the ploy had been more worrisome— flooding the airwaves with propaganda, trying to get as many of Steve's old friends to desert as possible. Jack said Hitler used to send operatives into cities he was about to capture, spreading propaganda and turning the populace against the city leaders. As much as she hated doing anything the horrible Nazi leader had done, it gave the plan the best possible chance of success. Jack hoped the deserters would join the Rippers. Then, whether the trick with the Pyros worked or not, he could force the rest of the Dragsters to join up, too—*after* Carter and his friends paid for what they'd done. *Blood for blood*, Jack said.

Lisa pounded the wheel in frustration. When her parents died, she thought she'd die too. It had been Greg who'd saved her—his sweet smile, his annoying brand of funny. He'd turned his own pain into a rescue mission and become her rock. It was a miracle they'd survived this long. The cruelest of blows if she lost him now.

She exited the interstate, and her thoughts drifted to Miguel. Until that last hourly check-in, nobody had known where he or his brother were. Then, an hour later, Greg shows up shot—and Miguel is there, too? Did he find Greg stumbling along a road somewhere? And where was Steve in all this?

Smelling a rat, Lisa parked at the turn just before Big Timber. She got out, slung her rifle over her shoulder, and checked her pistol. Sure, Greg could be hurt and bleeding up there, but she didn't like Miguel very much, and she trusted her instincts as to why.

Cautiously, she began the quarter mile trek of dirt road leading in, keeping to the side so she could slip behind a tree if someone drove by. She kept a steady pace and did her best to ignore the feeling her brother was dying nearby. Rushing into an ambush wouldn't help anyone.

When she came in sight of the cabins, she stopped and waited quietly, watching for any signs of movement. Nothing moved, the meadow was quiet. This deep in the hills, it grew dark early. There was still enough light to see clear to the other side, but that wouldn't last much longer.

Only the Skyline showed any activity—a thin trail of smoke from the chimney. The long shape of the school bus sat abandoned in the little parking lot for prospective cabin seekers. Behind the cabins, the half-circle of cars used for gas storage seemed a little thicker than last time. Two scavenging trucks were parked out front, but not the car Greg and Steve had taken for their mission. Either the car had come and gone or her brother had walked from Front

Royal with a bullet in his leg.

Or maybe it's all bullshit.

The longer she looked at the scene in front of her, the more satisfied she was with her cautious approach.

Lisa ranged wide around the meadow, avoiding the pond and the outhouse near the northern tree line. She angled behind the cabins at a far enough distance to feel safe, yet still be able to see if anyone came outside. Nobody did.

"Dammit," she said quietly, her worst fears confirmed. Up ahead, just behind the circle of gas cars, seven new cars were parked end to end, hiding in plain sight. All of them were sports cars with those silly checkered flags.

Seven cars—mostly two-doors—could carry seven people or twenty people. Lisa's gun had thirty rounds, no backup magazine, and iron sights. Difficult to aim in the lengthening shadows. Her pistol carried fifteen rounds and was even less accurate. She wasn't a great shot under ideal circumstances. She could hit the target, sure, but her shots tended to scatter, whereas Jack's were always close together.

It could be the kids in the cabin were tough, but she didn't think so. She still remembered the faces of the three she and Jack had scared off outside the library. Their innocent terror.

Lisa, on the other hand, was neither innocent nor afraid. She'd been in two firefights, and had trained with rifles and pistols. She understood just how devastating a rifle could be in the hands of a killer.

That's what she was, after all: *a killer.* She didn't shy from that fact, like Jack. What's more, she knew why.

She loved and missed her parents so much it sometimes took her breath away, but in the new way of the world, her mom may as well have been a stranger. Over the last few years, Lisa had spent a *lot* of time in the company of the Ferris family, and Jack's mom had lavished some of that doomy realism on her that she'd tried to instill in her son.

"Why are women physically weaker than men?" she'd once asked Lisa.

The answer had been as disturbing as it was insulting,

and Lisa had briefly contemplated telling her mother about it. Instead of that, she'd sought out Mrs. Ferris on hiking trips and other outings for more of the same.

Standing alone in that field of abandoned vehicles, Lisa mourned the girl that died with her parents and embraced the one that lived.

The door of the Skyline opened. Someone popped a head out and looked down the road, then ducked back and shut the door.

Though it was cold out, Lisa opened her knife and set to work cutting her pants down to shorts below the knees. Then she went to one of the Dragster cars, crawled underneath, and pounded a hole in the gas tank. It took her a while, but she eventually worked one of the strips into it. Hard to do, upside down with noxious gasoline dripping down her arm. Afterward, she went to three more and holed their tanks, too, not bothering to block them. She let them leak.

After her arm dried, she took out the matches used during the smoking process, lit a strip of cloth, and set it down near the first car. Though she'd managed to block the hole, a trickle of gas was still leaking out. She hoped it would be enough.

When blue and red flames spread out under the car, Lisa tore off toward the trout pond, running for her life.

A minute later, when nothing happened, she wondered if maybe the flames had gone out and she'd have to—

The car lifted off its back wheels in a terrific *WHUMP!* and dropped her concussively onto her back. The heat from the blast was scorching hot, and when her wits returned, she got up and frantically checked to see if she was on fire.

Satisfied she was all right, she readied her weapon and waited.

The front door opened, and several boys she didn't recognize spilled out clutching pistols. Lisa began firing, dropping five in no time at all, hitting them before they even saw her. More came, and more fell. Shooting from this close was easy, even with iron sights at dusk.

The few she'd missed fled back inside or ran behind the cabin. She flinched at the crack of returned fire and—

WHUMP!

Lisa fell sprawling again when the next car went up in a blast of flames.

Wits addled, bones aching, she stood again and brought her gun up. Or tried to. A boy came out of nowhere and kicked her a glancing blow to the head, and then she was down again. She shook it off and got a knee under her. Someone kicked her from behind and followed it with a painful kick to her side that knocked the wind out of her. A moment later, it seemed like everyone was kicking and punching her.

Helpless to stop the barrage, Lisa curled into a ball, covered her head, and waited for either their legs or her life to give out, whichever came first.

"Guys, stop!" Carter shouted. She recognized his voice from when they'd taken the grain and brought back Trisha. "Grab her arms and drag her inside. Get her guns, too."

The blows stopped, but Lisa's pain seemed only to grow.

THIRTY-TWO

The morning before Jack left on his clandestine mission into hostile territory doing Chosen One stuff, Greg and Steve snuck into Front Royal by way of a back road. Steve knew where all the Dragsters lived, and most didn't live near Carter. Only his favorites were so honored.

Greg taped handwritten notes to their doors:

Introducing Radio Free Front Royal! Broadcasting live on channel 19 all day today! Be sure to tune in for the latest news, sports, and entertainment! Make sure to tell Carter (because he can't read)!

Once the deliveries had been made, they pulled into the driveway of an abandoned house in the center of town and broke in through the back. Then they hauled in food, water, sleeping bags, and the equipment they'd need for the show.

"*You're* putting that stuff together," Steve said, eyeing the radio equipment dubiously.

"No sweat," Greg said. "So long as you do the talking. I get stage fright."

After Jack brought back that first CB, Lisa had taken to the technology like a long lost hobby, reading the manuals and everything. Since then, she'd managed to increase the range of the house units by an additional ten to fifteen miles through a variety of tricks.

As Jack was fond of saying, "Tough break, bro: your sis

got the beauty *and* the brains."

"Muscles too," Greg always said, mock sadly.

In truth, he was more proud of his sister than anything. Every time she did something cool, he technically shared in the credit. They had the same genes, didn't they? On those occasions when he felt like showing off *his* cerebral prowess, he did so in math, or looking through telescopes with his astronomy club, or writing short stories. After his parents died, he'd stopped writing. Too painful—his parents had been his only readers.

These days, there wasn't a whole lot of use for calculus, and the astronomy folks—mostly adults—were dead and gone from the Sickness. His sister and Jack only wanted to look at the moon, or Jupiter or Saturn, which got boring real fast. Deep sky stuff—*that's* where the action was. He'd tried to get Tony to find him a good telescope—a big cassegrain or dobsonian—but all he'd brought back was one of those cheap toys they sold at Walmart.

Steve interrupted his thoughts with a nudge. "You daydreaming or something? Be careful with that stuff— you'll get shocked." He was staring at the wires, batteries, and the CB on the table like it all might suddenly explode.

"Nah, I'm totally safe," Greg said, stacking the batteries side by side. "It's the voltage you have to worry about. If we screw up and put it in a series, it'll blow out the radio. So we stack them this way, see?" He connected them in parallel using thick copper wire, being careful not to complete the circuit with his other hand. "This way we get more amps for the same voltage. More amps means more range. Come on—let's go run the antenna."

The antenna was a five-foot-tall car-mounted unit with a magnet on the bottom. Great for clamping to the roof of the rusty shed in the back yard. After that, they connected it to the radio with a twenty-foot length of coaxial cable fished through a gap in the window.

Greg attached the final cables, turned it on, and smiled at the glowing display and static hiss coming from the built-in speaker.

Steve, who'd been cringing the whole time, said, "Holy cow. It worked!"

"Course it worked. Easiest thing in the world."

"Yeah, well ... electricity freaks me out."

Greg snorted. "You ready for the big show?"

Steve didn't answer immediately.

"Well?"

"Actually," he said cautiously, "can you do it?"

"I just risked my life attaching all those wires!" Greg said. "You said *you'd* be the DJ. Like I said: I get stage fright."

"Stage fright? I thought you were homeschooled. What kind of stage have *you* ever been on?"

Greg sighed. This was Lisa's doing, letting slip that they'd never been to public school. Since then, Olivia—lovely maiden of the green hair—had treated him differently. She used to smile sometimes and say, *hey, what's up?* Now all she said was, *hey.* No smiles, no question mark at the end.

"Okay, fine," Greg said, and took up the mic. "But if I suck at it, you're taking over."

"Deal," Steve said and tuned to channel 19.

Nothing but static.

"Testing one, two, three," Greg said and released the switch. More static. He squeezed it again. "One, two, three were the first numbers I ever learned. My grandpa—rest his wrinkly soul—told me they used to teach numbers like that when he was a kid, but now the numbers are all equal. That way, they don't get their feelings hurt. Before the Sickness, they were basically down to one number per school, and that was it. If you wanted a number *two*, you had to shut the door and turn on the fan."

He cut the mic and laughed out loud at his own joke.

Steve looked at him like he'd grown tentacles out of his head. "*What* the *hell* was *that?*"

Greg shrugged. "Gotta say something, right? If you can do better, give it a try."

Steve raised his hands in defeat and backed off.

It was still too early for primetime, so Greg left the radio on, curled up in his sleeping bag, and tried to get some sleep. Not so easy, because it was freezing, and they couldn't start a fire for fear of giving away their position.

Also, there was a dead body somewhere in the house. Not fresh—old and sour, and a little musty. Nasty things to look at, dead bodies, so they didn't go exploring.

Maybe two hours later, Greg woke suddenly with a start. He'd heard talking.

"Beats me," someone said on the radio. "Did everyone get one?"

"I got one," another voice said.

"Me too," said yet another. "Hello? Someone out there? Hello?"

The radio went silent. Greg looked over at Steve, who stared back in terror.

Stage fright, Greg thought smugly.

"All right," he said, "time to whip out the ol' guitar." He picked up a guitar they'd scavenged at some point, and which he fully intended to master one day. Olivia seemed like the type of girl who liked a guitar-playing man. "You hold the mic open while I let 'er rip. Okay?"

"Sure," Steve said, grabbing a chair.

Greg placed the strap over his neck and nodded for Steve to click the trigger.

"Hello, Front Royal!" he said, strumming the guitar theatrically, smiling at how awful it sounded. "As you can see, I can't really play this here gee-tar. But I'm gonna try anyway, because that's what the ladies like—a gee-tar-playin' man. Ah, the ladies ... Speaking of ladies, you know who used to be a lady but isn't anymore? Carter's mom!"

He strummed the guitar loudly for effect, like a rimshot off a snare drum.

"If there's one good thing about the Sickness," he said, "it rid the world of that horrible, ugly woman. *Oh come now*, you say. *Don't speak ill of the dead!* Normally, I'd never do that. But seriously, folks, is Carter's mom *really* dead, or is she just a few degrees cooler and a little bit prettier? I suppose you'd have to ask her ugly husband, Mr. Ugly. He married her, or so the court records say. On the way in, I had a look at those court records. Turns out Front Royal was the first town in the nation to legalize necrophilia!" He strummed the guitar again. "Now the bastard's parents can actually get married. Carter won't be a bastard anymore!"

Steve released the button, his face white as a sheet, and said, "What the hell are you doing? Carter's gonna kill us!"

From out of the little speaker, a voice said, "Um ... whoever you are, you shouldn't be saying stuff like that. He gets real mad if anyone, uh ... says stuff like that. Just saying."

Another voice broke in, deliberately high-pitched to disguise his voice: "I think it's funny as shit! Let her rip, kid!"

Greg smiled, pointed at the mic, and nodded. He strummed the guitar again.

"Before I tell you all of the various animals, minerals, and vegetables Carter's mom used to have sex with on a daily basis," he said in a deadly serious tone, "here's a few words from our sponsor, Jack Ferris, brilliant and fearless leader of the Rippers!"

He strummed the guitar for ten seconds, really getting into it.

"Jack Ferris is a great man, even though he's a teenager. He feeds his people the best food—even the little kids, who he bravely saved from murderers and wild animals. He taught us gun safety, and brought us books to read so we wouldn't grow up stupid like Carter's parents. Incidentally, Carter's parents are so stupid, when the Sickness came, they shot themselves in the head and lived. No brains. Get it?"

Greg strummed the guitar again.

"But back to Jack. Jack wanted me to tell you all about an amazing opportunity. You can join us at the farm after we kill Carter. Just stay out of the upcoming fight and you'll be fine. We plan to start school again for those who want to learn. All the adults are dead, and the world is messed up now, but Jack figures we can bring it back if we don't sit around being stupid like Carter's mom and dad. Jack wants us to raise cattle, not shoot them and eat their legs and leave the rest to rot. That's just wasteful. He wants to raise crops so we don't have to eat corn grain all winter. He wants to bring back electricity, clean water, and yes, even the Internet! All these things and more. If our parents could do it, why can't we? We're human, and humans are smart. Especially Jack."

Greg strummed his guitar a final time and nodded at Steve, who released the mic.

Carter's voice carried through the little speaker: "... *kill you, you son of a bitch!* We're gonna find you and then you're *dead!* Everyone get off this channel *now!* Anyone who listens to it is out of the gang!"

There was about half a minute of dead air. Then the concealed, high-pitched voice from before said, "Hey kid—tell us again how dumb Carter's mom is!"

Steve held the microphone like it was a bomb, his eyes very round.

Greg laughed. "Don't worry. He's running off less amperage than us. That's what the two batteries are for. We can drown him out easily. Go on, hit the button again. Let's do this."

For the rest of the day, Greg described the various members of Carter's colorful family. The Dragsters of Front Royal learned a great deal about Carter's dog-slash-half-sister Barky, the barking girl. They also learned about his half-brother, Poop Boy—half poop, half boy, and all charm. It turned out that Carter had about thirty different half-sisters and half-brothers, each of them with their own unique stories.

Sometime in the afternoon, Greg's voice started to get tired, and he signaled to cut the mic.

Steve shook his head in wonder. "Man, you got some lungs. You said you get stage fright!"

"I thought I did too," Greg said wonderingly. "I think it helps that nobody can see me but you. Cool, huh?"

"Yeah," he said. "But hey, I'm kind of hungry."

"Me too, and my voice is getting scratchy. Go on and hit it one more time."

Steve nodded.

"Okay, Front Royal," Greg said. "Time for me to shut this puppy down and eat some of that tasty Ripper food I told you about. Unless Jack shows up to kill Carter tonight, we'll be back tomorrow at nine for more fun!"

He strummed the guitar again loud and long, and that

was the end of their first day spreading propaganda in that small, dead town.

***

The next day, the Dragsters of Front Royal learned that Carter didn't just have a bunch of half-brothers and half-sisters. He also had half-*uncles*.

Sammy Sewage (half-uncle, half steaming pile of sewage) was captured by a group of well-meaning government scientists who'd heard how ugly Carter's mom was. They'd wanted to see if they could weaponize the family's ugly-DNA for use against good-looking terrorists.

Two hours and about twenty half-cousins, half-uncles, and half-grandmothers later, Greg was still going with no sign of letting up. He only stopped when Steve made distressed motions and closed the mic.

"I'm all cramped up," Steve said, flexing his fingers and rubbing his hand. "I keep switching back and forth, but I need a break."

Greg thought quickly. "I have an idea: tape the button down."

"Yeah," Steve said, nodding. "That's a good idea."

Then he remembered the tape was in the car.

"Be right back."

Steve slipped through the back door and around to the front. He peeked past the gate and saw nobody driving and no one on foot. Both very good signs. Quickly, he ran to the car, opened it, and searched frantically for the tape they'd used to post notices the day before.

He still couldn't believe that guy, Greg. He'd always seemed so nice. Chipper, upbeat, but overall, normal. Not brilliant and tough like his sister, and not cool and decisive like Jack. According to Molly, Olivia thought Greg was an annoying weirdo who wouldn't stop saying *hi* to her at every opportunity. Steve sort of wished the green-haired girl could listen to the show—*that'd* change her opinion. The dude was a genius.

If anyone told him Greg could rip insults out of thin air for hours and hours, he wouldn't have believed them. Back before the Sickness, people made millions of dollars on the Internet doing stuff like that.

He shook his head sadly. A miracle and a curse all mixed together, plain and simple.

Steve found the tape wedged under the passenger's seat. When he got out of the car, a little boy was standing at the end of the driveway looking at him. About seven years old, and not terribly skinny. Steve recognized him. The kid's older brother was in the gang.

"Go on, you little shit," Steve said. "Scram!"

The little boy ran off, and Steve went back inside.

***

"Okay, folks, where were we?" Greg said after taping the trigger down. "Oh yeah, I remember: Carter's mom, and whether or not she's an alien from the planet Puke-Theta-Z. Word has it she was the one that caused the Sickness when her face mutated the common cold virus in its tracks, causing it to run fleeing across the planet to get away ... But before we go there—and we *will* go *there*, I promise you—allow me to tell you a little more about our fearless leader Jack Ferris. Golden haired, wise of brow, tall of stature, and possessed of the Wisdom of Solomon. And unlike Carter, he's never had sex with his own mom. You remember Carter's mom, right? She's the alien from Puke-Theta-Z, who, as I just mentioned, caused the Sickness with her incredibly ugly face."

And so it went for the next few hours. Then the door burst open and Carter rushed in with a bunch of his friends, all of them armed and surprisingly angry.

As bad as that was, Greg was even more surprised at who was with them: Miguel and his brother, Paul.

THIRTY-THREE

They dragged Lisa through the living room, into the kitchen, and dropped her in a heap in front of the pantry. Someone had nailed boards over the door, which they quickly removed with a claw hammer. The door opened and she caught a glimpse of Greg with his shirt off and Steve, lying on the sacks of grain he'd brought the day he and Molly joined.

"Greg!" she shouted, and was thrust inside. The door slammed, followed by the sound of the boards being hammered back in place.

"Sis?" Greg said.

"Miguel said you got shot. Is it true?"

"Yeah. In the leg. It hurts. All because of that traitor. You know what? I never liked that guy. Now I know why. He used the special beep to sneak Carter and his friends in."

"Worry about that later," she said. "Tell me about your leg. Is it bleeding?"

Greg grunted and took a panting breath as he shifted around. "Not too much. I guess I'm lucky. I wrapped it in my shirt. The bullet's stuck deep, though. Hurts like a million bee stings. I need some of those pills Jack took after ... Hey, wait a minute, I heard gunshots outside. Was that you?"

"Yeah," she said bleakly.

"You okay, sis?"

"I'm pretty pissed off right now."

Greg snorted. "Who said you were pretty?"

She was glad it was dark so he couldn't see her smile. The fear in her heart when Miguel said he'd been shot was the worst she'd ever felt in her life. But here sat Greg, alive enough to make jokes.

Lisa reached up and felt her head. Her fingers came away sticky from a cut over her eye.

"Steve?" she said tentatively. She hadn't seen his face, but recognized his jacket.

"I don't think he's awake," Greg said. "He got beat up, but at least nobody shot him. Not yet."

"Well, that's some good news," she said. "Where are the children?"

"Carter stuck them in Jack's cabin." He swore. "He doesn't like little kids. He kicked one in front of me and laughed about it. Then Brad started yelling at him and he backed down."

That didn't make any sense. "Why does he care what Brad thinks? We're the enemy. Right?"

"Not totally. He wants to recruit them. That's why I'm still alive—to get to *you*. He wants you to join the Dragsters. Or did before you, um ... whatever it was you did outside."

That was nuts. She'd never join up with him. Not in a million years. She didn't think anyone else would, either. And when Carter realized that ...

"If the children are in Jack's cabin," she said, "where are Brad and the others?"

"No idea—I've been in here the whole time, except when the bastard murdered Trisha and beat up Steve. God, my leg hurts."

"*What?*" she said.

Greg didn't reply immediately. "Carter made us all watch it. He put Steve in a circle, called him a traitor, and took turns punching him. Trisha ..." There was a pause. "The son of a bitch called her a slut and shot her in the head. Right there. Said it was for running off with Jack."

She didn't know what to say. She wanted to cry, but if she did she worried she might not stop.

Poor Trisha.

They'd saved her from Carter, thinking they were doing the right thing, and now she was dead. Lisa hadn't gotten to know the girl, but she'd looked forward to long, snowy evenings around the fire after all the supplies were in and everyone was home and safe.

"Steve?" she said. "You okay?" She waited a few seconds. "How bad is he?"

Deeper in the gloom, about five feet away, Steve issued a low moan.

A second later, she realized something and felt a stab of fear. "Greg, what about Molly?"

"She's fine," he said. "Brad said if Carter killed her, may as well kill him, too. Everyone else said the same thing. Even some of the Dragsters. Carter wouldn't dare. Honestly, sis, I don't know anything else. If it's okay, I think I'm just gonna pass out for a while."

Lisa left him alone and settled back against the wall, struggling to find a position that didn't hurt too much. At first she tried to sleep, hoping it would take the pain with it, but occasional snatches of conversation outside dragged her back. Anything she learned could be of use. She could rest later.

An hour or so later, thumping sounds carried from the door as the nails were pried loose. The door creaked opened and the light turned on, blinding in its intensity after so long in the dark.

"Hah, you're not dead," Carter said. He looked directly at Lisa's cut and battered face for several seconds, as if taking her measure. "Count yourself lucky I don't shoot you too, after what you did to my men."

Steve groaned.

"And you can just shut up right now, Steve," he said hotly. "Only reason you're alive is because I'm killing you tomorrow—outside, when it's light. Maybe you too, funny guy. Kind of depends on your sister here. The spic says she's Jack's girlfriend. That right?"

"Let me help my brother. I need medical supplies."

"Shut up until I say you can talk." He looked from her to Greg. "Well, funny guy? Is she Jack's or what?"

Lisa's eyes had just about adjusted to the light. Greg's leg was wrapped in his shirt like he'd said, and there was dried blood around his nose and mouth. Steve had shifted at some point. His face was a mess of bruises, and both eyes had closed up.

"She's not anybody's," Greg said with some heat. "People don't belong to other people, you—"

"Yes!" Lisa said, drowning him out. "Jack's my boyfriend. Now what?"

Carter snorted. "I knew it. Consider yourself mine now. Do what I say and your brother lives. Come on, get up."

Lisa lay there uncomprehending. *His? His what?*

"I said get up!"

Carter reached down, grabbed her by the hair, and jerked her painfully to her feet. Greg struggled forward and got kicked in his bad leg, bringing forth a howl of pain.

"See this?" Carter said, brandishing a pistol and pressing it to Lisa's head. "Try it again, funny guy, and I'll shoot her."

Greg didn't do anything after that.

Carter pulled her roughly into the kitchen. A boy of about twelve or thirteen stood leaning against the countertop holding the hammer.

"Close it back up," Carter said.

"I'm starving," he said. "When can I eat?"

"When you close it back up. Now do it!"

The boy shook his head and grabbed a plank off the floor with nails sticking out of it.

Carter shoved Lisa into the living room with all the mattresses. The lights were on in there, too. Miguel must have shown him the generator out back. About ten teenagers, mostly boys, were lounging around on the mattresses, staring at her.

No, not just staring—glaring. All except one.

"Hi, Lisa," Miguel said in a high, light voice. He sprang off the closest mattress and approached with an anxious expression. "If you think about it, I had no choice. Jack's crazy—you know that. He can't lead us. All those little kids?" He shook his head. "And look what happened to Pete. You need a big group, like the Dragsters. These guys are cool, you'll see."

"You're a filthy backstabber, Miguel," she said calmly. "Get out of my sight before I ..." She paused, casting a furtive look at Carter, who looked amused. "Go lie in your bed, dead boy."

"Buzz off," Carter told him, and snorted when Miguel jumped back as if stung. Carter threw his arm around her. "Got a proposition for you, uh ... what's your name again?"

"Lisa," she said through gritted teeth.

He nodded. "That's right. And stop being so grumpy. Come on, let's go upstairs."

The boys on the mattresses gave knowing laughs and leered at her openly as she was led away, offering up suggestions like "stick it in her mouth" and "make her beg for it" and other disgusting things.

The only girl there ran over and said, "Where the hell you going with her? After what she did, why ain't you gonna shoot her?"

"Out of the way, Cassie," Carter said. "Like I told you a billion times, we're through."

Cassie was a stringy-haired girl with popping eyes, a weak chin, and a frown so deep it looked like she'd been born with it.

"No we ain't!" she said, and spit in Lisa's face, stunning her briefly.

"I said back off!" Carter roared and shoved her to the floor.

Tears streaming from her angry eyes, Cassie said, "First Molly, then Trisha. Now her? When you gonna see you got a *real* girl right here? Someone who actually loves you?" She glared at Lisa. "Go on and have a good time up there, stupid ugly slut. When I see you again, I'm gonna cut up your face and piss on it."

Cassie clambered to her feet and stalked angrily back to the others, who'd watched the exchange nervously.

Lisa noticed the girl didn't have a gun, but that didn't mean she couldn't get one.

Carter grabbed her arm, led her to the stairs, and

nudged her up the first few steps.

"Give it to her *one time*," he said, "and she goes crazy. Would have left her back in town, but she's with one of the guys now." He chuckled and shook his head. "*Supposed* to be. Some girls are like that, though."

Lisa wiped her face again and didn't reply.

Carter said, "This is a really cool place you guys have here. *Had* here." He laughed when loud pop music blared suddenly from the great room. "Got a generator and everything. We had one, too. Tried setting it up, and this one dude—forget his name—he fried himself pretty good. After that, nobody wanted to try again. But your spic friend with the loudmouth brother—forget his name, too—he said *you* know all about electricity. Is that true?"

"Yeah," she said. "It's ... uh ... easy. If you know what to do."

At the landing, he tugged her to the right and made her lead. "Come on, this way."

Together, they headed to the room she shared with Molly and Olivia. Her back itched the whole way.

Carter locked the door behind them and flipped the light switch. She turned around and saw he had a gun in his hand.

"So what, you're gonna execute me?"

"Nah," he said, smiling. "This is just to make sure of stuff. I can't believe you killed all those guys. You and Jack are totally badass, you know that? Kind of pisses me off, actually. I mean, you're just a girl. But I guess anyone can pull a trigger." He bit his lip in thought. "Still, they shouldn't have just ran out like that. I would have gone around back and approached from the side. But they didn't, I guess, and you popped them. I had to finish off this one girl because she wouldn't stop screaming. Didn't really like her, so it's cool." He motioned to the bed. "Go on, sit down."

She sat down.

"This you and Jack's room?" Carter said, looking around.

Clearly she hadn't done a good enough job hiding her feelings for Jack, if Miguel was telling stories. Despite the situation, she wanted to laugh at the idea of her sharing a room with a boy—at her age?

She hadn't meant to lead on poor Jack like that. She liked him a lot—a *whole* lot. But they had other priorities right now, and making kissy faces at each other wasn't one of them. Maybe later, after things calmed down and they could feed themselves without worrying about jerks like Carter. For now, the last thing she wanted was a baby on the way. Only an idiot added a medical emergency to the threat of starvation and random violence.

Instead of saying all that, Lisa said, "Yeah, we sleep in here. Together." Then she nodded her head for emphasis. "Every night."

Carter glared hotly and aimed his gun at the bed. "Did he do it with *Trisha* in here?"

She looked at him blankly for a moment, and then her eyes widened. "He didn't steal your girlfriend ... or whatever she was. You beat her up and she was sick of it, so she came back with us. That's it."

"Whatever," he said languidly. "I'm putting this away. If you try anything, you'll regret it. I'd like to think we can be friends. We *should* be friends. It makes the most sense. I mean, you're sort of pretty, and you know electricity. Also, just remember, I got your brother downstairs. I was real pissed off because of that shit he said about my mom, but I'm cooling down some. It helps that I got to shoot him. So what do you say?"

"Uh ... what?"

He sighed loudly. "You gonna try something if I put my gun away? You gonna be good?"

"Yeah, sure." She shook her head when his eyes narrowed. "Um, I mean no. I *will* be good. Whatever you want, Jesus."

Carter stared at her a few seconds, working it out, then holstered the gun and sat beside her.

"Easy, now," he said when she tried to scoot away. "I'm putting my arm around you, all right? Nothing more. Just being friendly."

Through an effort of will, she stopped moving and let him. She even managed not to cringe.

"See, now? That's not so bad," he said softly. "Don't worry, okay? I can see you worrying. Truth is, Trisha and Molly were mine all on their own. Just like Cassie downstairs, but she's not pretty enough for me to stick with steady. I never force girls to do it if they don't want to. I just kick them out. Or maybe someone in the gang wants them. I don't really pry into people's personal lives. But you're special. Know why?"

She shook her head. "No."

"Because you're his. *Jack's*. I'm still not gonna force it, even though I could." He took her chin in his hand and made her look at him. "You know I can, right? I won't, though. It's better if you want it, too. I'm gonna tell you why you'd want it. Just listen to my reasons. Okay?"

Lisa breathed steadily in and out, trying to control her hatred and disgust. Her head, back, and ribs hurt more than ever, and she felt like vomiting. Instead of that, she nodded. "Sure. I'm listening."

Carter smiled and smoothed her hair back, tucking it behind her ears. "Because of you and Jack and your asshole brother, we got openings in the gang now. Possibly for those friends of yours, especially that big guy ... dammit, I forget his name, too." He shook his head in disgust. "I really suck at names. Anyway, we need people. Half the gang split because of your brother and his stupid radio jokes." He took a deep breath and let it out. "They'll change their minds when I kill Jack. I figure he'll be here in a day or so. Or maybe that gang the spic came from will kill him."

She'd had enough. "Would you spit it out? What the hell do you want?"

"I want you to be my girlfriend," he said. "Just you and me, steady. But once we do it, that's it, you're mine. Not like Trisha, running off like that. That happens, I gotta kill you. So think real hard about it."

He smoothed her hair again, only this time he let his hand trail down her back. She stiffened when he went under her shirt, rubbing her back and feeling under her bra strap.

"Easy, now," he said quietly. "That's nice, right?"

Dutifully, she nodded.

"We can't keep the little kids," he said in a musing sort of tone. "But after your brother apologizes in front of everyone, well, he can live. Steve's gotta die, though. He's a backstabbing traitor, like the spic. We can kill him too, if you want. Would you like that?"

Lisa nodded her head. "Sounds great. Wonderful."

Carter smiled gently. "Just lie back and close your eyes. Don't worry about a thing. Leave everything to me."

THIRTY-FOUR

Eddie's plan was simple, and he didn't mind sharing with Jack.

"Centreville's used up," he said. "Everything's been stripped clean. The farther east you go the worse it gets. North's basically all little kids at the airport, and this crew down south is pretty dangerous. Think they got into some kind of military base or something. We never go there. But west ..." He shook his head. "Blaze was so stupid—he told us everything west was a waste of time and wouldn't let us look. Then you come along with all that food you stole. I'm thinking this other crew'll want it back, and I think turning you in will get me in tight with them. I'm sick of being hungry all the time."

"Me too," the kid on the left said. Richard. The other's name was Kyle.

"Why don't you bring more people and just attack?" Jack said, hoping to somehow salvage his plan. "Then you can take everything back and be in charge." So long as Eddie didn't know where the cabins or Freida's farm was, the Pyros still might solve his Dragster problem.

"What the heck would I do that for?" Eddie said, laughing. "That's how Blaze did things. Him and that psycho sister of his. My way's better. But listen, seriously: if you're cool, I'll put in a good word for you. Maybe when they get their stuff back they'll forgive you." He shrugged. "Best I can do. I'm actually really cool once you get to know me."

Jack nodded. "I see that now."

Eddie told Richard and Kyle to load up the back of the Humvee with the canned goods, snacks, and the rest of the prescription medicine. Afterward, he put Jack in the front-side passenger seat and made the others sit in the back.

"Can I have one of those snacks?" Richard said to Eddie.

"Me too?" Kyle said.

"Didn't you eat before we left?" Eddie said angrily.

The boys said they'd forgotten to, and Eddie was forced to relent.

"Make sure you throw the wrappers out," he said. "I don't want them thinking we ate their stuff. This is our ticket in. We can't screw it up."

Richard and Kyle wolfed their snacks down and threw the wrappers out the window.

Eddie backed down the ramp and then headed west on 66.

"Blaze said your gang's somewhere called Front Royal," he said about thirty minutes later. "I've heard of it. Didn't know where it was. Anyway, let me know where I gotta turn."

Jack still didn't know what to do and felt increasingly worried. If he'd held that piece of information back—the name of the town—he could have taken them to Warrenton, then said he had to go to the bathroom and made a run for it.

He tried not to swear. Eddie had already proven himself a killer. There wasn't any way to escape without getting shot or causing an accident. But maybe he could talk his way out of it—offer some value to Carter other than revenge.

It used to be warring nations would have peace talks. In Jack's case, he could offer a conditional surrender. Conditional, because he'd never reveal the location of the cabins, and he'd never betray his friends. But he was willing to offer a certain amount of dried beef—maybe some chopped wood or scavenged gear—in exchange for being left alone. Tribute, basically. Like in a real war. Then, come spring, he'd load everyone on the bus and find a new location—with their tails between their legs, sure, but alive, and not under anyone's thumb.

It wasn't a perfect plan, but it was the one he had. He'd figure out how to explain the whole *Eddie-thinks-I-stole-your-snacks* problem when it came up.

"All right," he said, pointing at the exit sign. "That's the one."

"Finally," Eddie said and slowed. He turned and looked behind him. "Kyle—gimme a pack of cookies. Chocolate, not oatmeal. And throw out the wrapper."

The streets of Front Royal were empty. Jack was wary. Surely the gang would be on alert after losing five of their people. But when Eddie drove past the headquarters, the cars were all gone. The shot up windows, Jack noted, were now covered over with cardboard.

Kyle and Richard got out and knocked on a few doors, but nobody answered.

Back in the Humvee, Eddie cast him a suspicious glance. "You sure this is the place?"

"Yeah, but I don't ..." Through the rearview mirror, Jack noticed a car pull out from a gas station parking lot, heading their way. "I think that's them."

"What the heck?" Eddie said, looking around and then back. "What should I do?"

"I don't know. You're in charge, remember?"

Eddie slowed down, drove through an intersection, and stopped. The car behind them stopped just inside the intersection and waited.

"Maybe you should get out," Kyle said. "See what they want."

Eddie turned around. "No. *You* get out and see. Go talk to them. And leave your gun on the seat. We're here as friends."

"But I don't *want* to get out. Why don't you make Richard for once? I always—"

Out of nowhere, Richard hit him with the back of his fist. When Kyle yelped he hit him again and shouted, "Get out of the stupid car, wimp!"

"But I don't *wanna!*" Kyle wailed, reluctantly opening the door.

Richard turned sideways in the seat and shoved him with both feet. Kyle fell into the street halfway and hung precariously by a loose seatbelt. Eddie, ever helpful, jerked the vehicle forward and Kyle fell the rest of the way. When he hit the brakes, the door snapped back, slammed shut, and he locked all the doors.

Kyle got up and pounded furiously on the windows, pulling door handles, and blubbering nonstop in terror.

Eddie lowered the back window an inch and yelled, "Just go see what they want, you big baby! We'll be right here!"

"Come on, let me in! Please! *Please!*"

They yelled back and forth for about a minute, and Jack's head—still not fully recovered from being bashed with a rock—began to throb. Eventually, Eddie backed toward the intersection, with Kyle keeping pace, staring at the waiting car and crying.

Abruptly, the car backed up a few feet, pulled a tight turn, and sped off down a different road.

"What the ...?" Eddie said. "Did you see that? I don't get it." He looked at Jack for an explanation and got a shrug in reply.

"I'm just a prisoner."

"Shut up," Eddie said. He unlocked the door for Kyle to get back in. "This place is weird, man."

They continued cautiously forward. More intersections, then a different car shot out of nowhere and blocked them. Eddie reversed and turned around—only to find his escape blocked by another car.

"I ain't getting out this time," Kyle said, covering his head when Richard tried to hit him again.

"Knock it off!" Eddie shouted. "*I'll* do it, you stupid wimps."

"Want me to hold your gun?" Jack said.

Eddie glared at him, cut the engine, and got out. He approached this newest car with his hands in the air. Just like before, when he got close, the car sped up and shot off. The first car was still there, though, blocking the other way.

Eddie swore and came back.

"Screw this. I'm getting out of here."

He started it up and sped back the way they'd come. They made it through three intersections before more cars zoomed in and blocked them. Grimly, he tried to lose them in a residential section. After a confusion of turns, he pulled onto one of the major roads bisecting the town.

"Which way's the interstate?" Eddie said.

"Back the way we came, then take a left," Jack said.

Eddie shook his head and kept going, taking more turns at random, passing dealerships and restaurants and office buildings. A few minutes later, four more cars pulled out and blocked the way, causing him to stop and turn around again. This time, the cars weren't content to wait and let them run away. They tore after them at high speed, easily catching the slower, bulkier vehicle. Then someone nudged them from behind. Then they did it again.

"Make them stop!" Kyle screamed.

"He's trying!" Richard yelled.

Eddie absorbed each bump as best he could, but they came harder and harder, causing him to fishtail. He jerked the wheel of the ponderous Humvee to keep it straight. A minute later, he took an unlucky hit that bumped them into a curb. The vehicle spun around in a circle and suddenly shut off. Two more cars roared in and they were surrounded.

Boys and girls jumped from every car pointing guns at them.

Jack knew he was well and truly screwed at this point. The Dragsters hadn't been content to communicate what they wanted. No, they wanted to play. Probably because they were bored. He knew how cruel bored kids could be.

"Jack, do something," Eddie said, pointing his pistol at him. "Go out there and talk to them. Tell them you're my prisoner for what you did. Please!"

"Fine," he said, and got out with his hands raised.

A girl with blond hair rushed forward and pointed a revolver at his face.

"Hello," he said. "My name's—"

"Don't care what your name is, dummy," she said, and

shot a round over his head.

The various Dragsters laughed, pointed, and fired more shots into the air. Yelling and crying from the Humvee added to the weirdness of the situation. Despite all that, he felt oddly calm.

"As I was saying, my name's Jack. I think Carter wants me alive, at least for a while, so uh ..." He couldn't believe what he was about to say. "Take me to your leader."

A boy with a pistol-gripped shotgun whistled for attention. "You say your name's Jack? Jack what?"

"Jack Ferris?" he said. "I, uh, stole some of your grain—real sorry about that, by the way. I'm here to—"

"Wait a minute," the boy said, coming forward with his gun pointed thoughtlessly at him, finger on the trigger. "You're *the* Jack Ferris? From the Rippers? Greg's gang?"

What the ...?

"The real Jack's got golden hair," the girl said, pointing at him. "*Golden* haired, that's what Greg said. His hair's blond."

Another said, "Golden hair *is* blond hair, you idiot."

An argument abruptly sprang up about what degree of blond constituted golden.

"Check if he's got a radio," someone said at one point. "Maybe he heard about it there."

"What's this about?" Jack said, mystified and a little irritated. He wanted to get to his meeting with Carter and be done with it. "Why's my hair so important?"

The boy with the shotgun walked over to the passenger door and tapped on it. The window rolled down and Eddie said, "What?"

"Just wanna look in your car a minute," the boy said, peering inside. "Thanks." He turned back to the crowd. "Doesn't have no radio. Gotta be him."

Jack narrowed his eyes. A nagging suspicion began to tug at him. "What exactly did Greg say to you people on the radio?"

The girl cracked a smile and said, "Shit—what *didn't* he say. Tore Carter a new asshole, that's what he did. We're what's left of the gang. We're done taking orders from that jerk anymore." She smiled apologetically. "We thought you were them. No offense."

"So, Jack, what are you doing here?" the one with the shotgun said. He pointed at the Humvee. "And who are those guys? I'm Larry, by the way."

He held out his hand. Jack shook it, not missing a beat.

"The one in front was going to turn me in to Carter," he said. "His name's Eddie, and he's a backstabbing killer. The two in the back, I don't know."

"Is that right?" Larry said in a flat voice. He walked to the Humvee and tapped on the window.

"What?" Eddie said.

"Out of the car," Larry said. "You two in the back—stay put."

Eddie got out, his whole demeanor meek. Then he came around and stood where everyone could see him.

"Jack says you're a backstabbing killer," Larry said. "And we're with Jack."

Then he blasted Eddie in the chest with the shotgun.

THIRTY-FIVE

"Why are women physically weaker than men?" Jack's mom, Mrs. Ferris, had said when they stopped to refill their water from a stream. The boys and Mr. Ferris were a ways off, sitting on rocks and relaxing. Typical male behavior—lazing around while the women did all the work.

The Mitchell twins and the Ferris family were hiking in Dolly Sods, West Virginia, working their way to an overlook they'd camped at the previous year. Lisa's parents couldn't go because ... well, the truth was both were overweight, and it was a five mile hike up and down hills. Jack's parents, in their sixties, were healthy and trim, and could manage the trek almost as well as the kids.

"I don't know about that, Mrs. Ferris," Lisa said. "I'm stronger than Greg. And I can crush an apple in one hand. Jack can't even do that. And I always win when we wrestle." She laughed. "No offense, but even with all that karate, Jack's sort of a wimp."

Mrs. Ferris laughed too. "You're still young. When they hit puberty, they'll produce more testosterone, and that'll stimulate muscle growth. By the time they're twenty, they'll be at least twice as strong as you if they don't do anything but sit around, and a lot stronger if they exercise."

Lisa didn't think that was fair, or necessarily true. She'd seen women on TV run super fast and lift weights that even her dad couldn't pick up.

"What if I exercise too? Wouldn't I get stronger if I started now? Then could I keep up with them?"

"I'm sorry, no," Mrs. Ferris said sadly. "Not in sheer physical strength, at least. The strongest man in the world will always be stronger than the strongest woman. You *could* outrun a man if you had to, but only if he's out of shape and you're in *good* shape. But again, biology's against us. The fastest man in the world will always be faster than the fastest woman. In this case, it's more because of the way our hips are structured, and because of the differences in the way men and women distribute weight."

She looked hard at Lisa, and her face grew deadly serious. "If you're ever in a fight with a man, unless you get very lucky or have some other advantage, he's probably going to win."

Lisa didn't say anything for a time, letting the unsettling thought digest. Briefly, she considered not talking to Mrs. Ferris anymore. For an adult, she was actually pretty weird, as well as sort of cold. Jack said his whole childhood was based around his parents dying the day he turned eighteen. How messed up was that?

She couldn't help herself. She had to know the answer.

"All right. So why *are* girls weaker than boys?"

Mrs. Ferris paused before answering, as if choosing the best words for her audience.

"Size and strength in animals often tracks closely with monogamy and polygamy. Do you know those words?"

Lisa nodded. She loved reading, and always had a dictionary handy when she did. She particularly liked grown-up books, though she had to hide them under her bed if they had S-E-X in them. Not from her mom, but from her dad. He was prudish about stuff like that.

Mrs. Ferris said, "Polygamous animals, like chimps and gorillas, tend to have larger males. Monogamous animals, like gibbons and beavers, exhibit no such sexual dimorphism. Why do you think that is?"

Lisa shrugged, feeling less and less comfortable with the conversation, but not wanting to be rude now that she'd committed to it.

"I'll give you two reasons," Mrs. Ferris said. "One: males are forced to compete with each other for access to females. When they fight, the bigger ones usually win, and they get to mate."

Lisa frowned. "But that's not true about humans. Humans get married. They're—*we're*—monogamous."

"Tell that to any invading army since the dawn of history. Or any frat boy, or lonely barroom drunk."

Lisa didn't know much about drunks or frat boys, but she got the point. "So what's the other reason?"

"Just this: weak females are easier to dominate. If strong men and weak females tend to have more babies, a pattern will eventually develop."

Lisa nodded slowly. "You mean evolution, I'm learning about that now. Mom says we believe in God, so we don't believe in evolution. But Dad thinks God *made* evolution. They don't really talk about it much." She frowned in thought. "I don't know what to believe. But why do weak girls have to ... um ... keep on being weak? We'd just get eaten by lions easier. Right?"

"Without parents or a vigilant community," Mrs. Ferris said, "boys would get eaten by lions too. You're talking about competitive advantage. But there are other forces at work—sexual selection, culture, environment. In the end, though, it's all a numbers game."

Lisa was really confused now. Numbers game? What was this, math?

"Think of it this way," Mrs. Ferris said. "Do you know what a human being really is? At its most basic level?"

"A person? Um ... someone?"

Mrs. Ferris smiled gently. "Yes, in a sense. In another sense, a *human* is simply a way for human DNA to make more human DNA—a curious byproduct of a chemical reaction that happened three-and-a-half billion years ago." At Lisa's shocked, faintly offended expression, she added, "Unless of course we were *created*. As far as that goes, I'm more likely to agree with your father than your mother."

Lisa pondered what she'd heard and clipped another bottle to the water filter.

Over on the rocks, the boys were laughing out loud about something, blissfully ignorant of the meaning of life. She loved her brother, but he could never be serious. She couldn't imagine either him or Jack trying to dominate a girl. Still, she wasn't completely naive. She watched the news sometimes and knew not every boy was the same. She also knew what *dominate* meant, even if Mrs. Ferris wasn't saying the word.

Unexpectedly, she felt like crying. "Why are you telling me all this terrible stuff?"

"Because I want you to be prepared," Mrs. Ferris said. "We women don't have to be victims. There are things we can do to protect ourselves."

Lisa wiped her eyes. "Yeah, like what?"

"Like you said, we can exercise."

"But you said that wouldn't help."

"Not true—I said it won't make us equal. But it *will* help. Another numbers game, but we can skew the results if we try. If you're walking alone one night, chances are you won't be jumped by an Olympic swimmer, right?"

Lisa nodded. "Yeah, I suppose."

"So if you're stronger than he expects, you'll have a better chance. If you're healthy—and you know how to fight—you can use your body far more effectively. You can increase the odds of survival."

After that, Lisa felt more at ease. She felt even better when, the following week, Mrs. Ferris invited her to the gym.

At first, Mrs. Ferris started her on stretches, running on the treadmill, and lifting weights. She said most women didn't like weights because they were afraid of growing big, ugly muscles, even though that was biologically impossible without anabolic steroids.

Despite the work she was putting in, Lisa wasn't blind. She saw the burly men in the gym, and cringed at how much they were lifting—sometimes twenty or thirty times what she could. Heck, she could barely lift up the free weight bar with ten-pound plates on it. And here she'd thought she was pretty strong.

"If you can surprise someone," Mrs. Ferris said, "you

can end the fight sometimes even before it begins. Hurt the bastard and run away, then trust your cardio training. Most of these meatheads will fall over gasping if they have to run five feet. You don't need to beat them to a pulp to win. You only need to outlast them."

One day, they didn't lift weights or run on the treadmill. Instead, they attended a self-defense class, which Mrs. Ferris paid for with her own money on the condition that Lisa hide it from her parents. Not entirely ethical, Lisa knew, but she also knew her mother would have forbidden her to go. Her parents also didn't know she and Greg had gone shooting at the range with Jack, and with luck they never would.

The defense class was taught by a former mixed martial arts fighter and emphasized boxing, jiu-jitsu, and dirty fighting. Lisa loved it, because ever since Mrs. Ferris said she was just human DNA trying to make more human DNA, she'd felt something close to helpless—adrift in an unfair universe of violent men who could do what they wanted no matter how she felt.

There were several women in the class, and only a couple of girls and boys. As the weeks went by, she looked forward to training against the boys because she was able to beat them more times than not. And when she went home and tried the moves on her brother, she wiped the floor with him.

Now, two years later, Lisa looked back on those days at the gym and the only thing she wished is that she'd trained even harder.

***

"Just leave everything to me," Carter had said, and gently eased her down onto the bed.

He touched her chest with his fingers and groped clumsily.

"Wait," Lisa whispered. "Let me ... um ... I need to get comfortable."

"Sure, no problem," he said, overly agreeable. He had a look in his eyes she'd never seen before from anyone. A little like hunger and hate, mixed together.

Lisa arranged her legs beneath him, one on either side

of his waist, then took his left hand in hers and kissed it.

He leaned down to kiss her on the mouth and she shied away, saying, "Not yet, don't ruin it."

Carter's jaw clenched with impatience. She kissed his fingers again and spread her legs wider and he relaxed.

"What are you doing?" he said when she adjusted her right leg up high and sort of angled it sideways.

"I saw it on the Internet," she said. "You're gonna love it."

"Huh? Saw what?"

Before she was forced to kiss his nasty fingers again, Lisa slipped her leg from beneath his arm, up around his neck, and then clamped down with her left leg. Simultaneously, she pulled his right arm straight with both hands and squeezed her legs together. Carter yelped in shock. She squeezed harder to cut off his airflow, lest he alert anyone downstairs. He struck out with his left arm, flailing to hit something, but only landed a few ineffectual punches to her side.

Lisa was great at squeezing. *She* was the girl that could crush apples in her bare hands when she was twelve. *She* could beat up her brother and Jack—karate or no karate. Sure, the strongest man in the world would always beat the strongest women. But Carter wasn't a man—he was just a boy, not to mention a bully who probably won most fights because his opponents were too scared to fight back.

Well, he'd caught a double dose of bad luck in Lisa. Not only wasn't she scared, she *enjoyed* fighting back.

A moment came where Carter stopped batting against her with his free hand and began scrabbling at his side. Lisa's eyes widened in alarm—he was going for his gun!

Rather than let that happen, she did the unthinkable— she rolled sideways off the bed, pulling him with her, trusting in blind luck for a safe landing. They landed, and it sure didn't feel safe or lucky the way her vision swam down a funnel of fading light. She'd landed on her bruised back, and the breath was knocked clear out of her. Carter issued a weak groan and gasped raggedly for air. She still had hold of his arm, though her legs had shifted a little.

Before he could yell, she pulled back harder and

squeezed, arching off her back for a tighter grip. Holding the pose, she squeezed like her life depended on it—which it did—and hoped nobody downstairs had heard them fall.

After what seemed like hours, but was probably only a minute, Carter's body turned limp in her perfectly performed triangle choke. Still she held on, choking him with everything she had, now panting and sweating from exertion, her inflamed back and legs screaming in agony. When she couldn't hold on any longer, she let go and fell back gasping for breath with the boy lying grossly between her legs.

"Was it good for you, asshole?" she muttered.

She crawled backwards on her elbows and lay flat. A minute passed and her eyes snapped open. She'd almost fallen asleep. Her whole body felt like a big, giant sore, and all she wanted to do was sleep. Instead of that, she got to her knees and checked Carter's pulse—still there, and somehow he was still breathing.

Lisa got up, grabbed one of the pillows off the bed, and shucked it free of the pillowcase. She twisted the pillowcase in her hands like a rope, then sat behind Carter and wrapped it twice around his throat. Once again, she mustered her hard-earned strength and squeezed. For more leverage, she twisted it around her foot halfway and leaned back. In time, her hands began to burn and she let go, giving them a break. When they felt better, she resumed strangling him.

After he was finally dead, she let go, liberated the gun from his corpse, and stood up.

Lisa's whole body shook, and she was as tired as she'd ever been in her life. But she was armed, she was desperate, and sleep could wait.

Upon checking the magazine, she swore quietly. There were only three rounds left. The idiot was carrying a nearly empty gun. There were ten of them downstairs, including that crazy girl, Cassie, and that traitor, Miguel.

Quietly, Lisa left the room and crossed to the landing. She needn't have tiptoed—they were still playing their dumb music.

She made her way down the stairs and peeked into the

great room. Some were sleeping, others talking, and two were playing a card game. Cassie was pacing and looking at the ceiling, shaking her head and muttering to herself.

"Would you sit down already?" someone said.

"Mind your own business!" she shouted.

Lisa eased back and crept to the kitchen, then to the pantry. She saw two boards with nails sticking out of them resting on the floor. Another board was hammered across the door, and a claw hammer lay on the counter next to a box of nails. A couple of strong kicks from the other side would have knocked the board free. If Carter had seen it, he probably would have yelled or threatened someone or whatever bullies like that did.

After a quick look to ensure nobody was coming, Lisa pried it loose and opened the door.

Greg flinched in terror, then smiled when he saw she was alone.

"I'll help you up," she whispered, staring at his leg. "Whatever you do, don't scream."

When he was on his feet—mewling softly in agony—he gasped out, "We gotta get Steve, too. Can't leave my wingman."

Cursing the time it was taking, but knowing she couldn't just leave the poor boy here for them to slaughter, she tried to help Steve to his feet. It was hard because his legs and arms were like jelly, and he moaned loudly when she tried to lift him. She was about to suggest they leave him anyway, try to free the others and come back, but then someone said, "I *thought* I heard something. Got you now, you ugly slut!"

The door slammed behind them. Lisa let Steve go and slammed it with her shoulder. It held fast. She twisted the knob and pushed. It gave about six inches, but slammed shut again. Now the doorknob wouldn't move—Cassie was holding it from her side and screaming for help.

The doorknob was more decorative than functional, not meant for heavy duty. Lisa twisted it hard and heard a snap. After that, it moved without resistance, the internals clearly broken.

Lisa heard more voices, then hammering as each of the

boards was secured with *way* more nails than before.

"Trapped again," Lisa said.

With nothing to do but wait, she pulled the gun free of her waistband and slumped down against the wall.

THIRTY-SIX

"It's really cool meeting you, Jack Ferris," Larry said, shaking his hand again. Despite being a killer, he was one of the few people Jack had met after the Sickness who shook hands without prompting. Tony always did that head-nod thing, and Brad was big into fist bumps.

"It's cool meeting you too, Larry. All of you."

Everyone came around and touched him on the shoulder or smiled or nodded at him or said hello. They didn't call him *Jack*, but rather *Jack Ferris*. For the first time in his life, he felt like a celebrity.

Soon, he learned he wasn't nearly the celebrity that Greg was. They kept asking about him. Who was he really? What was he like? Did he used to be on YouTube? Stuff like that.

Eventually, they told him what had happened.

Greg's only job had been to go into town and broadcast about the "Rippers," their delicious food, and their plans for the future. A long shot, and sort of a backup plan if Jack's mission failed. It turned out Greg hadn't just been successful—he'd pulled off a miracle. Most of the Dragsters had decided to ditch Carter and his cronies and had essentially run them out of town.

"Glad we ain't at war no more," Larry said. "It was starting to get messy, huh?"

Jack forced a smile he didn't feel. He'd attacked these

259

people the other night, and he worried someone here cared about one of the ones he'd shot.

"Yeah," Jack said. "Messy."

"We need a better leader, and Greg said you're amazing. Everyone's sick of grain. Whenever we get meat, it rots before we can finish it. Then we gotta drive even *farther* next time. There's another group out west we used to trade stuff with, but they won't let us come near anymore." He spit. "That was all Carter."

Great, more stupid gangs.

"Cool," Jack said. "So where's Greg? Is he still here?"

Larry pulled a sad, almost scared look, like he wanted to say something but needed special permission.

"What is it?" Jack said.

"The thing is, Carter's pretty easy to piss off. And Greg— much as I like him—well, the thing is what he was saying about Carter ... and Carter's *mom* ..."

"Ripped him and his whole stupid family a new one," another finished for him. "Guess that's why you guys are *Rippers*. Get it?"

Some of them laughed and Larry shushed them.

"I know he's your friend and all," Larry continued, "but someone from your gang came here and told Carter your plan to sick the Pyros on him. Cool plan, by the way."

"*What?* Who?"

Larry filled him in.

Thanks to Paul's distinctive motormouth, Larry didn't have to say Miguel's name for Jack to know who it was. He seethed over the betrayal. The slimy backstabber. He wanted to strangle the kid, but that'd have to wait.

Larry coughed. "Anyway, they found Greg and Steve earlier today. Someone said Carter shot Greg in the leg and took him prisoner." He paused in thought. "Or maybe the arm. It's hard to tell what's true right now."

Jack swore, chewing on the shame that came from putting his friends in danger. But he hadn't seen a body yet. Until he did, he wouldn't give up hope.

"Where's Carter now?"

Larry nodded. "The traitor brought him and his friends back to your place. Not the farm—somewhere else. I know they're your friends and all, but Carter's pretty mean, and he still has like twenty people with him. You could just stay here. We can send someone up to talk to them. Like Will, over there. Everyone likes Will."

Will smiled at Jack and waved a little howdy-do wave.

Jack considered the idea, weighing the pros and cons. If he sent a messenger up—an *envoy*—Carter would rightly feel he was in a position of power, and that Jack was scared of him. He had to assume the worst—that Carter might use the opportunity to further twist the screws by hurting his friends, regardless of whether they reached an agreement later.

He shook his head. "I can't just sit here knowing they're in trouble. And I'd really appreciate it if you guys would help me—help *Greg*. Carter's not dumb. If we go up there armed to the teeth, all of us together, he'll give in and let them go."

"And if he doesn't?" the girl from before said.

"Then I'll have to make him."

"*We'll* make him," she said, and everyone cheered when she shot her gun in the air.

Some of the others shot their guns in the air, too. He bit his lip and held off telling them how dangerous that was.

Before they set out, Richard—who'd been quiet the whole time, along with Kyle—spoke up. "What about us?"

Jack frowned in thought. "We'll talk about that later. For now, you're sticking with me."

***

On the way out of town, someone crashed into a ditch and had to be rescued. Thirty minutes later, Jack and the Dragsters got to the dirt road leading to Big Timber. His heart skipped a beat when he saw Lisa's favorite car parked where the asphalt ended. He got out and looked inside, but she wasn't there. He gazed all around and into the woods, but didn't see her. She was supposed to be at the farm— with Tony, Freida, and Carla. But it looked like she'd come here for some reason, parked, and decided to walk up. The question was, why?

Larry looked out the window of a two-door with a huge stuffer on the hood and said, "What's up, chief?"

"I don't know yet," Jack said, and got back in the Humvee.

They set out again. A few minutes later, they pulled into the little parking lot in front of the sales trailer. Though it was now after dark, the sky was lit by the fires of several burning cars out beyond the Skyline model. The electric lights were on in the cabin.

While Jack watched, the door to the Paul Bunyan opened up, and someone pointed a flashlight their way.

Jack jumped out of the Humvee and said, "Hey, wait!" but the figure was already running toward the Skyline. Whoever it was banged on the door frantically. When it opened, a long wedge of light speared down to the pond and disappeared when it closed.

Jack took a moment to look around the clearing, the little dock by the pond, and the two scavenging trucks. He didn't see Lisa anywhere, and decided she was probably inside. If so, that meant Carter had her.

Or maybe he's killed her already.

Before Jack could beat himself up over the hateful thought, Larry and the other Dragsters got out of their cars and ran over to join him at the edge of the lot.

"Pretty sure that was Dwayne running," Larry said. "Look at those fires, would you? Holy shit burgers!" He whistled and shook his head. "Carter and his boys parked over there—you see that line of cars? That's Cassie's Corvette there at the end. Wonder what the hell happened."

Jack wondered too, but not about the cars. "Who's Dwayne?"

"One of Carter's chumps. Seriously, don't worry about him."

Jack *was* worried about him. About everything, really, but it was never enough. Something always got missed, and then bad stuff like this happened. "Be right back."

He went to one of the Dragster cars, reached through the window, and picked up the CB microphone. He tuned to the channel he and his friends used and said, "Anyone there?"

Quietly, he waited, trying to stay calm, wishing the

Dragsters would shut up for a minute. They were yelling, laughing, wrestling, and generally acting like idiots.

"Anyone? Carter?"

He waited again, giving it a good ten seconds. The rule was, the radio in the cabin had to be on all the time. Either they weren't answering or the unit was off.

With Brad's help, Lisa had run the big antenna to the roof and connected multiple batteries together for more amperage. That was how they could reach the farm over the hills across however many miles. He knew the ones in the cars wouldn't carry that far, but he was desperate. He needed people he could trust.

Jack clicked the mic and said, "Freida? Tony?"

Still nothing.

Resignedly, he returned to Larry and the others. "Where's Will at?"

"Right here," Will said from the back of the group, doing his little howdy-ho wave. The boy had scraggly black hair and a friendly, patient expression.

Jack called him forward. "Larry said those people inside think you're cool. Is that true?"

Will laughed modestly. "Man, I dunno. I guess, sure. Ain't cool to say you're cool."

A couple of them laughed.

Before Jack could reply, the door to the Skyline opened again and two people came out. Then three people. Then four. They stared toward the parking lot, aiming flashlights.

Behind him, one of Jack's friendly Dragsters reached through a window and honked a horn—then all of them ran to their cars and started honking horns. Not normal horns, either. They were big, loud Yankee Doodle horns or tunes from famous movies or pop songs. The effect, all at once under the fire-lit sky, was menacing and strange, and he felt suddenly insecure in his newfound friendship. The boys and girls of Front Royal were savage, in their way. And he knew if they ever turned on him he'd be dead as quick as they'd killed Eddie.

The horns' effect on the group outside the Skyline was electric. In one boy's haste to run inside, he collided with a girl coming out, and both of them went down. Another dropped a flashlight, scrabbled wildly for it, and jumped over his downed friends before dashing inside. His friends got up and ran in behind him, then slammed the door shut. In another time and place, Jack would have laughed.

"Will," he said, "how do you feel about going there and talking to them? See if they'll come out?"

"W-what?"

"If they let my friends go unharmed, they can leave too. No one needs to get hurt."

"You really mean that?"

Jack shrugged, staring at the burning cars, thinking of Pete and Mandy. "Carter's dead if I see him. Don't tell them that, though."

Will swallowed. "Uh, I'm not sure it's a good idea for me to—"

Larry clapped him on the back and said, "Jesus Christ, grow some balls. Don't be a fraidy cat." He laughed good-naturedly.

A girl in the crowd said, "Then why don't *you* do it?"

"Because he's a fraidy cat!" someone yelled and honked his Yankee Doodle horn again.

Everyone laughed at that—even Larry.

"Come on, man," Larry said. "They all like you in there. You'll be fine." He crossed his heart. "I promise."

Will smiled weakly. "Man, I don't know why I'm doing this."

Everyone watched with bated breath as Will walked cautiously over to the Skyline. Every once in a while he'd stop and look back, only to get jeered at and waved forward by his friends. When he got to the door, he raised his fist to knock and the door flew open. He screamed once, and two people pulled him inside, vanishing him as if he'd never been there.

"He'll be fine," Larry said, sounding a little less sure of himself.

The other Dragsters lost interest as soon as Will was out of sight. A minute later, the girl who'd first accosted Jack was standing next to the bus, waving for attention. "Everyone, hey, check it out. Someone's in the bus! I hear yelling!"

***

Jack didn't see anyone through the windows, but it was also pretty dark out. With a sinking feeling in his gut, he ran over and pushed inside, prepared for anything but what he saw.

"What the ...?"

"Jack?" Olivia said fearfully, squinting at him from the floor of the bus. "Is that you?"

Lying or sitting in the aisle were Olivia, Brad, Molly, and Paul. Their hands were handcuffed to the bottoms of the seats. Clutched in Brad's free arm was his baby brother Tyler, swaddled in blankets.

"Yeah, it's me," Jack said. "What are you doing here? What happened?"

Olivia opened her mouth to explain, and then Paul said, "Oh my God, Jack, you wouldn't believe it! There was all kinds of shooting and then *explosions*—big, huge *explosions* like you wouldn't believe! I thought the world was exploding. Where's my brother? Carter made me stay in here and Miguel said he'd talk to him and get me out, but now I'm super worried about him because of the *explosions*. You wouldn't believe it, they were so loud. The whole bus shook! I couldn't believe—"

Brad, Olivia, and Molly yelled, "*Would you shut up?*" at the same time, and the kid closed his mouth.

"Brad," Jack said, "how's little Tyler doing?"

Brad frowned. "He's fine, but it's too cold out, and I'm cramped as hell. If I get out of here, I swear I'll ..." He bit his lip. That was the funny thing about Brad—he never actually cursed around Tyler. "That son of a ... man, he better *hope* I never get out."

Jack didn't have to ask who he meant. "Right. Where's Greg?"

"Greg got shot," Molly said. "In the leg. It looked like he might be okay with some kind of help. I mean ... if it doesn't get infected. Jesus, Jack, I'm sorry. Steve's hurt, too. They beat him up pretty bad. Because of me."

She covered her face and burst into tears.

As sad as he was to hear about Steve, a wave of relief

265

flooded through him on hearing Greg wasn't dead. Any hope was better than no hope. "What about the children?"

"Locked in your cabin," she said in a hoarse voice, wiping her eyes. "But Jack—Carter killed Trisha. Made us all watch, too. I'm sorry."

Red, enveloping rage rose up in him like a volcano, and he reached out to steady himself. It was all he could do to keep from pulling his recently recovered pistol and storming the place right now, but all that'd do was get him killed and leave his friends with one less person to help.

"Me too," he said lamely, hating how it sounded. "For everything. Give me a minute. I'll see if someone can help with those cuffs."

Jack found Larry, brought him onto the bus, and explained the situation. Even though Jack introduced him as a friend, his friends looked at the Dragster nervously.

"Everyone carries tools," Larry said. "Mostly to be cool. I'll get someone started on it. I bet we can cut through where the seats bolt down, or maybe unscrew them." He shook his head. "I totally forgot he had those handcuffs. Carter looted the police station way back when. Too bad we don't have that tear gas he took—we could bust in like Call Of Duty. That'd be so boss."

Jack clapped him on the shoulder. "Yeah. You said it. Thanks, man."

Maybe five minutes later, Will returned, troubled but unhurt.

"Well?" Jack said.

"Uh ... man, I don't know what, uh ... how to say it." He looked at Larry and the others as if seeking friendly faces. "First off, Greg's still alive." A few people cheered, but were quickly shushed to let him speak. "So anyway, there's this girl named Lisa. That's Greg's sister. She damn near killed half of everyone who came here with Carter. Then get this—she went and *killed Carter*."

Shocked gasps filled the air.

Larry said, "What do you mean killed him?"

"She killed Carter. That's what they said, and I didn't see him anywhere. They're super pissed about it, too. They were about to kill her, but now they're waiting. They got her locked up somewhere and—"

Whatever he said was lost in the jumble of shocked and excited conversation. Nobody seemed upset, really—just surprised, and possibly happy about the new development. For his part, Jack was torn between vicious joy and concern for his friends.

Cutting through the din, he said, "You know where they have her?"

"No idea," Will said. "Think she's with Greg and Steve, though, the way they talked. They ain't giving them up, either. I told them what you said. They said they don't trust you on account of what you did to Ray." He stared at his shoes, not meeting his eye. "This one kid—Mexican or something—he said you promised to let Ray go and then shot him dead. Now they won't come out unless you ..." He moved closer to Larry as if seeking protection. "Unless you go in yourself. Unarmed."

THIRTY-SEVEN

Would it have been so hard to get handcuffs of your own and just hold Ray a few days? Did you really have to kill him?

Jack had been so angry when he did it. Ray had been in on Mandy and Pete's murders, he was sure of it. Justice had to be served—a message sent. He'd recognized the importance of meeting Carter's aggression with the same level of force and then topping that with a crushing blow.

Minus the detour through weirdness and Hell with Blaze and the Pyros, everything had gone just fine. Better than fine, if Larry and his friends outside were any indication. And then Miguel happened.

Despite seeming calm to Larry and the others, Jack was furious.

Dammit, Miguel. You backstabber. Why did I trust you?

If only the stupid know-it-all had kept his mouth shut. Then his friends would be safe, and Carter gone or severely weakened.

While the crowd watched, Jack pulled his gun and handed it directly to Will. He didn't care about safety anymore. The crowd voiced their collective good wishes. He didn't care about that either. In fact, he felt empty. He didn't even have Carter to hate now. He may as well have aged ninety-nine years, so little did the world around him seem to matter. All that was left was a desire to save his friends, get them somewhere safe, and then ride out the wave of violence and death that had plagued him since losing his parents.

Without looking back, he made his way to the Skyline. He almost tried the knob, but then knocked instead. The door opened, and rough hands dragged him inside.

Jack found himself in the great room surrounded by nine boys including Miguel, and a girl with a weak chin and a perpetual scowl. Most were as old as Jack, give or take, and all were armed except Miguel and the girl.

"So you're the famous *Jack Ferris*," the girl said, sneering through the name.

The rest glowered at him with hard eyes.

Jack detected another emotion living side-by-side with the hatred: *fear*. Fear was good. He could use that.

"Okay," he said, "tell me where my friends are and everyone lives."

"Why don't we just kill him?" a fat kid said.

Jack blinked in amazement. The boy wasn't just a little plump in the face, like Tony and some of the Pyros. He was the first honest-to-goodness fat kid Jack had seen since before the Sickness.

The girl said, "Because he's got those idiots outside brainwashed, that's why. They don't know what a snake he is."

"You killed my sister, you son of a bitch!" said a dirty-faced kid with a hairlip. He pulled his gun and pointed it. The girl grabbed his arm, twisting it to the side, and it went off.

The blast was shockingly loud, causing his ears to ring, and for a brief moment everyone was staring around to see who'd been hit.

When it became clear everyone was fine, the girl yelled, "Give me that, you idiot!" and pulled it from his hand.

Jack pondered the killed-my-sister comment, then realized: *ah ... the girl from the house the other night, with the flashlight.*

The boy yelled, "You're not supposed to have a gun,

Cassie! Carter said so. Give it back!"

He reached for her, and she shot it over his head.

Everyone crouched, including Jack.

"I'm keeping it!" she shouted. "Carter didn't want me having one because he was afraid I'd kill him. I might have, too, but now he's dead. So just back off!"

Keeping his face impassive, Jack said, "I'm sorry about your sister. What do you expect when you come murdering my friends? And now Trisha." He shook his head. "One of your own people."

The fat one said, "Shut up!" and hit him in the face, staggering him against the wall, where he slipped and fell.

Sudden pounding on the door froze them, and nobody said anything.

Miguel went to the door and shouted, "What do you want?"

"What's all that shooting?" Larry shouted from the other side. "Did you shoot Jack?"

The fat kid nudged him with his foot. "Tell him we didn't shoot you."

Jack got up slowly, taking his time, letting their fear build. Then he said, "I'm fine, Larry. You don't have to come in and kill them like we said. Give me a few more minutes."

There was a brief pause from the other side. "Sure, Jack. You got it. Just like you said."

"Thanks, Larry."

Jack turned around and faced a different sort of room than the one he'd walked into. He knew he needed to build on that before they caught their balance.

"So, as you can see," he said, "those guys are on my side now. And they're perfectly willing to come in here and wipe you out if that's what you want. But unlike Carter—"

"Don't you say his name!" the girl shouted and pointed her gun at him.

Jack tensed, ready for the bullet that would end all his troubles, but it didn't come.

"Sorry," he said, hands raised. "Didn't know it was a sore spot. Look, I don't enjoy killing. I'm actually sick of it. But then he had my friends killed. Then I got mad, and then *you-know-who* got mad back. See? That's how wars are started. So we had a war. But here's our chance to turn all that off and go back to normal."

Miguel shook his head. "Oh, wow, just listen to you. You expect us to believe you after what you did to Ray? You sounded the same way! Then you shot him. You're just a murderer, that's all you are."

Rather than back down, Jack said, "I'll shoot anyone who hurts my friends, and that's the truth. As far as I know, none of you killed Pete and Mandy. And Carter— sorry—he's the one who hurt Greg. As far as I'm concerned"—he raised his hands peacefully—"you're all free to go. Or even join me. Let's just end this."

Cassie and the others exchanged glances, each trying to gauge what the other was thinking while still seeming tough and in control. Miguel looked thoughtful.

"Stay here," the fat kid said and told the others to follow him.

Jack watched them go into one of the downstairs bedrooms. Apparently they weren't worried about him getting away, which was comforting. He tried to listen in, but couldn't hear anything except the girl yelling at them. She wanted to keep him hostage so they could get away.

If that happened, he wouldn't go. All they'd do was kill him and the others once they were safe.

To pass the time, he looked around the room where the children usually slept. Mattresses had been arranged in a fun, flower-shaped pattern on the floor, with photos and keepsakes gathered in boxes beside each one. Over against the far wall was the radio—usually glowing like a nightlight 24/7, and now turned off. He considered sneaking over to call the farm, but didn't. The most it would do was scare them, and by now they were probably scared enough from no one answering their check-ins.

Whatever would happen would be decided soon, one way or the other.

Jack flinched when the girl ran out of the bedroom, tears streaking her dirty cheeks. Three boys grabbed her— she'd been trying to get to the kitchen. They dragged her past Jack and threw her onto one of the mattresses, scattering a box of toys in the process. He noticed she didn't have her gun anymore.

The one whose sister Jack had killed said, "Cassie, sit down and act mature! We got no choice!"

He must really want to live.

That was good, because Jack did too.

"Okay, Jack, we'll do it your way," the fat kid said. "Brian, Dwayne, go let 'em out."

Two of them went to the kitchen. Then came the sound of boards clattering on the floor.

Jack couldn't keep the smile from his face. It was going to work out after all.

Then, moments later, all hell broke loose.

***

Lisa was bad at waiting. She considered shooting the door, but all that would do was let everyone know she was armed and waste her three precious bullets in the process. So she forced herself to relax.

Maybe five minutes later, she heard a blood-curdling scream from Cassie, who must have discovered Carter's body. Then came a loud argument between her and Miguel. Lisa could guess what it was about. Cassie wanted to execute her, and Miguel—for all his faults—was trying to stop her.

Okay, so maybe I won't kill him when I get out of here.

Didn't mean she couldn't shoot him in the leg, though.

After that, there was a series of slamming doors, followed by ...

"What the hell?" Greg said.

"Quiet," she said.

From somewhere outside, barely heard through the thick cabin walls, came a bunch of weird, Yankee Doodle tunes. Ten quiet minutes later, a gunshot banged from somewhere in the cabin, possibly the great room. She wondered who'd died. Cassie? Miguel? One of her friends?

They heard a second shot.

Several minutes passed. Worried for her friends, she was about to try kicking her way out when she heard noises coming from the door. Someone was prying the board loose—coming to kill them next. It was now or never.

A boy opened the door and said, "All right, you. Come on, we're—"

Lisa shot him in the face and rushed out. She aimed at a second boy but held her shot. He wore a holstered gun and was holding a hammer. He dropped the hammer and raised his hands.

Quickly, she grabbed the pistol off the dead kid. Semi-automatic. No idea if it was chambered. She shot the kid with his hands up to find out, then grunted in satisfaction.

She could still feel their taunts as she'd been led upstairs with Carter, the disgusting things they'd said—telling him to "stick it in her mouth" and then laughing at her. Then that girl had spit in her face.

Lisa embraced her hatred, her fear, her pain, knowing she couldn't hesitate in what she had to do, however barbaric. Not if she wanted to save her brother.

With a wordless shout of rage, she rounded the corner and started firing.

***

Jack stood dumbstruck when Lisa flew around the corner with a gun in each hand. She shot the kid with the hairlip and then another boy, twice—once with each gun.

The fat kid's eyes seemed to bug out of his head. He pulled his weapon and aimed at her—then fired wildly when Jack tackled him to the ground. Jack punched him hard in the jaw and wrenched the pistol from his hand.

Armed now, he turned just in time to receive a glancing blow to the head with the stool Olivia used when she told stories to the children.

Jack fell back, dazed, but didn't drop the gun. He pointed at Cassie, ready to pull the trigger, and then paused when he saw the fear in her eyes.

"Find a place to hide," he said and moved to stand.

Faster than he could blink, she reared back and hit him with the stool again, catching him on his hastily raised arm.

Really? he thought, crab-walking backward to get away.

Her eyes were crazy with rage, and she was actually drooling. She followed him, swinging with everything she had. Jack kicked her hard in the leg, bringing a yelp of pain and taking her down.

Over near the kitchen, Lisa kept shooting. The fat kid got to his feet and ran for the door—only to fall back when Larry slammed it open and swept in with his pistol-gripped shotgun.

Jack aimed and shot a different kid just as he was drawing down on Lisa. At the blast, she looked over, and her eyes widened. "Jack? Oh, God, you're here!"

"Everyone stop!" he yelled, clambering to his feet and running foolishly into the middle of the fray, arms outstretched for calm. "Stop shooting! Hold your fire!"

Behind him, Larry's shotgun boomed through the room, tickling the bones in Jack's chest. He'd shot the fat kid while he was down.

"Larry, dammit, enough already!"

For a moment, Larry looked angry, then he shook his head. "I was just helping."

Miguel was cowering with two others behind an upturned table.

Cassie sat rocking on the floor, clutching her knee and not looking at anyone.

***

Outside in the field, they found the bodies of five boys and two girls, Trisha among them. Carter was dead upstairs. Two boys had died in the kitchen. There were four dead in the great room, now hazy with gun smoke. The whole place smelled of blood and excrement and would for several days.

An hour later, the Rippers and Dragsters, former and ex, came together and stacked their dead in a van that hadn't caught fire. Then they burned them. All stood in attendance, though nothing was said.

Of the dead, there were too many. Of words, there were too few.

EPILOGUE

Paul and Miguel didn't wait around to be thrown out—they were gone before the morning, as were Cassie and the two surviving boys from Carter's group.

Richard and Kyle were beside themselves with worry that Jack would reveal their part in Blaze's murder. Jack assured them he wouldn't, provided they escorted him back to their base—with Tony and a few Dragsters.

Jack didn't like the idea of some kid taking his sword and stabbing someone, and wanted to retrieve it. He also wanted to make friends with the next leader. He had no interest in bringing the gang of murderous thieves into his own group. But if he could forge an alliance, they'd be a useful friendly force in the east. To that end, he'd ply them with as much grain as needed to keep them happy and healthy through the winter. He'd also meet with the group at the airport—to ensure they were really taking care of the children Blaze had brought them. Who knew, maybe they could trade a few things. Like those stun guns the Pyro's dead leader had mentioned.

That night after the battle, Lisa pulled the bullet out of Greg's leg with a pair of sanitized needle-nosed pliers. Over the next few months, he'd recover nicely. Steve would too, though his nose had been broken and set by unskilled hands. Pain medication was in high demand that winter, and Jack had to take them both aside to ensure it wasn't becoming a habit.

Most of Larry's Dragsters chose to stay at the cabins and now called themselves Rippers. They claimed the Saskatchewan, it being the biggest and coolest building there. Everyone answered to Jack, but they also deferred to Larry. Rather than worry about it like some paranoid dictator, Jack took advantage of it and passed orders through him, as well as the other leaders: Lisa, Greg, Brad, Tony, Olivia, Molly, and Steve. Each was given the official rank of "Captain" and moved into the Paul Bunyan with him. A small cabin, compared to the others, but it still had a lot of unused space.

A large group of children from Front Royal were brought to Big Timber—mostly little sisters and brothers. Molly took them under her wing and put them in the Abe Lincoln on hastily scavenged mattresses.

Somewhere along the way, Olivia and Greg became quite the item. It helped that the former Dragsters fell over themselves trying to chat him up whenever they could. He was even more popular than that one kid, Will.

Freida and Carla had livestock to take care of, and didn't want to leave. Jack was fine with that, but asked that they keep at least two guards from the cabins with them at all times. They happily agreed.

The snow came down heavily in January, and again in February. Nobody froze, and they didn't starve. There was still a lot to do, but there always had been. There were gun safety classes and scavenging runs and plans for farming. There were rabbit hutches to build and more cattle to find. Horses, too. And for the first time since starting out with Pete that cold day in November, Jack felt they actually had a chance to not just survive, but thrive.

The sentiment was comforting. And for the next several months, it was even true.

ABOUT THE AUTHOR

John L. Monk lives in Virginia, USA, with his wife, Dorothy. A writer with a degree in cultural anthropology, he boldly does the dishes, roots out evil wherever it lurks, and writes his own stunts.

Made in the USA
Lexington, KY
09 September 2016